PENGUIN POETRY LIBRARY

WILLIAM BLAKE: SELECTED POETRY

William Blake was born in Broad Street in 1757, the son of a London hosier. Having attended Henry Parr's drawing school in the Strand, he was in 1772 apprenticed to Henry Basire, engraver to the Society of Antiquaries, and later was admitted as a student to the Royal Academy, where he exhibited in 1780. He married Catherine Boucher in 1782 and in 1783 published *Poetical Sketches*. The first of his 'illuminated books' was *Songs of Innocence* (1789), which, like *The Book of Thel* (published in the same year), has as its main themes the celebration of innocence and its inviolability.

Blake sets out his ideas more fully in his chief prose work, *The Marriage of Heaven and Hell* (1791), which proclaims his lifelong belief in the moral primacy of the imagination. But in *Songs of Experience* (1794) he recognizes the power of repression, and in a series of short narrative poems he looks for mankind's redemption from oppression through a resurgence of imaginative life. By 1797 he was ready for epic; *Vala* was never finished, but in *Milton* and *Jerusalem* he presents his renewed vision of reconciliation among the warring fragments of humanity. Other striking poems of his middle years are the lyrics of the Pickering Manuscript, and *The Everlasting Gospel*, but in the last years of his life he expressed himself in drawing rather than poetry.

Little of Blake's work was published in conventional form. He combined his vocations as poet and graphic artist to produce books that are visually stunning. He also designed illustrations of works by other poets and devised his own technique for producing large watercolour illustrations and colour-printed drawings. Blake died in 1827, 'an Old Man feeble & tottering but not in Spirit & Life not in the Real Man The Imagination which Liveth for Ever'.

WILLIAM BLAKE:
SELECTED POETRY

Edited by
W. H. Stevenson

PENGUIN BOOKS

PENGUIN BOOKS

Published by the Penguin Group
Penguin Books Ltd, 27 Wrights Lane, London W8 5TZ, England
Penguin Books USA Inc., 375 Hudson Street, New York, New York 10014, USA
Penguin Books Australia Ltd, Ringwood, Victoria, Australia
Penguin Books Canada Ltd, 10 Alcorn Avenue, Toronto, Ontario, Canada M4V 3B2
Penguin Books (NZ) Ltd, 182–190 Wairau Road, Auckland 10, New Zealand

Penguin Books Ltd, Registered Offices: Harmondsworth, Middlesex, England

First published 1988
7 9 10 8

Printed in England by Clays Ltd, St Ives plc
Filmset in 9 on 11 pt Aldus

CONTENTS

INTRODUCTION

Two of the most famous poems in the language are William Blake's. Everyone has met the 'Tyger, tyger, burning bright' at one time or another. 'And did those feet . . .' is sung with great gusto in halls and at concerts all round the country. At the same time, Blake is one of the most obscure of poets; few of the singers reflect on what he meant by the 'bow of burning gold', or the 'arrows of desire'. But they feel its impetus, and that is surely what Blake would have wanted.

Blake is one of the most powerful lyric writers in English. His images may be biblical, or literary, or the stuff of dreams. His style is often deceptively conventional. But he writes with a cryptic economy that creates, in the nightmare vividness of 'The Tyger', or the fervour and drive of 'And did those feet . . .', a force rarely found in others, and never surpassed.

But it is the difficulty of Blake's poetry, rather than the vividness, that has captured the commentators. They have sought high and low in the mystical philosophies, or in the politics, of East and West for the 'key' to his work. It is true that he has a habit of allusiveness that is certainly obscure. In the famous song, for example, England is 'clouded' by spiritual blindness more than by cumuli, and the 'Satanic mills' are the shackles of the mind, of which the Industrial Revolution is only one manifestation. The difficulty is not to be solved by finding a missing key. It is something less systematic; the problem of Blake himself.

'I know I am inspired!' is the foundation of his obscurity as well as of the dynamic enthusiasm. He was ambitious for fame; he longed for, even demanded, an audience as enthusiastic as himself, to build the Jerusalem he was looking for in England's green and pleasant land. He was after all writing at a time when the Age of Reason was turning into an Age of Enthusiasm. But he had a naive, almost arrogant confidence in the power of his own inspiration. Burning with its fire, convinced that to hear him must be to applaud, he failed to realize that he must also address himself to the minds of his audience before they could hear him. He never made any concessions to them, and as a result they made none to him. He sought to project his inner enthusiasms on to the public, but chose one method after another that ensured that his audience would regard his enthusiasms, not as inspiration, but as mere eccentricity or worse.

Blake was a touchy man. He was not a solitary; he had many friends, but seems not to have been an easy collaborator. It is significant that his 'illuminated printing' enabled him to print works without assistance. But this trait sorted badly with his ambition to be heard. At Felpham, in 1800, the complacent Hayley tried to take him in hand, and was roundly cursed for his pains. At one level, he was right to point out that Blake's obstinate concentration on higher things kept him poor, but he was incapable of understanding Blake, or he would have seen that this was essential to him.

Blake's life might seem uneventful, but his inner life was so exciting that it did not matter. His enthusiasm lifted him out of London into Jerusalem – or rather, brought Jerusalem into London and turned a rainbow over Hyde Park into a gateway to heaven. Blake's enthusiasms are not the Toad-like crazes of a perpetually unsatisfied man, but the developing insights of someone with a wide-ranging mind responding to life's rejections of his hopes, not by losing hope, but by rebuilding it. And each stage has its own artistic correlative.

It is therefore no use trying to understand Blake by means of a key. No one scheme fits all his works; each stage grows out of the one preceding it. Each enthusiasm gives a striking new turn to his legend and its imagery, but the new is always superimposed on the old. If we can understand the series of enthusiasms, we can begin to find our way through the difficulties of his works.

The product of his first enthusiasm is the foundation of all the rest; it reveals him, not as the preacher of doctrines of free innocence, or as a mystical thinker, but as that typical eighteenth-century figure, the inventor. In other hands his invention might well have succeeded: the re-creation in modern guise of the medieval illuminated book, text and design together as a unity, but using new techniques to make reproduction feasible.

Illustrated books were much in demand, but not easy to produce. Blake was writing poetry; how better to see it published than in the style of the medieval illuminated book, a hand-made, unique work of art? As poet and artist, he could create the whole work, and the result would be as fine as an illuminated manuscript. But there was no need for the work to remain unique; as an engraver he had the skill and the means to hand to make multiple copies. He called it 'illuminated printing'. He transferred his design and text on to the plate – not in reversed script, as an engraver must normally do. After etching away the unwanted material, the plate became one large piece of type, to be inked and printed on his engraver's press. Many of the plates, especially in the *Songs*, *America* and *Europe*, fulfil his hopes and make one artistic unity, poem and design.

He must have thought his fortune was made. True, it was a clumsy process by our standards, and did not produce a very well-defined or legible text, but it satisfied Blake's needs, and he used it as long as he wrote poetry. It might well have made him a success, if he had produced works that the public wanted to see. But apart from *Songs of Innocence*, a children's poetry book which might well have found a market, he used it almost entirely for his own ideological campaign. Even this might have succeeded – Shelley found an audience – but Blake's books used an idiom that even his friends found hard to hear.

In his readiness to invent new techniques, Blake was typical of his age. And, like William Morris seventy years later, he was just as typical in his fascination with the medieval. Gothic stories and melodramas of castles, knights, monks and fair ladies were already popular enough for Jane Austen to parody in *Northanger Abbey*. Matthew Lewis's notorious soft-porn *The Monk* sold very well indeed. Scott, not Wordsworth, became the favourite poet of the age.

Blake, unfortunately, was captured, not by the clarity and humour of Chaucer, much as he admired him, but by the cloudy pseudo-medievalism of Chatterton and Ossian. This kind of writing is most suitable for escapist literature, but Blake used it for most of his work in 'illuminated printing', to convey his most urgent messages. Apart from the *Songs* (1789–94), virtually all his completed books are such gothic legends. Grandiose, superhuman figures gesticulate across his pages; and since they crowd past, not to entertain us but to evangelize, bearing names we have never heard of and associations we can only slowly grasp, it is not surprising that Blake's major poetry, far from bringing him fame, brought only ridicule. When later he added to his myth the fumblings of antiquaries who identified Eastern religions with ancient Britain, linked the Syrian mother-goddess with Avebury and the Druids with the biblical patriarchs, even his best friends found it almost impossible to follow his imaginative flights; and so do we.

When Blake's first great enthusiasm gripped him, the world was in the ferment of revolution. But Blake was convinced that art, the works of the imagination, not political revolution, were the key to its renovation. In the first group of legends (1789–93), from *Thel* to *America*, Blake presents his case: the indestructibility of innocence. The soul that freely follows its imaginative instincts will be innocent and virtuous; nature protects this innocence, and the only sin is to allow one's nature to be perverted by law and custom. Free love is the only true love; law destroys both love and freedom.

Freedom could not come about except through the imagination. The Bible presented a view, not of freedom, love, innocent happiness and (above all) imagination, but of law. Other myth-makers had followed suit. The world's images were all wrong. Blake would put this right with a series of narrative poems in the new medium, to illustrate – not prove – the nature of imaginative truth. Political revolution was not in itself the antidote to tyranny, but a symptom of mankind's awakening to the freedom of the spirit. In the exercise of the imagination, the purity and inviolability of innocence would reveal itself. The need for law, and tyranny itself, would not wither at the hand of war, but at the breath of the free imagination.

It did not happen, and the next books, including the *Songs of Experience* and *Urizen*, are devoted to discovering what had gone wrong. Typically, Blake did not reject his beliefs, but went on to improve them. Now he understood that it was too simple to see the world's problems as the hostility of evil minds against good, the tyrant threatening the innocent imagination. A new vision and a new enthusiasm emerges: the plan of a great epic, *Vala*, written on the back of proofs of his *Night Thoughts* designs.

In this new vision of the ideal world, all beings are united in one perfect Human Form. After the Fall – which as always in Blake is a failure of the imagination – the Human is fragmented, and hostility arises between his now separated elements. None of these elements is perfectly good or evil; the creatures of the earlier myth, Orc, Urizen and Los, are now all damaged pieces of the Universal Human Form, and none will be complete without the rest. From this time on,

Urizen, the great evil of *America*, becomes less hated and more pitied. Even Vala, the female form who is at first blamed for the disintegration, is at last regenerated.

But another enthusiasm arrives, close on the heels of the Immortal Man. It is time once more for a restatement of the vision and the third development of the myth, not this time through disillusionment but because, by the time Blake went to Felpham in 1800, his images had taken on a new colouring. Markedly Christian language begins to creep into *Vala*, which eventually collapses under the strain. Even before Felpham, Blake had used the phrase, 'We who call ourselves Christians'. Now the belief grows into its own images which must be incorporated into the myth.

It is a complex development. The Druids of ancient Britain are identified with the patriarchs of the Bible, and the Giant Albion – the spirit of Britain – is identified with the Israel of the Bible. Thus Albion is the Holy Land, London is Jerusalem, and Jesus did indeed walk (in the truth of the imagination) across these hills. The solution to the disintegration of man is reconciliation through forgiveness, and the reconciliation of Christ and Albion brings about the reunion of the disintegrated Eternal Human, who appears then as Christ himself. It is not enough now, as in *The Marriage of Heaven and Hell*, to find one's own imaginative life. The Human Form Divine will not be re-created until the whole nation, the whole of mankind, the whole of the universe, is drawn together; but this can begin in the smallest of single actions. Blake has returned to the idealistic hope of *America*, but now his thought is less simple and more mystical; yet, as the pages of *Jerusalem* show, no less radical.

Thus each new enthusiasm reshapes the legend of his poems. As Blake refines his beliefs, he refines his myth too. The function of Orc and Urizen in *America* is quite plain; one fights for freedom, the other for law. In *Urizen* it is not so simple, and by *Vala* and *Milton* they have had to be altered almost out of recognition, but they are never quite abandoned. Blake was not by instinct a narrative poet. He tended to 'improve' his longer poems by a process of accumulation rather than by following the demands of the narrative. His mind was like an untidy desk. He threw nothing away, and often used old material for new tasks. One never knows what one will find. The reader ploughing through pages full of 'dismal howling woe' comes across an unexpected line of startling beauty which only Blake could have written.

It is easy to dismiss Blake as a 'primitive', an artist whose attraction resides in his naivety, which is lost when the work becomes heavy and charmless. This also is too simple. There is an odd contradiction at the heart of Blake's writing. He repeatedly called for art to concern itself with the 'minute particulars' of life: 'To Generalise is to be an idiot!' he scribbled in the margin of Reynolds's *Works*. On the other hand, he criticized Wordsworth for paying too much attention to the details of nature at the expense of inner realities. More important, much of his poetry disregards his own rule. Words like 'howling' and 'dismal' appear far too often. His lyrics are usually marvels of conciseness, but he chose to express his dearest beliefs, not as 'Minute Particulars', but as cloudy, generalized figures representing eternal states of humanity. Milton ceases to be a seventeenth-century poet and becomes a State of Los, the eternal spirit of the imagination. From first to last, Blake champions the imagination; but the great flaw in his works is not too much free imagination, but too much misplaced convention. At his greatest, minutiae become eternal; at his worst, the eternal becomes a scheme.

Here, if anywhere, lies the key to Blake. He was not a 'Romantic' writer, whatever that is; he was neo-classic by training and inclination. He had no time for classical myth, but that is irrelevant. His instinct was to create, not symbols out of mystical tradition, nor vivid observations of human life, but representative figures to embody both the inner nature of the subject and the artist's response to it. When he failed, he became obscure or tedious – often both. When he succeeded, he created a kind of magic of which no other English poet has been capable.

It is easy to point out that, among lyric collections, the *Songs* are unmatched for sustained power in small compass. There is scarcely a single uncertain note in *Experience*, and even *Innocence* has a strength which one slowly comes to appreciate. Blake's typical images come from the mind, not from life. The 'midnight Harlot's curse' of 'London' is an exception, and the Blossom that becomes a Sick Rose is more typical. His greatness as a lyricist lies in the vividness of the emotional force with which he imbues these abstract images.

But it is even more remarkable to observe Blake's greatness, however spasmodic and unpredictable, in the longer works. He did not know how to handle situations or develop a plot, nor was he very interested. His long poems are made up of a mixture of inspiration, pig-headedness, evangelical fervour, and profound imagery. He blundered into greatness, just as he too often blundered away from it. Yet there are many occasions, as his mythical figures move across the abyss, when all the elements come together, and then he produces poetry of a unique kind of genius. No one else has written anything resembling Enion's lament in *Vala* (p. 120); the vision of Satan in *Milton* (p. 188); the journey of Los through London (p. 223). All these leave the reader in something more than admiration; in wonderment.

It is easy to see what the elements are: a formal set-piece after the fashion of the neo-classical genre paintings with which Blake was familiar; stylized, old-fashioned 'poetical' language leaning heavily on the Bible; the abstract images drawn more from dreams than from observation. And often, designs of the same specification. It is much less easy to show how these come together so that the formality of the set-piece becomes the necessary vehicle for the very personal emotions of this passionate man. The surrealist quality of the images partly explains why they are so vivid, but there is an emotional power in their vividness that surrealism rarely touches. Above all, it is the ability to mould these images, arising from the depths of the mind of an impulsive, fiery man, into the framework provided by conventional, even trite materials that creates such unexpected greatness.

CHRONOLOGY

1757	William Blake born, 28 November.
1767	Goes to Parr's drawing school.
1772	Apprenticed to James Basire, engraver.
1779	Admitted as student at the Royal Academy.
1782	Marries Catherine Boucher, 18 August.
1783	*Poetical Sketches* printed.
1784	'An Island in the Moon' (satirical sketches, with some verses).
1788	*All Religions are One*, and *There is No Natural Religion*: three miniature tracts, Blake's first essays in 'illuminated printing'.
1788–9	*Tiriel* (a tragic-mythic narrative, not printed); *Songs of Innocence; Thel.*
1790–91	*The French Revolution*, a visionary narrative, set in letterpress but not published. Blake moves to Hercules Buildings, Lambeth.
1793	A prospectus advertises *The Marriage of Heaven and Hell, Visions of the Daughters of Albion, America,* etc.
1794	*Songs of Innocence and of Experience*; *Europe*; *Urizen.*
1795	*Song of Los* (composed of *Africa* and *Asia*); *Book of Ahania*; *Book of Los* (see p. 280, pl. 24.10n below).
1796	Blake at work on engravings for Young's *Night Thoughts* (published 1797). Writing of *Vala* begins on discarded proof sheets.
1798	Wordsworth and Coleridge publish *Lyrical Ballads*, first edition.
1800	Because of Blake's poverty, Flaxman arranges for him to go to Felpham, Sussex, as protégé of William Hayley.
1800–1803	Work on *Vala, Milton*, and lyrics (including the Pickering manuscript). Blake quarrels with Hayley, who tries to steer him to more lucrative work and discourages the poetry.

1803	Warrant for Blake's arrest, on 12 August, for alleged seditious words during a quarrel with Trooper Scholfield. Acquitted in January 1804.
	Returns to London in September, to 17 South Molton Street.
1804	The date 1804 appears on title pages of *Milton* and *Jerusalem* (but see 1810, 1820).
1805–7	Disputes with Cromek, his publisher.
1806	B. H. Malkin publishes some of Blake's lyrics; first publication not by Blake himself.
1806–7	Stothard paints *The Canterbury Pilgrims*. Blake believed Stothard had stolen the idea from him.
1809	Blake has an exhibition of his work; though visited by Southey and Hunt, it is a failure. Blake's period of greatest poverty begins.
1810	The first two copies (45 plates) of *Milton* probably printed; two others (50 plates) followed after 1815.
1818	*The Everlasting Gospel*.
1819	Meets John Varley. Blake begins to attract the company of appreciative young artists.
1820	*Jerusalem* printed; woodcuts for Thornton's *Virgil*.
1821	Blake moves to 3 Fountain Court, Strand.
1822	*The Death of Abel*, a scene in dramatic verse: Blake's last book in 'illuminated printing'.
1821–5	Series of *Job* designs for Linnell.
1824	Meets Samuel Palmer.
1825–7	Work on Dante drawings.
1827	Blake dies, 12 August.
1831	Catherine Blake dies, 18 October.

NOTE ON THE TEXT

The aim of this selection is to present the best, and the most characteristic, of Blake's poetry. I have omitted the juvenilia, and the longer poems which Blake himself did not choose to engrave, except for *Vala* and *The Everlasting Gospel*, which cannot be ignored. The *Songs* are included entire, as are the most important of the Lambeth books. *Milton* and *Jerusalem* are Blake's most ambitious poems and must receive serious attention, although they are too long to be included complete. *Jerusalem* can only be represented by extracts showing the main themes of the poem throughout its length, but I have tried to produce a shortened version of *Milton* which will give a sense of the work as a whole. Finally, one cannot represent Blake without a selection of the manuscript pieces, including the best of the discarded poems from *Songs of Experience*, the Pickering manuscript, and some of the revealing epigrams of the years 1800 to 1810.

Blake's punctuation and spelling are quite idiosyncratic, and in his manuscripts there are long stretches with no punctuation at all. I have therefore changed or added punctuation, but only to what seemed a necessary minimum, while the original spellings are retained as far as possible. Raised commas (which Blake himself often included in his finished works) are added in such words as 'wat'ry' and 'brandish'd' to coincide as nearly as possible with contemporary practice, and for the same reason his many capitals are left largely untouched. In this way I hope to have clarified the poetry, while retaining the original flavour of Blake's works.

Marginal figures in square brackets, thus: [16], indicate the beginning of a plate engraved by Blake, on a page in the manuscript concerned. The use of square brackets for certain headings indicates that they are editorial. Between lines, an asterisk denotes that a passage has been omitted; where there is no asterisk, the space is Blake's.

Introduction

Piping down the valleys wild
Piping songs of pleasant glee,
On a cloud I saw a child,
And he laughing said to me:

Pipe a song about a Lamb:
So I piped with merry chear.
Piper, pipe that song again –
So I piped: he wept to hear.

Drop thy pipe, thy happy pipe,
Sing thy songs of happy chear: 10
So I sung the same again
While he wept with joy to hear.

Piper, sit thee down and write
In a book that all may read –
So he vanish'd from my sight
And I pluck'd a hollow reed,

And I made a rural pen
And I stain'd the water clear
And I wrote my happy songs,
Every child may joy to hear. 20

The Ecchoing Green

The Sun does arise
And make happy the skies,
The merry bells ring
To welcome the Spring:
The skylark and thrush
The birds of the bush
Sing louder around
To the bells' chearful sound,

While our sports shall be seen
On the Ecchoing Green. 10

Old John with white hair
Does laugh away care
Sitting under the oak
Among the old folk.
They laugh at our play,
And soon they all say:
Such, such were the joys
When we all girls & boys
In our youth-time were seen
On the Ecchoing Green 20

Till the little ones weary
No more can be merry,
The sun does descend,
And our sports have an end:
Round the laps of their mothers
Many sisters and brothers,
Like birds in their nest,
Are ready for rest:
And sport no more seen
On the darkening Green. 30

The Lamb

Little Lamb, who made thee?
Dost thou know who made thee?
Gave thee life & bid thee feed
By the stream & o'er the mead:
Gave thee clothing of delight,
Softest clothing, wooly, bright:
Gave thee such a tender voice,
Making all the vales rejoice:
Little Lamb who made thee,
Dost thou know who made thee?

Little Lamb, I'll tell thee,
Little Lamb, I'll tell thee:
He is called by thy name
For he calls himself a Lamb.
He is meek & he is mild,
He became a little child:
I a child & thou a lamb,
[n]We are called by his name:
Little Lamb God bless thee,
Little Lamb God bless thee! 20

The Shepherd

How sweet is the Shepherd's sweet lot!
From the morn to the evening he strays;
He shall follow his sheep all the day
And his tongue shall be filled with praise.

For he hears the lambs innocent call,
And he hears the ewes tender reply.
He is watchful when they are in peace,
For they know that their Shepherd is nigh.

Infant Joy

I have no name
I am but two days old –
What shall I call thee?
I happy am
[n]Joy is my name –
Sweet joy befall thee!

Pretty joy!
Sweet joy but two days old,
Sweet joy I call thee:
Thou dost smile, 10
I sing the while:
Sweet joy befall thee!

[n]*The Little Black Boy*

My mother bore me in the southern wild,
And I am black, but O! my soul is white;
White as an angel is the English child,
But I am black as if bereav'd of light.

My mother taught me underneath a tree
And sitting down before the heat of day,
She took me on her lap and kissed me,
And pointing to the east began to say:

Look on the rising sun: there God does live
And gives his light, and gives his heat away: 10
And flowers and trees and beasts and men recieve
Comfort in morning, joy in the noon day.

And we are put on earth a little space,
That we may learn to bear the beams of love:
And these black bodies and this sunburnt face
Is but a cloud, and like a shady grove:

For when our souls have learn'd the heat to bear
The cloud will vanish; we shall hear his voice,
Saying: Come out from the grove, my love & care,
And round my golden tent like lambs rejoice. 20

Thus did my mother say and kissed me:
And thus I say to little English boy;
When I from black and he from white cloud free,
And round the tent of God like lambs we joy,

I'll shade him from the heat, till he can bear
To lean in joy upon our father's knee:
And then I'll stand and stroke his silver hair,
And be like him and he will then love me.

Laughing Song

When the green woods laugh with the voice of joy
And the dimpling stream runs laughing by,
When the air does laugh with our merry wit,
And the green hill laughs with the noise of it,

When the meadows laugh with lively green,
And the grasshopper laughs in the merry scene,
When Mary and Susan and Emily
With their sweet round mouths sing 'Ha, Ha, He!'

When the painted birds laugh in the shade,
Where our table with cherries and nuts is spread, 10
Come live & be merry, and join with me,
To sing the sweet chorus of 'Ha, Ha, He!'

Spring

Sound the Flute!
Now it's mute.
Birds delight
Day and Night,
Nightingale
In the dale
Lark in Sky
Merrily,
Merrily Merrily to welcome in the Year.

Little Boy 10
Full of joy,
Little Girl
Sweet and small;
Cock does crow
So do you,
Merry voice
Infant noise
Merrily Merrily to welcome in the Year.

Little Lamb,
Here I am, 20
Come and lick
My white neck.
Let me pull
Your soft Wool,
Let me kiss
Your soft face:
Merrily Merrily we welcome in the Year.

[n]*A Cradle Song*

Sweet dreams form a shade
O'er my lovely infant's head;
Sweet dreams of pleasant streams
By happy silent moony beams.

Sweet sleep with soft down
Weave thy brows an infant crown:
Sweet sleep Angel mild,
Hover o'er my happy child.

Sweet smiles in the night
Hover over my delight: 10
Sweet smiles, Mother's smiles,
All the livelong night beguiles.

Sweet moans, dovelike sighs,
Chase not slumber from thy eyes.
Sweet moans, sweeter smiles,
All the dovelike moans beguiles.

Sleep sleep happy child,
All creation slept and smil'd:
Sleep sleep, happy sleep,
While o'er thee thy mother weep. 20

Sweet babe in thy face
Holy image I can trace:
Sweet babe once like thee,
Thy maker lay and wept for me,

Wept for me, for thee, for all,
When he was an infant small.
Thou his image ever see
Heavenly face that smiles on thee,

Smiles on thee on me on all:
Who became an infant small. 30
Infant smiles are his own smiles:
Heaven & earth to peace beguiles.

Nurse's Song

When the voices of children are heard on the green
And laughing is heard on the hill,
My heart is at rest within my breast
And everything else is still.

Then come home, my children, the sun is gone down
And the dews of night arise:
Come, come, leave off play, and let us away
Till the morning appears in the skies.

No, no, let us play, for it is yet day
And we cannot go to sleep, 10
Besides, in the sky the little birds fly
And the hills are all cover'd with sheep.

Well, well, go & play till the light fades away
And then go home to bed.
The little ones leaped & shouted & laugh'd
And all the hills ecchoed.

[n]*Holy Thursday*

'Twas on a Holy Thursday, their innocent faces clean,
The children walking two & two in red & blue & green:
Grey-headed beadles walk'd before with wands as white as snow,
Till into the high dome of Paul's they like Thames' waters flow.

what a multitude they seem'd these flowers of London
town,
Seated in companies they sit with radiance all their own.
The hum of multitudes was there, but multitudes of lambs:
Thousands of little boys & girls raising their innocent hands.

Now like a mighty wind they raise to heaven the voice of
song,
Or like harmonious thunderings the seats of heaven among. 10
Beneath them sit the aged men, wise guardians of the poor:
Then cherish pity lest you drive an angel from your door.

The Blossom

Merry Merry Sparrow
Under leaves so green,
A happy Blossom
Sees you swift as arrow
Seek your cradle narrow
Near my Bosom.

Pretty Pretty Robin
Under leaves so green,
A happy Blossom
Hears you sobbing sobbing 10
Pretty Pretty Robin
Near my Bosom.

[n]*The Chimney Sweeper*

When my mother died I was very young,
And my father sold me while yet my tongue
Could scarcely cry 'weep weep! weep weep!'
So your chimneys I sweep & in soot I sleep.

There's little Tom Dacre, who cried when his head
That curl'd like a lamb's back was shav'd, so I said,
Hush Tom, never mind it, for when your head's bare
You know that the soot cannot spoil your white hair.

And so he was quiet, & that very night
As Tom was asleeping he had such a sight, 10
That thousands of sweepers, Dick Joe Ned & Jack,
Were all of them lock'd up in coffins of black;

And by came an Angel who had a bright key,
And he open'd the coffins & set them all free.
Then down a green plain, leaping laughing they run
And wash in a river and shine in the Sun.

Then naked & white, all their bags left behind,
They rise upon clouds and sport in the wind.
And the Angel told Tom if he'd be a good boy,
He'd have God for his father & never want joy. 20

And so Tom awoke and we rose in the dark
And got with our bags & our brushes to work.
Tho' the morning was cold, Tom was happy & warm,
So if all do their duty, they need not fear harm.

[n]*The Divine Image*

To Mercy, Pity, Peace and Love
All pray in their distress;
And to these virtues of delight
Return their thankfulness.

For Mercy, Pity, Peace and Love
Is God, our father dear,
And Mercy, Pity, Peace and Love
Is Man, his child and care.

For Mercy has a human heart,
Pity a human face, 10
And Love the human form divine,
And Peace the human dress.

Then every man, of every clime
That prays in his distress,
Prays to the human form divine
Love, Mercy, Pity, Peace.

And all must love the human form,
In heathen, Turk or Jew:
Where Mercy, Love & Pity dwell
There God is dwelling too. 20

Night

The sun descending in the west
The evening star does shine,
The birds are silent in their nest,
And I must seek for mine.
The moon like a flower
In heaven's high bower,
With silent delight
Sits and smiles on the night.

Farewell, green fields and happy groves,
Where flocks have took delight: 10
Where lambs have nibbled, silent moves
The feet of angels bright;
Unseen they pour blessing
And joy without ceasing,
On each bud and blossom,
And each sleeping bosom.

They look in every thoughtless nest,
Where birds are cover'd warm;
They visit caves of every beast,
To keep them all from harm: 20
If they see any weeping
That should have been sleeping
They pour sleep on their head,
And sit down by their bed.

When wolves and tygers howl for prey,
They pitying stand and weep;
Seeking to drive their thirst away,
And keep them from the sheep.

But if they rush dreadful,
The angels, most heedful 30
Recieve each mild spirit
New worlds to inherit.

And there the lion's ruddy eyes
Shall flow with tears of gold,
And pitying the tender cries,
And walking round the fold,
Saying: wrath by his meekness
And by his health, sickness
Is driven away
From our immortal day. 40

And now beside thee bleating lamb
I can lie down and sleep;
Or think on him who bare thy name,
Graze after thee and weep.
For wash'd in life's river
My bright mane for ever
Shall shine like the gold
As I guard o'er the fold.

A Dream

Once a dream did weave a shade
O'er my Angel-guarded bed,
That an ⁿEmmet lost its way
Where on grass methought I lay.

Troubled wilder'd and forlorn,
Dark benighted travel-worn,
Over many a tangled spray
All heart-broke I heard her say:

O, my children! do they cry,
Do they hear their father sigh? 10
Now they look abroad to see,
Now return and weep for me.

Pitying, I drop'd a tear:
But I saw a glow-worm near,
Who replied: What wailing wight
Calls the watchman of the night?

I am set to light the ground,
While the beetle goes his round:
Follow now the beetle's hum,
Little wanderer hie thee home. 20

On Another's Sorrow

Can I see another's woe
And not be in sorrow too?
Can I see another's grief,
And not seek for kind relief?

Can I see a falling tear,
And not feel my sorrow's share?
Can a father see his child
Weep, nor be with sorrow fill'd?

Can a mother sit and hear
An infant groan an infant fear: 10
No, no, never can it be!
Never, never can it be!

And can he who smiles on all
Hear the wren with sorrows small,
Hear the small bird's grief & care
Hear the woes that infants bear;

And not sit beside the nest
Pouring pity in their breast;
And not sit the cradle near
Weeping tear on infant's tear: 20

And not sit both night & day,
Wiping all our tears away?
O no, never can it be!
Never, never can it be!

He doth give his joy to all,
He becomes an infant small:
He becomes a man of woe,
He doth feel the sorrow too.

Think not thou canst sigh a sigh
And thy maker is not by; 30
Think not thou canst weep a tear
And thy maker is not near.

O! he gives to us his joy
That our grief he may destroy:
Till our grief is fled & gone
He doth sit by us and moan.

The Little Boy Lost

Father, father, where are you going?
O do not walk so fast.
Speak father, speak to your little boy
Or else I shall be lost.

The night was dark, no father was there,
The child was wet with dew.
The mire was deep, & the child did weep
And away the vapour flew.

The Little Boy Found

The little boy lost in the lonely fen,
Led by the wand'ring light,
Began to cry but God ever nigh
Appear'd like his father in white.

He kissed the child & by the hand led
And to his mother brought,
Who in sorrow pale thro' the lonely dale
Her little boy weeping sought.

SONGS OF EXPERIENCE

Introduction

Hear the voice of the Bard!
Who Present, Past & Future sees
Whose ears have heard
The Holy Word
That walk'd among the ancient trees,

Calling the lapsed Soul
And weeping in the evening dew:
That might controll
The starry pole,
And fallen fallen light renew! 10

O Earth, O Earth return!
Arise from out the dewy grass:
Night is worn,
And the morn
Rises from the slumberous mass.

Turn away no more:
Why wilt thou turn away?
The starry floor
The wat'ry shore
Is giv'n thee till the break of day. 20

Earth's Answer

Earth rais'd up her head,
From the darkness dread & drear.
Her light fled:
Stony dread!
And her locks cover'd with grey despair.

Prison'd on wat'ry shore
Starry Jealousy does keep my den:
Cold and hoar
Weeping o'er
I hear the Father of the ancient men. 10

Selfish father of men
Cruel, jealous selfish fear!
Can delight
Chain'd in night
The virgins of youth and morning bear?

Does spring hide its joy
When buds and blossoms grow?
Does the sower
Sow by night,
Or the plowman in darkness plow? 20

Break this heavy chain
That does freeze my bones around.
Selfish! vain,
Eternal bane!
That free Love with bondage bound.

Nurse's Song

When the voices of children are heard on the green
And whisp'rings are in the dale,
The days of my youth rise fresh in my mind,
My face turns green and pale.

Then come home my children, the sun is gone down
And the dews of night arise:
Your spring & your day are wasted in play
And your winter and night in disguise.

See 'Nurse's Song' in *Songs of Innocence*, p. 27

The Fly

Little Fly,
Thy summer's play
My thoughtless hand
Has brush'd away.

Am not I
A fly like thee?
Or art not thou
A man like me?

For I dance
And drink & sing, 10
Till some blind hand
Shall brush my wing.

If thought is life
And strength and breath;
And the want
Of thought is death;

Then am I
A happy fly,
If I live,
Or if I die. 20

The Tyger

Tyger, Tyger, burning bright,
In the forests of the night:
What immortal hand or eye,
Could frame thy fearful symmetry?

In what distant deeps or skies
Burnt the fire of thine eyes?
On what wings dare he aspire?
What the hand dare sieze the fire?

And what shoulder, & what art
Could twist the sinews of thy heart? 10
And when thy heart began to beat,
[n]What dread hand? & what dread feet?

What the hammer? what the chain,
In what furnace was thy brain?
What the anvil? what dread grasp
Dare its deadly terrors clasp?

When the stars threw down their spears
And water'd heaven with their tears,
Did he smile his work to see?
Did he who made the Lamb make thee? 20

Tyger, Tyger, burning bright
In the forests of the night:
What immortal hand or eye
Dare frame thy fearful symmetry?

See 'The Lamb' in *Songs of Innocence*, p. 22

[n]*The Little Girl Lost*

In futurity
I prophetic see
That the earth from sleep
(Grave the sentence deep)

Shall arise and seek
For her maker meek:
And the desart wild
Become a garden mild.

In the southern clime
Where the summer's prime 10
Never fades away,
Lovely Lyca lay.

Seven summers old
Lovely Lyca told;
She had wander'd long,
Hearing wild birds' song.

Sweet sleep come to me
Underneath this tree;
Do father, mother weep –
'Where can Lyca sleep?' 20

Lost in desart wild
Is your little child:
How can Lyca sleep
If her mother weep?

If her heart does ake,
Then let Lyca wake;
If my mother sleep
Lyca shall not weep.

Frowning frowning night,
O'er this desart bright 30
Let thy moon arise,
While I close my eyes.

Sleeping Lyca lay;
While the beasts of prey
Come from caverns deep,
View'd the maid asleep.

The kingly lion stood
And the virgin view'd,
Then he gambol'd round
O'er the hallow'd ground: 40

Leopards, tygers play
Round her as she lay;
While the lion old
Bow'd his mane of gold,

And her bosom lick,
And upon her neck
From his eyes of flame
Ruby tears there came;

While the lioness
Loos'd her slender dress, 50
And naked they convey'd
To caves the sleeping maid.

The Little Girl Found

All the night in woe
Lyca's parents go:
Over vallies deep,
While the desarts weep.

Tired and woe-begone,
Hoarse with making moan:
Arm in arm seven days
They trac'd the desart ways.

Seven nights they sleep
Among shadows deep: 10
And dream they see their child
Starv'd in desart wild.

Pale thro' pathless ways
The fancied image strays,
Famish'd, weeping, weak
With hollow piteous shriek.

Rising from unrest,
The trembling woman prest
With feet of weary woe;
She could no further go. 20

In his arms he bore
Her, arm'd with sorrow sore;
Till before their way
A couching lion lay.

Turning back was vain,
Soon his heavy mane
Bore them to the ground,
Then he stalk'd around,

Smelling to his prey,
But their fears allay, 30
When he licks their hands;
And silent by them stands.

They look upon his eyes
Fill'd with deep surprise:
And wondering behold
A spirit arm'd in gold,

On his head a crown,
On his shoulders down
Flow'd his golden hair;
Gone is all their care. 40

Follow me, he said,
Weep not for the maid;
In my palace deep
Lyca lies asleep.

Then they followed,
Where the vision led:
And saw their sleeping child
Among tygers wild.

To this day they dwell
In a lonely dell, 50
Nor fear the wolvish howl,
Nor the lion's growl.

Cp. 'A Little Girl Lost', p. 48

The Clod & the Pebble

Love seeketh not itself to please,
Nor for itself hath any care;
But for another gives its ease,
And builds a Heaven in Hell's despair.

So sang a little Clod of Clay,
Trodden with the cattle's feet:
But a Pebble of the brook
Warbled out these metres meet:

Love seeketh only Self to please,
To bind another to its delight; 10
Joys in another's loss of ease,
And builds a Hell in Heaven's despite.

The Little Vagabond

Dear Mother, dear Mother, the Church is cold,
But the Ale-house is healthy & pleasant & warm;
Besides I can tell where I am used well;
Such usage in heaven will never do well.

But if at the Church they would give us some Ale,
And a pleasant fire, our souls to regale;
We'd sing and we'd pray all the live-long day,
Nor ever once wish from the Church to stray,

Then the Parson might preach & drink & sing,
And we'd be as happy as birds in the spring: 10
And modest dame Lurch, who is alway at Church,
Would not have bandy children nor fasting nor birch.

And God like a father rejoicing to see
His children as pleasant and happy as he:
Would have no more quarrel with the Devil or the Barrel
But kiss him & give him both drink and apparel.

Holy Thursday

Is this a holy thing to see,
In a rich and fruitful land,
Babes reduced to misery,
Fed with cold and usurous hand?

Is that trembling cry a song?
Can it be a song of joy?
And so many children poor?
It is a land of poverty!

And their sun does never shine,
And their fields are bleak & bare, 10
And their ways are fill'd with thorns:
It is eternal winter there.

For where-e'er the sun does shine,
And where-e'er the rain does fall,
Babe can never hunger there,
Nor poverty the mind appall.

See 'Holy Thursday' in *Songs of Innocence*, p. 27

A Poison Tree

I was angry with my friend,
I told my wrath, my wrath did end.
I was angry with my foe:
I told it not, my wrath did grow:

And I water'd it in fears,
Night & morning with my tears;
And I sunned it with smiles,
And with soft deceitful wiles.

And it grew both day and night,
Till it bore an apple bright, 10
And my foe beheld it shine,
And he knew that it was mine,

And into the garden stole,
When the night had veil'd the pole:
In the morning glad I see
My foe outstretch'd beneath the tree.

The Angel

I Dreamt a Dream! what can it mean?
And that I was a maiden Queen,
Guarded by an Angel mild;
Witless woe was ne'er beguil'd!

And I wept both night and day
And he wip'd my tears away,
And I wept both day and night
And hid from him my heart's delight.

So he took his wings and fled:
Then the morn blush'd rosy red: 10
I dried my tears & arm'd my fears
With ten thousand shields and spears.

Soon my Angel came again:
I was arm'd, he came in vain:
For the time of youth was fled
And grey hairs were on my head.

See 'A Dream' in *Songs of Innocence*, p. 31

The Sick Rose

O Rose, thou art sick;
The invisible worm
That flies in the night
In the howling storm:

Has found out thy bed
Of crimson joy;
And his dark secret love
Does thy life destroy.

See 'The Blossom' in *Songs of Innocence*, p. 28

[n]*To Tirzah*

Whate'er is born of mortal birth
Must be consumed with the Earth
To rise from Generation free;
Then what have I to do with thee?

The Sexes sprung in Shame & Pride
Blow'd in the morn: in evening died:
But Mercy chang'd Death into Sleep;
The Sexes rose to work & weep.

Thou Mother of my Mortal Part
With cruelty didst mould my Heart, 10
And with false self-deceiving tears
Didst bind my Nostrils, Eyes & Ears,

Didst close my Tongue in senseless clay
And me to Mortal Life betray:
The death of Jesus set me free;
Then what have I to do with thee?

[n]*The Voice of the Ancient Bard*

Youth of delight, come hither:
And see the opening morn,
Image of truth new-born:
Doubt is fled & clouds of reason,
Dark disputes & artful teazing.
Folly is an endless maze,
Tangled roots perplex her ways,
How many have fallen there!
They stumble all night over bones of the dead;
And feel they know not what but care; 10
And wish to lead others when they should be led.

My Pretty Rose Tree

A flower was offer'd to me;
Such a flower as May never bore,
But I said, I've a Pretty Rose-tree,
And I passed the sweet flower o'er.

Then I went to my Pretty Rose-tree;
To tend her by day and by night,
But my Rose turn'd away with jealousy:
And her thorns were my only delight.

Ah! Sun-flower

Ah Sun-flower! weary of time
Who countest the steps of the Sun;
Seeking after that sweet golden clime
Where the traveller's journey is done,

Where the Youth pined away with desire,
And the pale Virgin shrouded in snow;
Arise from their graves and aspire
Where my Sun-flower wishes to go.

The Lilly

The modest Rose puts forth a thorn:
The humble Sheep, a threat'ning horn:
While the Lilly white shall in Love delight,
Nor a thorn nor a threat stain her beauty bright.

The Garden of Love

I went to the Garden of Love,
And saw what I never had seen:
A Chapel was built in the midst,
Where I used to play on the green.

And the gates of this Chapel were shut,
And *Thou shalt not* writ over the door;
So I turn'd to the Garden of Love
That so many sweet flowers bore,

And I saw it was filled with graves,
And tomb-stones where flowers should be: 10
And Priests in black gowns were walking their rounds,
And binding with briars my joys & desires.

A Little Boy Lost

Nought loves another as itself
Nor venerates another so,
Nor is it possible to Thought
A greater than itself to know:

And Father, how can I love you,
Or any of my brothers more?
I love you like the little bird
That picks up crumbs around the door.

The Priest sat by and heard the child,
In trembling zeal he siez'd his hair: 10
He led him by his little coat;
And all admir'd the Priestly care.

And standing on the altar high,
Lo, what a fiend is here! said he:
One who sets reason up for judge
Of our most holy Mystery.

The weeping child could not be heard,
The weeping parents wept in vain:
They strip'd him to his little shirt,
And bound him in an iron chain, 20

And burn'd him in a holy place,
Where many had been burn'd before:
The weeping parents wept in vain,
Are such things done on Albion's shore?

Infant Sorrow

My mother groan'd! my father wept,
Into the dangerous world I leapt:
Helpless, naked, piping loud;
Like a fiend hid in a cloud.

Struggling in my father's hands,
Striving against my swadling bands;
Bound and weary I thought best
To sulk upon my mother's breast.

See 'Infant Joy' in *Songs of Innocence*, p. 23

ⁿ*The School Boy*

I love to rise in a summer morn,
When the birds sing on every tree;
The distant huntsman winds his horn,
And the sky-lark sings with me.
O! what sweet company.

But to go to school in a summer morn
O! it drives all joy away:
Under a cruel eye outworn,
The little ones spend the day,
In sighing and dismay. 10

Ah! then at times I drooping sit,
And spend many an anxious hour.
Nor in my book can I take delight,
Nor sit in learning's bower,
Worn thro' with the dreary shower.

How can the bird that is born for joy
Sit in a cage and sing?
How can a child when fears annoy
But droop his tender wing
And forget his youthful spring? 20

O! father & mother, if buds are nip'd,
And blossoms blown away,
And if the tender plants are strip'd
Of their joy in the springing day
By sorrow and care's dismay,

How shall the summer arise in joy
Or the summer fruits appear
Or how shall we gather what griefs destroy
Or bless the mellowing year,
When the blasts of winter appear. 30

London

I wander thro' each charter'd street,
Near where the charter'd Thames does flow,
And mark in every face I meet
Marks of weakness, marks of woe.

In every cry of every Man,
In every Infant's cry of fear,
In every voice, in every ban,
The mind-forg'd manacles I hear.

How the Chimney-sweeper's cry
Every black'ning Church appalls, 10
And the hapless Soldier's sigh
Runs in blood down Palace walls:

But most thro' midnight streets I hear
How the youthful Harlot's curse
Blasts the new-born Infant's tear,
And blights with plagues the Marriage hearse.

A Little Girl Lost

Children of the future Age,
Reading this indignant page:
Know that in a former time
Love! sweet Love! was thought a crime.

In the Age of gold,
Free from winter's cold;
Youth and maiden bright,
To the holy light
Naked in the sunny beams delight.

Once a youthful pair 10
Fill'd with softest care,
Met in garden bright,
Where the holy light
Had just remov'd the curtains of the night.

There in rising day,
On the grass they play:
Parents were afar;
Strangers came not near,
And the maiden soon forgot her fear.

Tired with kisses sweet 20
They agree to meet,
When the silent sleep
Waves o'er heavens deep;
And the weary tired wanderers weep.

To her father white
Came the maiden bright:
But his loving look,
Like the holy book
All her tender limbs with terror shook.

Ona! pale and weak! 30
To thy father speak!
O the trembling fear!
O the heavy care!
That shakes the blossoms of my hoary hair!

The Chimney Sweeper

A little black thing among the snow
Crying 'weep 'weep! in notes of woe:
Where are thy father & mother? say?
They are both gone up to the church to pray.

Because I was happy upon the heath
And smil'd among the winter's snow:
They clothed me in the clothes of death
And taught me to sing the notes of woe.

And because I am happy, & dance & sing
They think they have done me no injury: 10
And are gone to praise God & his Priest & King
Who make up a heaven of our misery.

See 'The Chimney Sweeper' in *Songs of Innocence*, p. 28

The Human Abstract

Pity would be no more
If we did not make somebody Poor;
And Mercy no more could be
If all were as happy as we:

And mutual fear brings peace,
Till the selfish loves increase,
Then Cruelty knits a snare,
And spreads his baits with care.

He sits down with holy fears,
And waters the ground with tears: 10
Then Humility takes its root
Underneath his foot.

Soon spreads the dismal shade
Of Mystery over his head;
And the Catterpiller and Fly
Feed on the Mystery.

And it bears the fruit of Deceit,
Ruddy and sweet to eat;
And the Raven his nest has made
In its thickest shade. 20

The Gods of the earth and sea
Sought thro' Nature to find this Tree:
But their search was all in vain:
There grows one in the Human Brain.

See 'The Divine Image' in *Songs of Innocence*, p. 29

[n] *A Divine Image*

Cruelty has a Human Heart
And Jealousy a Human Face:
Terror, the Human Form Divine
And Secrecy, the Human Dress.

The Human Dress is forged Iron,
The Human Form, a fiery Forge;
The Human Face, a Furnace seal'd,
The Human Heart, its hungry Gorge.

NOTEBOOK POEMS: LAMBETH

Never pain to tell thy love
Love that never told can be,
For the gentle wind does move
Silently invisibly.

I told my love, I told my love
I told her all my heart:
Trembling cold in ghastly fears
Ah she doth depart!

Soon as she was gone from me
A traveller came by 10
Silently invisibly:
O was no deny.

I fear'd the fury of my wind
Would blight all blossoms fair & true,
And my sun it shin'd & shin'd
And my wind it never blew:

But a blossom fair or true
Was not found on any tree,
For all blossoms grew & grew
Fruitless false, tho' fair to see.

I saw a chapel all of gold
That none did dare to enter in,
And many weeping stood without
Weeping mourning worshipping.

I saw a serpent rise between
The white pillars of the door
And he forc'd & forc'd & forc'd,
Down the golden hinges tore,

And along the pavement sweet
Set with pearls & rubies bright 10
All his slimy length he drew,
Till upon the altar white

Vomiting his poison out
On the bread & on the wine –
So I turn'd into a sty
And laid me down among the swine.

A Cradle Song

Sleep Sleep, beauty bright,
Dreaming o'er the joys of night:
Sleep Sleep: in thy sleep
Little sorrows sit & weep.

Sweet Babe, in thy face
Soft desires I can trace,
Secret joys & secret smiles
Little pretty infant wiles.

As thy softest limbs I feel
Smiles as of the morning steal 10
O'er thy cheek & o'er thy breast
Where thy little heart does rest.

O the cunning wiles that creep
In thy little heart asleep:
When thy little heart does wake,
Then the dreadful lightnings break

From thy cheek & from thy eye
O'er the youthful harvests nigh:
Infant wiles & infant smiles
Heaven & Earth of peace beguiles. 20

I asked a thief to steal me a peach
He turned up his eyes:
I ask'd a lithe lady to lie her down
Holy & meek she cries –

As soon as I went
An angel came,
He wink'd at the thief
And smil'd at the dame –

And without one word said
Had a peach from the tree 10
And still as a maid
Enjoy'd the lady.

"In a Mirtle Shade

Why should I be bound to thee
O my lovely mirtle tree?
Love, free love cannot be bound
To any tree that grows on ground.

O how sick & weary I
Underneath my mirtle lie,
Like to dung upon the ground
Underneath my mirtle bound.

Oft my mirtle sigh'd in vain
To behold my heavy chain: 10
Oft my father saw us sigh
And laugh'd at our simplicity:

So I smote him & his gore
Stain'd the roots my mirtle bore:
But the time of youth is fled
And grey hairs are on my head.

An Answer to the Parson

Why of the sheep do you not learn peace?
Because I don't want you to shear my fleece.

Experiment

Thou hast a lap full of seed
And this is a fine country:
Why dost thou not cast thy seed
And live in it merrily?

Shall I cast it on the sand
And turn it into fruitful land?
For on no other ground
Can I sow my seed
Without tearing up
Some stinking weed. 10

Riches

The countless gold of a merry heart
The rubies & pearls of a loving eye;
The indolent never can bring to the mart,
Nor the secret hoard up in his treasury.

If you trap the moment before it's ripe
The tears of repentance you'll certainly wipe:
But if once you let the ripe moment go
You can never wipe off the tears of woe.

Eternity

He who binds to himself a joy
Does the winged life destroy:
But he who kisses the joy as it flies
Lives in eternity's sun rise.

I heard an Angel singing
When the day was springing:
Mercy Pity Peace
Is the world's release.

Thus he sung all day
Over the new mown hay
Till the sun went down
And haycocks looked brown.

I heard a Devil curse
Over the heath & the furze: 10
Mercy could be no more
If there was nobody poor

And pity no more could be
If all were as happy as we.
At his curse the sun went down
And the heavens gave a frown.

Down pour'd the heavy rain
Over the new reap'd grain,
And Miseries' increase
Is Mercy Pity Peace. 20

Silent Silent Night
Quench the holy light
Of thy torches bright.

For possess'd of Day
Thousand spirits stray
That sweet joys betray.

Why should joys be sweet
Used with deceit
Nor with sorrows meet?

But an honest joy 10
Does itself destroy
For a harlot coy.

Are not the joys of morning sweeter
Than the joys of night,
And are the vig'rous joys of youth
Ashamed of the light?

Let age & sickness silent rob
The vineyards in the night,
But those who burn with vig'rous youth
Pluck fruits before the light.

Love to faults is always blind
Always is to joy inclin'd,
Lawless wing'd & unconfin'd
And breaks all chains from every mind.

Deceit to secresy confin'd
Lawful cautious & refin'd
To every thing but interest blind
And forges fetters for the mind.

The Wild Flower's Song

As I wander'd the forest
The green leaves among
I heard a wild flower
Singing a song:

I slept in the earth
In the silent night
I murmur'd my fears
And I felt delight.

In the morning I went
As rosy as morn 10
To seek for new Joy
But I met with scorn.

Why should I care for the men of Thames
Or the cheating waves of charter'd streams
Or shrink at the little blasts of fear
That the hireling blows into my ear?

Tho' born on the cheating banks of Thames
Tho' his waters bathed my infant limbs,
The [n]Ohio shall wash his stains from me
I was born a slave but I go to be free.

The sword sung on the barren heath
The sickle in the fruitful field:
The sword he sung a song of death
But could not make the sickle yield.

Abstinence sows sand all over
The ruddy limbs & flaming hair,
But Desire Gratified
Plants fruits of life & beauty there.

An old maid early, ere I knew
Ought but the love that on me grew:
And now I'm cover'd o'er & o'er
And wish that I had been a Whore.

O I cannot cannot find
The undaunted courage of a Virgin Mind:
For Early I in love was crost
Before my flower of love was lost.

The look of love alarms
Because 'tis fill'd with fire:
But the look of soft deceit
Shall Win the lover's hire.

The Fairy

Come hither my sparrows
My little arrows
If a tear or a smile
Will a man beguile:
If an amorous delay
Clouds a sunshiny day,
If the step of a foot
Smites the heart to its root
'Tis the marriage ring
Makes each fairy a king. 10

So a fairy sung.
From the leaves I sprung:
He leap'd from the spray
To flee away.
But in my hat caught
He soon shall be taught:
Let him laugh let him cry
He's my butterfly
For I've pull'd out the Sting
Of the marriage ring. 20

THE BOOK OF THEL

Thel's Motto

Does the Eagle know what is in the pit,
Or wilt thou go ask the Mole?
Can Wisdom be put in a silver rod,
Or Love in a golden bowl?

I

[1] The daughters of Mne Seraphim led round their sunny
flocks,
All but the youngest: she in paleness sought the secret air,
To fade away like morning beauty from her mortal day:
Down by the river of Adona her soft voice is heard,
And thus her gentle lamentation falls like morning dew:—

O life of this our spring! why fades the lotus of the water?
Why fade these children of the spring, born but to smile &
fall?
Ah! Thel is like a wat'ry bow, and like a parting cloud,
Like a reflection in a glass; like shadows in the water:
Like dreams of infants, like a smile upon an infant's face, 10
Like the dove's voice, like transient day, like music in the air.
Ah! gentle may I lay me down, and gentle rest my head,
And gentle sleep the sleep of death, and gentle hear the voice
Of him that walketh in the garden in the evening time.

The Lilly of the valley breathing in the humble grass
Answer'd the lovely maid and said: I am a wat'ry weed,
And I am very small and love to dwell in lowly vales;
So weak, the gilded butterfly scarce perches on my head:
Yet I am visited from heaven, and he that smiles on all
Walks in the valley, and each morn over me spreads his hand 20
Saying: rejoice thou humble grass, thou new-born lilly
flower,
Thou gentle maid of silent valleys, and of modest brooks:

For thou shalt be clothed in light, and fed with morning
manna:
Till summer's heat melts thee beside the fountains and the
springs
To flourish in eternal vales: then why should Thel complain,
[2] Why should the mistress of the vales of Har utter a sigh?

She ceas'd & smil'd in tears, then sat down in her silver
shrine.

Thel answer'd: O thou little virgin of the peaceful valley,
Giving to those that cannot crave, the voiceless, the o'ertired,
Thy breath doth nourish the innocent lamb, he smells thy
milky garments, 30
He crops thy flowers, while thou sittest smiling in his face,
Wiping his mild and meekin mouth from all contagious
taints.
Thy wine doth purify the golden honey, thy perfume,
Which thou dost scatter on every little blade of grass that
springs
Revives the milked cow, & tames the fire-breathing steed.
But Thel is like a faint cloud kindled at the rising sun:
I vanish from my pearly throne, and who shall find my place?

Queen of the vales, the Lilly answer'd: Ask the tender cloud,
And it shall tell thee why it glitters in the morning sky,
And why it scatters its bright beauty thro' the humid air; 40
Descend O little Cloud, & hover before the eyes of Thel.

The Cloud descended, and the Lilly bow'd her modest head
And went to mind her numerous charge among the verdant
grass.

II

[3] O little Cloud, the virgin said, I charge thee tell to me
Why thou complainest not when in one hour thou fade
away:
Then we shall seek thee, but not find: ah! Thel is like to
thee;
I pass away, yet I complain, and no one hears my voice.

The Cloud then shew'd his golden head & his bright form emerg'd,
Hovering and glittering on the air before the face of Thel.

O virgin know'st thou not, our steeds drink of the golden springs
Where Luvah doth renew his horses: Look'st thou on my youth,
And fearest thou, because I vanish and am seen no more,
Nothing remains: O maid, I tell thee, when I pass away 10
It is to tenfold life, to love, to peace, and raptures holy:
Unseen descending, weigh my light wings upon balmy flowers,
And court the fair-eyed dew to take me to her shining tent:
The weeping virgin trembling kneels before the risen sun,
Till we arise link'd in a golden band and never part,
But walk united, bearing food to all our tender flowers.

Dost thou, O little Cloud? I fear that I am not like thee,
For I walk through the vales of Har, and smell the sweetest flowers;
But I feed not the little flowers: I hear the warbling birds,
But I feed not the warbling birds; they fly and seek their food. 20
But Thel delights in these no more because I fade away;
And all shall say, Without a use this shining woman liv'd,
Or did she only live to be at death the food of worms?

The Cloud reclin'd upon his airy throne and answer'd thus:

Then if thou art the food of worms, O virgin of the skies,
How great thy use, how great thy blessing! Every thing that lives,
Lives not alone nor for itself: fear not, and I will call
The weak worm from its lowly bed, and thou shalt hear its voice.
Come forth, worm of the silent valley, to thy pensive queen.

The helpless worm arose, and sat upon the Lilly's leaf, 30
And the bright Cloud sail'd on, to find his partner in the vale.

III

[4] Then Thel astonish'd view'd the Worm upon its dewy bed.

Art thou a Worm? Image of weakness, art thou but a Worm?
I see thee like an infant wrapped in the Lilly's leaf:
Ah! weep not, little voice, thou canst not speak; but thou
canst weep.
Is this a Worm? I see thee lay helpless & naked, weeping,
And none to answer, none to cherish thee with mother's
smiles.

The Clod of Clay heard the Worm's voice, & rais'd her
pitying head:
She bow'd over the weeping infant, and her life exhal'd
In milky fondness: then on Thel she fix'd her humble eyes.

O beauty of the vales of Har, we live not for ourselves; 10
Thou seest me the meanest thing, and so I am indeed,
My bosom of itself is cold, and of itself is dark;

[5] But he that loves the lowly pours his oil upon my head,
And kisses me, and binds his nuptial bands around my breast,
And says: Thou mother of my children, I have loved thee,
And I have given thee a crown that none can take away:
But how this is, sweet maid, I know not, and I cannot know;
I ponder, and I cannot ponder; yet I live and love.

The daughter of beauty wip'd her pitying tears with her
white veil,
And said: Alas! I knew not this, and therefore did I weep: 20
That God would love a Worm I knew, and punish the evil
foot
That wilful bruis'd its helpless form: but that he cherish'd it
With milk and oil, I never knew; and therefore did I weep,
And I complain'd in the mild air, because I fade away,
And lay me down in thy cold bed, and leave my shining lot.

Queen of the vales, the matron Clay answer'd, I heard thy
sighs,
And all thy moans flew o'er my roof, but I have call'd them
down.

Wilt thou, O Queen, enter my house? 'Tis given thee to
enter
And to return; fear nothing, enter with thy virgin feet.

IV

[6] The eternal gates' terrific porter lifted the northern bar:
Thel enter'd in & saw the secrets of the land unknown.
She saw the couches of the dead, & where the fibrous roots
Of every heart on earth infixes deep its restless twists:
A land of sorrows & of tears where never smile was seen.

She wander'd in the land of clouds thro' valleys dark,
list'ning
Dolours & lamentations: waiting oft beside a dewy grave
She stood in silence, list'ning to the voices of the ground,
Till to her own grave plot she came & there she sat down;
And heard this voice of sorrow breathed from the hollow pit: 10

Why cannot the Ear be closed to its own destruction?
Or the glist'ning Eye to the poison of a smile?
Why are Eyelids stor'd with arrows ready drawn,
Where a thousand fighting men in ambush lie?
Or an Eye of gifts & graces show'ring fruits & coined gold?
Why a Tongue impress'd with honey from every wind?
Why an Ear, a whirlpool fierce to draw creations in?
Why a Nostril wide inhaling terror, trembling, & affright?
Why a tender curb upon the youthful burning boy?
Why a little curtain of flesh on the bed of our desire? 20

The Virgin started from her seat & with a shriek
Fled back unhinder'd, till she came into the vales of Har.

THE MARRIAGE OF HEAVEN AND HELL

[2] *The Argument*

Rintrah roars, & shakes his fires in the burden'd air:
Hungry clouds swag on the deep.

Once meek, and in a perilous path
The just man kept his course along
The vale of death.
Roses are planted where thorns grow
And on the barren heath
Sing the honey bees.

Then the perilous path was planted,
And a river and a spring 10
On every cliff and tomb;
And on the bleached bones
[n]Red clay brought forth:

Till the villain left the paths of ease
To walk in perilous paths, and drive
The just man into barren climes.

Now the sneaking serpent walks
In mild humility:
And the just man rages in the wilds
Where lions roam. 20

Rintrah roars, & shakes his fires in the burden'd air:
Hungry clouds swag on the deep.

[3] As [n]a new heaven is begun, and it is now thirty-three years since its advent: the Eternal Hell revives. And lo! Swedenborg is the Angel sitting at the tomb: his writings are the linen clothes folded up. Now is the dominion of [n]Edom, & the return of Adam into Paradise: see Isaiah xxxiv & xxxv Chap.

Without Contraries is no progression. Attraction and Repulsion, Reason and Energy, Love and Hate, are necessary to Human existence.

From these contraries spring what the religious call Good & Evil. Good is the passive that obeys Reason. Evil is the active springing from Energy. 10

Good is Heaven. Evil is Hell.

[4] *The Voice of the Devil*

All Bibles or sacred codes have been the causes of the following Errors:

1. That Man has two real existing principles, Viz: a Body & a Soul.

2. That Energy, call'd Evil, is alone from the Body; & that Reason, call'd Good, is alone from the Soul.

3. That God will torment Man in Eternity for following his Energies.

But the following Contraries to these are True:

1. Man has no Body distinct from his Soul; for that call'd Body is a portion of Soul discern'd by the five Senses, the chief inlets of Soul in this age. 10

2. Energy is the only life and is from the Body: and Reason is the bound or outward circumference of Energy.

3. Energy is Eternal Delight.

*

[5] Those who restrain desire, do so because theirs is weak enough to be restrained; and the restrainer or reason usurps its place & governs the unwilling.

And being restrain'd it by degrees becomes passive till it is only the shadow of desire.

The history of this is written in Paradise Lost, & the Governor or Reason is call'd Messiah.

And the original Archangel or possessor of the command of the heavenly host, is call'd the Devil or Satan, and his children are call'd Sin & Death. 10

But in the Book of Job, Milton's Messiah is call'd [n]Satan:

For this history has been adopted by both parties.

It indeed appear'd to Reason as if Desire was cast out; but

[6] the Devil's account is, that the Messiah fell, & formed a heaven of what he stole from the Abyss.

This is shewn in the Gospel, where he prays to the Father to send the comforter or Desire; that Reason may have Ideas to build on: the Jehovah of the Bible being no other than he who dwells in flaming fire. Know that after Christ's death, he became Jehovah.

But in Milton, the Father is Destiny, the Son a Ratio of the five senses, & the Holy-ghost, Vacuum!

Note: The reason Milton wrote in fetters when he wrote of Angels & God, and at liberty when of Devils & Hell, is because he was a true Poet and of the Devil's party without knowing it. 10

A Memorable Fancy

As I was walking among the fires of hell, delighted with the enjoyments of Genius, which to Angels look like torment and insanity, I collected some of their Proverbs, thinking that as the sayings used in a nation mark its character, so the Proverbs of Hell show the nature of Infernal wisdom better than any description of buildings or garments.

When I came home; on the abyss of the five senses, where a flat sided steep frowns over the present world, I saw a mighty Devil folded in black clouds, hovering on the sides of the rock; 20
[7] with ⁿcorroding fires he wrote the following sentence now percieved by the minds of men, & read by them on earth:

How do you know but ev'ry Bird that cuts the airy way,
Is an immense world of delight, clos'd by your senses five?

Proverbs of Hell

In seed time learn, in harvest teach, in winter enjoy.
Drive your cart and your plow over the bones of the dead.
The road of excess leads to the palace of wisdom.
Prudence is a rich, ugly old maid courted by Incapacity.
He who desires but acts not, breeds pestilence.

The cut worm forgives the plow. 10
Dip him in the river who loves water.
A fool sees not the same tree that a wise man sees.
He whose face gives no light, shall never become a star.
Eternity is in love with the productions of time.
The busy bee has no time for sorrow.
The hours of folly are measur'd by the clock, but of wisdom, no clock can measure.
All wholesome food is caught without a net or a trap.
Bring out number, weight & measure in a year of dearth.
No bird soars too high, if he soars with his own wings.
A dead body revenges not injuries. 20
The most sublime act is to set another before you.
If the fool would persist in his folly he would become wise.
Folly is the cloke of knavery.
Shame is Pride's cloke.

[8] Prisons are built with stones of Law, Brothels with bricks of Religion.
The pride of the peacock is the glory of God.
The lust of the goat is the bounty of God.
The wrath of the lion is the wisdom of God.
The nakedness of woman is the work of God.
Excess of sorrow laughs. Excess of joy weeps.
The roaring of lions, the howling of wolves, the raging of the stormy sea, and the destructive sword, are portions of eternity too great for the eye of man.
The fox condemns the trap, not himself.
Joys impregnate. Sorrows bring forth.
Let man wear the fell of the lion, woman the fleece of the sheep. 10
The bird a nest, the spider a web, man friendship.
The selfish, smiling fool, & the sullen, frowning fool shall be both thought wise, that they may be a rod.
What is now proved was once only imagin'd.
The rat, the mouse, the fox, the rabbet watch the roots; the lion, the tyger, the horse, the elephant watch the fruits.
The cistern contains: the fountain overflows.
One thought fills immensity.

Always be ready to speak your mind, and a base man will avoid you.

Every thing possible to be believ'd is an image of truth.

The eagle never lost so much time as when he submitted to learn of the crow.

[9] The fox provides for himself, but God provides for the lion.

Think in the morning. Act in the noon. Eat in the evening. Sleep in the night.

He who has suffer'd you to impose on him, knows you.

As the plow follows words, so God rewards prayers.

The tygers of wrath are wiser than the horses of instruction.

Expect poison from the standing water.

You never know what is enough unless you know what is more than enough.

Listen to the fool's reproach! it is a kingly title!

The eyes of fire, the nostrils of air, the mouth of water, the beard of earth.

The weak in courage is strong in cunning. 10

The apple tree never asks the beech how he shall grow; nor the lion, the horse, how he shall take his prey.

The thankful reciever bears a plentiful harvest.

If others had not been foolish, we should be so.

The soul of sweet delight can never be defil'd.

When thou seest an Eagle, thou seest a portion of Genius; lift up thy head!

As the catterpiller chooses the fairest leaves to lay her eggs on, so the priest lays his curse on the fairest joys.

To create a little flower is the labour of ages.

Damn braces: Bless relaxes.

The best wine is the oldest, the best water the newest.

Prayers plow not! Praises reap not! 20

Joys laugh not! Sorrows weep not!

[10] The head Sublime, the heart Pathos, the genitals Beauty, the hands & feet Proportion.

As the air to a bird or the sea to a fish, so is contempt to the contemptible.

The crow wish'd every thing was black, the owl that every thing was white.

Exuberance is Beauty.

If the lion was advised by the fox, he would be cunning.

Improvement makes strait roads: but the crooked roads without Improvement are roads of Genius.

Sooner murder an infant in its cradle than nurse unacted desires.

Where man is not, nature is barren.

Truth can never be told so as to be understood, and not be believ'd.

Enough! or Too much. 10

[11] The ancient Poets animated all sensible objects with Gods or Geniuses, calling them by the names and adorning them with the properties of woods, rivers, mountains, lakes, cities, nations, and whatever their enlarged & numerous senses could percieve.

And particularly they studied the genius of each city & country, placing it under its mental deity:

Till a system was formed, which some took advantage of & enslav'd the vulgar by attempting to realize or abstract the mental deities from their objects: thus began Priesthood; 10

Choosing forms of worship from poetic tales.

And at length they pronounc'd that the Gods had order'd such things.

Thus men forgot that All deities reside in the human breast.

[12] *A Memorable Fancy*

The Prophets Isaiah and Ezekiel dined with me, and I asked them how they dared so roundly to assert that God spoke to them; and whether they did not think at the time that they would be misunderstood, & so be the cause of imposition.

Isaiah answer'd: I saw no God, nor heard any, in a finite organical perception; but my senses discover'd the infinite in everything, and as I was then perswaded, & remain confirm'd, that the voice of honest indignation is the voice of God, I cared not for consequences, but wrote.

Then I asked: does a firm perswasion that a thing is so, make it so? 10

He replied: All poets believe that it does, & in ages of imagination this firm perswasion removed mountains; but many are not capable of a firm perswasion of any thing.

Then Ezekiel said: The philosophy of the east taught the first principles of human perception: some nations held one principle for the origin, & some another; we of Israel taught that the Poetic Genius (as you now call it) was the first principle and all the others merely derivative, which was the cause of our despising the Priests & Philosophers of other 20 [13] countries, and prophecying that all Gods would at last be proved to originate in ours & to be the tributaries of the Poetic Genius; it was this that our great poet, King David, desired so fervently & invokes so pathetic'ly, saying by this he conquers enemies & governs kingdoms; and we so loved our God, that we cursed in his name all the deities of surrounding nations, and asserted that they had rebelled: from these opinions the vulgar came to think that all nations would at last be subject to the Jews.

This, said he, like all firm perswasions, is come to pass; for 10 all nations believe the Jews' code and worship the Jews' god, and what greater subjection can be?

I heard this with some wonder, & must confess my own conviction. After dinner I ask'd Isaiah to favour the world with his lost works; he said none of equal value was lost. Ezekiel said the same of his.

I also asked Isaiah what made him go naked and barefoot three years? he answer'd: the same that made our friend Diogenes, the Grecian.

I then asked Ezekiel why he eat dung, & lay so long on his 20 right & left side? he answer'd, the desire of raising other men into a perception of the infinite: this the North American tribes practise, & is he honest who resists his genius or conscience only for the sake of present ease or gratification?

[14] The ancient tradition that the world will be consumed in fire at the end of six thousand years is true, as I have heard from Hell.

For the cherub with his flaming sword is hereby commanded to leave his guard at tree of life: and when he does, the whole creation will be consumed and appear infinite and holy, whereas it now appears finite & corrupt.

This will come to pass by an improvement of sensual enjoyment.

But first the notion that man has a body distinct from his soul is to be expunged; this I shall do by printing in the 10 infernal method, by corrosives, which in Hell are salutary and medicinal, melting apparent surfaces away, and displaying the infinite which was hid.

If the doors of perception were cleansed every thing would appear to man as it is, infinite.

For man has closed himself up, till he sees all things thro' narrow chinks of his cavern.

[15] *A Memorable Fancy*

I was in a Printing house in [n]Hell, & saw the method in which knowledge is transmitted from generation to generation.

In the first chamber was a Dragon-Man, clearing away the rubbish from a cave's mouth; within, a number of Dragons were hollowing the cave.

In the second chamber was a Viper folding round the rock & the cave, and others adorning it with gold, silver and precious stones.

In the third chamber was an Eagle with wings and feathers of air; he caused the inside of the cave to be infinite; around 10 were numbers of Eagle-like men who built palaces in the immense cliffs.

In the fourth chamber were Lions of flaming fire, raging around & melting the metals into living fluids.

In the fifth chamber were Unnam'd forms, which cast the metals into the expanse.

There they were reciev'd by Men who occupied the sixth chamber, and took the forms of books & were arranged in libraries.

[16] The Giants who formed this world into its sensual existence and now seem to live in it in chains, are in truth the causes of its life & the sources of all activity: but the chains are the cunning of weak and tame minds which have power to resist energy; according to the proverb, the weak in courage is strong in cunning.

Thus one portion of being is the Prolific, the other the Devouring: to the devourer it seems as if the producer was in his chains; but it is not so, he only takes portions of existence and fancies that the whole. 10

But the Prolific would cease to be Prolific unless the Devourer as a sea recieved the excess of his delights.

Some will say: Is not God alone the Prolific? I answer: God only Acts & Is, in existing beings or Men.

These two classes of men are always upon earth, & they [17] should be enemies: whoever tries to reconcile them seeks to destroy existence.

Religion is an endeavour to reconcile the two.

Note: "Jesus Christ did not wish to unite, but to seperate them, as in the Parable of sheep and goats! & he says: I came not to send Peace, but a Sword.

Messiah or Satan or Tempter was formerly thought to be one of the Antediluvians who are our Energies.

A Memorable Fancy

An Angel came to me and said: O pitiable foolish young man! O horrible! O dreadful state! consider the hot burning 10 dungeon thou art preparing for thyself to all eternity, to which thou art going in such career.

I said: perhaps you will be willing to shew me my eternal lot, & we will contemplate together upon it; and see whether your lot or mine is most desirable.

So he took me thro' a stable & thro' a church & down into the church vault at the end of which was a mill: thro' the mill we went, and came to a cave; down the winding cavern we groped our tedious way till a void boundless as a nether sky appear'd beneath us, & we held by the roots of trees and hung 20 over this immensity; but I said: if you please, we will commit ourselves to this void, and see whether providence is here also; if you will not I will: but he answer'd: do not presume O young man, but as we here remain behold thy lot which will soon appear when the darkness passes away.

[18] So I remain'd with him, sitting in the twisted root of an oak; he was suspended in a fungus which hung with the head downward into the deep.

By degrees we beheld the infinite Abyss, fiery as the smoke of a burning city; beneath us at an immense distance was the sun, black but shining; round it were fiery tracks on which revolv'd vast spiders, crawling after their prey, which flew or rather swum in the infinite deep, in the most terrific shapes of animals sprung from corruption: & the air was full of them, & seem'd composed of them; these are Devils, and are called Powers of the air. I now asked my companion which was my eternal lot? he said: between the black & white spiders. 10

But now, from between the black & white spiders a cloud and fire burst and rolled thro' the deep, black'ning all beneath, so that the nether deep grew black as a sea & rolled with a terrible noise: beneath us was nothing now to be seen but a black tempest, till looking east between the clouds & the waves, we saw a cataract of blood mixed with fire, and not many stones' throw from us appear'd and sunk again the scaly fold of a monstrous serpent. At last, to the east, distant about three degrees, appear'd a fiery crest above the waves: slowly it reared like a ridge of golden rocks, till we discover'd two globes of crimson fire, from which the sea fled away in clouds of smoke; and now we saw it was the head of Leviathan; his forehead was divided into streaks of green & purple like those on a tyger's forehead: soon we saw his mouth & red gills hang just above the raging foam, tinging the black deep with beams [19] of blood, advancing toward us with all the fury of a spiritual existence. 20

My friend the Angel climb'd up from his station into the mill: I remain'd alone, & then this appearance was no more, but I found myself sitting on a pleasant bank beside a river by moonlight, hearing a harper, who sung to the harp; & his theme was: The man who never alters his opinion is like standing water, & breeds reptiles of the mind.

But I arose, and sought for the mill, & there I found my Angel, who surprised, asked me, how I escaped? 10

I answer'd: All that we saw was owing to your metaphysics: for when you ran away, I found myself on a bank by moonlight, hearing a harper. But now we have seen my eternal lot, shall I shew you yours? He laugh'd at my proposal; but I by force suddenly caught him in my arms, & flew westerly thro' the night, till we were elevated above the earth's shadow: then I flung myself with him directly into the body of the sun; here I clothed myself in white, & taking in my hand Swedenborg's volumes, sunk from the glorious clime, and passed all the planets till we came to Saturn; here I stay'd to rest & then 20 leap'd into the void between Saturn & the fixed stars.

Here, said I, is your lot, in this space: if space it may be call'd. Soon we saw the stable and the church, & I took him to the altar and open'd the Bible, and lo! it was a deep pit, into which I descended driving the Angel before me; soon we saw [20] seven houses of brick; one we enter'd: in it were a number of monkeys, baboons, & all of that species, chain'd by the middle, grinning and snatching at one another, but witheld by the shortness of their chains: however, I saw that they sometimes grew numerous, and then the weak were caught by the strong, and with a grinning aspect, first coupled with, & then devour'd, by plucking off first one limb and then another, till the body was left a helpless trunk: this after grinning & kissing it with seeming fondness, they devour'd too; and here & there I saw one savourily picking the flesh off of his own tail; as the 10 stench terribly annoy'd us both we went into the mill, & I in my hand brought the skeleton of a body, which in the mill was Aristotle's Analytics.

So the Angel said: thy phantasy has imposed upon me, & thou oughtest to be ashamed.

I answer'd: we impose on one another, & it is but lost time to converse with you whose works are only Analytics.

Opposition is true Friendship.

[21] I have always found that Angels have the vanity to speak of themselves as the only wise; this they do with a confident insolence sprouting from systematic reasoning.

Thus Swedenborg boasts that what he writes is new, tho' it is only the Contents or Index of already publish'd books.

A man carried a monkey about for a shew, & because he was a little wiser than the monkey grew vain, and conciev'd himself as much wiser than seven men. It is so with Swedenborg: he shews the folly of churches, & exposes hypocrites, till he imagines that all are religious, & himself 10
[22] the single one on earth that ever broke a net.

Now hear a plain fact: Swedenborg has not written one new truth. Now hear another: he has written all the old falshoods.

And now hear the reason. He conversed with Angels who are all religious, & conversed not with Devils who all hate religion, for he was incapable thro' his conceited notions.

Thus Swedenborg's writings are a recapitulation of all superficial opinions and an analysis of the more sublime – but no further.

Have now another plain fact. Any man of mechanical 10
talents may from the writings of [n]Paracelsus or Jacob Behmen, produce ten thousand volumes of equal value with Swedenborg's, and from those of Dante or Shakespear an infinite number.

But when he has done this, let him not say that he knows better than his master, for he only holds a candle in sunshine.

A Memorable Fancy

Once I saw a Devil in a flame of fire, who arose before an Angel that sat on a cloud, and the Devil utter'd these words: The worship of God is: Honouring his gifts in other men, each
[23] according to his genius, and loving the greatest men best: those who envy or calumniate great men hate God, for there is no other God.

The Angel hearing this became almost blue, but mastering

himself he grew yellow, & at last white, pink, & smiling, and then replied:

Thou Idolater! is not God One? & is not he visible in Jesus Christ? and has not Jesus Christ given his sanction to the law of ten commandments? and are not all other men fools, sinners, & nothings? 10

The Devil answer'd: bray a fool in a morter with wheat, yet shall not his folly be beaten out of him: if Jesus Christ is the greatest man, you ought to love him in the greatest degree; now hear how he has given his sanction to the law of ten commandments: did he not mock at the sabbath, and so mock the sabbath's God? murder those who were murder'd because of him? turn away the law from the woman taken in adultery? steal the labour of others to support him? bear false witness when he omitted making a defence before Pilate? covet when he pray'd for his disciples, and when he bid them shake off the 20 dust of their feet against such as refused to lodge them? I tell you, no virtue can exist without breaking these ten command-[24] ments. Jesus was all virtue, and acted from impulse, not from rules.

When he had so spoken, I beheld the Angel, who stretched out his arms embracing the flame of fire, & he was consumed and arose as Elijah.

Note: This Angel, who is now become a Devil, is my particular friend; we often read the Bible together in its infernal or diabolical sense, which the world shall have if they behave well.

I have also "the Bible of Hell, which the world shall have 10 whether they will or no.

One Law for the Lion & Ox is Oppression.

[25] *A Song of Liberty*

1. The Eternal Female groan'd! it was heard over all the Earth.

2. Albion's coast is sick silent; the American meadows faint!

3. Shadows of Prophecy shiver along by the lakes and the

rivers and mutter across the ocean. France, rend down thy dungeon!

4. Golden Spain, burst the barriers of old Rome!

5. Cast thy keys, O Rome, into the deep down falling, even to eternity down falling.

6. And weep. 10

7. In her trembling hands she took the new born terror, howling:

8. On those infinite mountains of light now barr'd out by the Atlantic sea, the new born fire stood before the starry king!

9. Flag'd with grey brow'd snows and thunderous visages, the jealous wings wav'd over the deep.

10. The speary hand burned aloft, unbucklěd was the shield; forth went the hand of jealousy among the flaming hair, and [26] hurl'd the new born wonder thro' the starry night.

11. The fire, the fire is falling!

12. Look up! look up! O citizen of London, enlarge thy countenance! O Jew, leave counting gold! return to thy oil and wine. O African! black African! (go, winged thought, widen his forehead.)

13. The fiery limbs, the flaming hair, shot like the sinking sun into the western sea.

14. Wak'd from his eternal sleep, the hoary element roaring fled away: 10

15. Down rush'd, beating his wings in vain, the jealous king; his grey brow'd councellors, thunderous warriors, curl'd veterans, among helms, and shields, and chariots, horses, elephants, banners, castles, slings, and rocks,

16. Falling, rushing, ruining! buried in the ruins, on Urthona's dens.

17. All night beneath the ruins; then, their sullen flames faded, emerge round the gloomy King.

18. With thunder and fire, leading his starry hosts thro' the [27] waste wilderness, he promulgates his ten commands, glancing his beamy eyelids over the deep in dark dismay,

19. Where the son of fire in his eastern cloud, while the morning plumes her golden breast,

20. Spurning the clouds written with curses, stamps the stony

law to dust, loosing the eternal horses from the dens of night, crying

Empire is no more! and now the lion & wolf shall cease.

Chorus

Let the Priests of the Raven of dawn no longer, in deadly black, with hoarse note curse the sons of joy. Nor his accepted brethren whom, tyrant, he calls free, lay the bound or build the roof. Nor pale religious letchery call that virginity that wishes but acts not!

For every thing that lives is Holy.

from
VISIONS OF THE DAUGHTERS OF ALBION

The Eye sees more than the Heart knows.

The Argument

I loved Theotormon
And I was not ashamed,
I trembled in my virgin fears
And I hid in Leutha's vale!

I plucked Leutha's flower,
And I rose up from the vale;
But the terrible thunders tore
My virgin mantle in twain.

[1]

Visions

Enslav'd, the Daughters of Albion weep: a trembling lamentation
Upon their mountains; in their valleys, sighs toward America.

For the soft soul of America, Oothoon, wander'd in woe,
Along the vales of Leutha seeking flowers to comfort her;
And thus she spoke to the bright Marygold of Leutha's vale:

Art thou a flower! art thou a nymph! I see thee now a flower;
Now a nymph! I dare not pluck thee from thy dewy bed?

The Golden nymph replied; pluck thou my flower, Oothoon the mild:
Another flower shall spring, because the soul of sweet delight
Can never pass away. She ceas'd & clos'd her golden shrine. 10

Then Oothoon pluck'd the flower saying, I pluck thee from
thy bed
Sweet flower, and put thee here to glow between my breasts;
And thus I turn my face to where my whole soul seeks.

Over the waves she went in wing'd exulting swift delight,
And over Theotormon's reign took her impetuous course.

Bromion rent her with his thunders: on his stormy bed
Lay the faint maid, and soon her woes appall'd his thunders
hoarse.

Bromion spoke: Behold this harlot here on Bromion's bed,
And let the jealous dolphins sport around the lovely maid;
Thy soft American plains are mine, and mine thy north &
south: 20
Stampt with my signet are the swarthy children of the sun:
They are obedient, they resist not, they obey the scourge:
Their daughters worship terrors and obey the violent:
[2] Now thou maist marry Bromion's harlot, and protect the
child
Of Bromion's rage, that Oothoon shall put forth in nine
moons' time.

Then storms rent Theotormon's limbs; he roll'd his waves
around,
And folded his black jealous waters round the adulterate pair.
Bound back to back in Bromion's caves terror & meekness
dwell.

At entrance Theotormon sits, wearing the threshold hard
With secret tears; beneath him sound like waves on a desart
shore
The voice of slaves beneath the sun, and children bought with
money,
That shiver in religious caves beneath the burning fires
Of lust, that belch incessant from the summits of the earth. 10

Oothoon weeps not: she cannot weep! her tears are locked up;
But she can howl incessant, writhing her soft snowy limbs,
And calling Theotormon's Eagles to prey upon her flesh:

I call with holy voice! kings of the sounding air,
Rend away this defiled bosom that I may reflect.
The image of Theotormon on my pure transparent breast.

The Eagles at her call descend & rend their bleeding prey;
Theotormon severely smiles, her soul reflects the smile;
As the clear spring mudded with feet of beasts grows pure & smiles.

The Daughters of Albion hear her woes, & eccho back her sighs. 20

Why does my Theotormon sit weeping upon the threshold,
And Oothoon hovers by his side, perswading him in vain?
I cry, arise O Theotormon! for the village dog
Barks at the breaking day, the nightingale has done lamenting,
The lark does rustle in the ripe corn, and the Eagle returns
From nightly prey, and lifts his golden beak to the pure east;
Shaking the dust from his immortal pinions to awake
The sun that sleeps too long. Arise, my Theotormon I am pure,
Because the night is gone that clos'd me in its deadly black.
They told me that the night & day were all that I could see; 30
They told me that I had five senses to inclose me up.
And they inclos'd my infinite brain into a narrow circle.
And sunk my heart into the Abyss, a red round globe hot burning
Till all from life I was obliterated and erased.
Instead of morn arises a bright shadow, like an eye
In the eastern cloud: instead of night a sickly charnel house,
That Theotormon hears me not! to him the night and morn
Are both alike: a night of sighs, a morning of fresh tears;
[3] And none but Bromion can hear my lamentations . . .

*

Silent I hover all the night, and all day could be silent.
If Theotormon once would turn his loved eyes upon me;
How can I be defil'd when I reflect thy image pure?

Sweetest the fruit that the worm feeds on, & the soul prey'd
on by woe,
The new wash'd lamb ting'd with the village smoke & the
bright swan
By the red earth of our immortal river: I bathe my wings.
And I am white and pure to hover round Theotormon's
breast.

*

[4] . . . Then Bromion said, and shook the cavern with his
lamentation:

Thou knowest that the ancient trees seen by thine eyes have
fruit;
But knowest thou that trees and fruits flourish upon the
earth
To gratify senses unknown? trees beasts and birds unknown:
Unknown, not unperciev'd, spread in the infinite microscope,
In places yet unvisited by the voyager, and in worlds
Over another kind of seas, and in atmospheres unknown:
Ah! are there other wars, beside the wars of sword and fire?
And are there other sorrows, beside the sorrows of poverty?
And are there other joys, beside the joys of riches and ease? 10
And is there not one law for both the lion and the ox?
And is there not eternal fire, and eternal chains?
To bind the phantoms of existence from eternal life?

Then Oothoon waited silent all the day, and all the night,
[5] But when the morn arose, her lamentation renew'd,

*The Daughters of Albion hear her woes, & eccho back her
sighs.*

O Urizen! Creator of men! mistaken Demon of heaven:
Thy joys are tears! thy labour vain, to form men to thine
image.
How can one joy absorb another? are not different joys
Holy, eternal, infinite! and each joy is a Love.

Does not the great mouth laugh at a gift? & the narrow
eyelids mock

At the labour that is above payment; and wilt thou take the
ape
For thy councellor? or the dog, for a schoolmaster to thy
children?
Does he who contemns poverty, and he who turns with
abhorrence 10
From usury, feel the same passion or are they moved alike?
How can the giver of gifts experience the delights of the
merchant?
How the industrious citizen the pains of the husbandman.
How different far the fat fed hireling with hollow drum,
Who buys whole corn fields into wastes, and sings upon the
heath:
How different their eye and ear! how different the world to
them!
With what sense does the parson claim the labour of the
farmer?
What are his nets & gins & traps, & how does he surround
him
With cold floods of abstraction, and with forests of solitude,
To build him castles and high spires, where kings & priests
may dwell. 20
Till she who burns with youth, and knows no fixed lot, is
bound
In spells of law to one she loaths: and must she drag the chain
Of life, in weary lust! must chilling murderous thoughts
obscure
The clear heaven of her eternal spring? to bear the wintry
rage
Of a harsh terror, driv'n to madness, bound to hold a rod
Over her shrinking shoulders all the day; & all the night
To turn the wheel of false desire: and longings that wake her
womb
To the abhorred birth of cherubs in the human form
That live a pestilence & die a meteor & are no more:
Till the child dwell with one he hates, and do the deed he
loaths 30

And the impure scourge force his seed into its unripe birth
Ere yet his eyelids can behold the arrows of the day.

Does the whale worship at thy footsteps as the hungry dog?
Or does he scent the mountain prey, because his nostrils wide
Draw in the ocean? does his eye discern the flying cloud
As the raven's eye? or does he measure the expanse like the
vulture?
Does the still spider view the cliffs where eagles hide their
young?
Or does the fly rejoice because the harvest is brought in?
Does not the eagle scorn the earth & despise the treasures
beneath?
But the mole knoweth what is there, & the worm shall tell it
thee. 40
Does not the worm erect a pillar in the mouldering church
yard?
[6] And a palace of eternity in the jaws of the hungry grave?
Over his porch these words are written: Take thy bliss O
Man!
And sweet shall be thy taste & sweet thy infant joys renew!

Infancy, fearless, lustful, happy! nestling for delight
In laps of pleasure; Innocence! honest, open, seeking
The vigorous joys of morning light; open to virgin bliss!
Who taught thee modesty, subtil modesty! child of night &
sleep?
When thou awakest, wilt thou dissemble all thy secret joys
Or wert thou not awake when all this mystery was disclos'd?
Then com'st thou forth a modest virgin, knowing to
dissemble 10
With nets found under thy night pillow, to catch virgin joy,
And brand it with the name of whore; & sell it in the night,
In silence, ev'n without a whisper, and in seeming sleep.
Religious dreams and holy vespers, light thy smoky fires;
Once were thy fires lighted by the eyes of honest morn:
And does my Theotormon seek this hypocrite modesty?
This knowing, artful, secret, fearful, cautious, trembling
hypocrite.

Then is Oothoon a whore indeed! and all the virgin joys
Of life are harlots: and Theotormon is a sick man's dream
And Oothoon is the crafty slave of selfish holiness. 20
But Oothoon is not so, a virgin fill'd with virgin fancies
Open to joy and to delight where ever beauty appears:
If in the morning sun I find it, there my eyes are fix'd
[7] In happy copulation; if in evening mild, wearied with work
Sit on a bank and draw the pleasures of this free-born joy.

The moment of desire! the moment of desire! The virgin
That pines for man shall awaken her womb to enormous joys
In the secret shadows of her chamber; the youth shut up from
The lustful joy, shall forget to generate & create an amorous image
In the shadows of his curtains and in the folds of his silent pillow.
Are not these the places of religion? the rewards of continence?
The self enjoyings of self denial? Why dost thou seek religion?
Is it because acts are not lovely, that thou seekest solitude? 10
Where the horrible darkness is impressed with reflections of desire.

Father of Jealousy, be thou accursed from the earth!
Why hast thou taught my Theotormon this accursed thing?
Till beauty fades from off my shoulders darken'd and cast out,
A solitary shadow wailing on the margin of non-entity.

I cry, Love! Love! Love! happy happy Love! free as the mountain wind!
Can that be Love, that drinks another as a sponge drinks water?
That clouds with jealousy his nights, with weepings all the day:
To spin a web of age around him, grey and hoary! dark!
Till his eyes sicken at the fruit that hangs before his sight. 20

Such is self-love that envies all! a creeping skeleton
With lamplike eyes watching around the frozen marriage
bed.

But silken nets and traps of adamant will Oothoon spread,
And catch for thee girls of mild silver, or of furious gold;
I'll lie beside thee on a bank & view their wanton play
In lovely copulation bliss on bliss with Theotormon:
Red as the rosy morning, lustful as the first born beam,
Oothoon shall view his dear delight, nor e'er with jealous
cloud
Come in the heaven of generous love; nor selfish blightings
bring.

Does the sun walk in glorious raiment on the secret floor 30
[8] Where the cold miser spreads his gold? or does the bright
cloud drop
On his stone threshold? does his eye behold the beam that
brings
Expansion to the eye of pity? or will he bind himself
Beside the ox to thy hard furrow? does not that mild beam
blot
The bat, the owl, the glowing tyger, and the king of night.
The sea fowl takes the wintry blast for a cov'ring to her
limbs:
And the wild snake, the pestilence to adorn him with gems &
gold.
And trees, & birds, & beasts, & men, behold their eternal
joy.

Arise you little glancing wings, and sing your infant joy!
Arise and drink your bliss, for every thing that lives is holy! 10

Thus every morning wails Oothoon: but Theotormon sits
Upon the margin'd ocean conversing with shadows dire.

*The Daughters of Albion hear her woes, & eccho back her
sighs.*

AMERICA

a Prophecy

[1] *Preludium*

The shadowy daughter of Urthona stood before red Orc.
When fourteen suns had faintly journey'd o'er his dark abode;
His food she brought in iron baskets, his drink in cups of iron;
Crown'd with a helmet & dark hair the nameless female stood;
A quiver with its burning stores, a bow like that of night,
When pestilence is shot from heaven; no other arms she need:
Invulnerable tho' naked, save where clouds roll round her loins
Their awful folds in the dark air; silent she stood as night;
For never from her iron tongue could voice or sound arise;
But dumb till that dread day when Orc assay'd his fierce embrace. 10

Dark virgin; said the hairy youth: thy father stern abhorr'd
Rivets my tenfold chains while still on high my spirit soars:
Sometimes an eagle screaming in the sky, sometimes a lion,
Stalking upon the mountains, & sometimes a whale I lash
The raging fathomless abyss; anon a serpent folding
Around the pillars of Urthona, and round thy dark limbs,
On the Canadian wilds I fold, feeble my spirit folds.
For chain'd beneath I rend these caverns; when thou bringest food
I howl my joy! and my red eyes seek to behold thy face
In vain! these clouds roll to & fro, & hide thee from my sight. – 20

[2] Silent as despairing love, and strong as jealousy,
The hairy shoulders rend the links, free are the wrists of fire;

Round the terrific loins he siez'd the panting struggling womb;
It joy'd: she put aside her clouds & smiled her first-born smile;
As when a black cloud shews its lightnings to the silent deep.

Soon as she saw the terrible boy then burst the virgin cry:

I know thee, I have found thee, & I will not let thee go;
Thou art the image of God who dwells in darkness of Africa;
And thou art fall'n to give me life in regions of dark death.
On my American plains I feel the struggling afflictions 10
Endur'd by roots that writhe their arms into the nether deep:
I see a serpent in Canada, who courts me to his love;
In Mexico an Eagle, and a Lion in Peru;
I see a Whale in the South-sea, drinking my soul away.
O what limb rending pains I feel! thy fire & my frost
Mingle in howling pains, in furrows by thy lightnings rent;
This is eternal death; and this the torment long foretold.

*

[3] *A Prophecy*

The Guardian Prince of Albion burns in his nightly tent,
Sullen fires across the Atlantic glow to America's shore:
Piercing the souls of warlike men, who rise in silent night;
Washington, Franklin, Paine & Warren, Gates, Hancock & Green,
Meet on the coast glowing with blood from Albion's fiery Prince.

Washington spoke: Friends of America, look over the Atlantic sea;
A bended bow is lifted in heaven, & a heavy iron chain
Descends link by link from Albion's cliffs across the sea to bind
Brothers & sons of America, till our faces pale and yellow;
Heads deprest, voices weak, eyes downcast, hands work-bruis'd, 10

Feet bleeding on the sultry sands, and the furrows of the whip
Descend to generations that in future times forget. –

The strong voice ceas'd; for a terrible blast swept over the heaving sea;
The eastern cloud rent; on his cliffs stood [n]Albion's wrathful Prince,
A dragon form clashing his scales at midnight he arose,
And flam'd red meteors round the land of Albion beneath:
His voice, his locks, his awful shoulders, and his glowing eyes
[4] Appear to the Americans upon the cloudy night.

Solemn heave the Atlantic waves between the gloomy nations,
Swelling, belching from its deeps red clouds & raging Fires!

Albion is sick! America faints! enrag'd the Zenith grew.
As human blood shooting its veins all round the orbed heaven
Red rose the clouds from the Atlantic in vast wheels of blood
And in the red clouds rose a Wonder o'er the Atlantic sea;
Intense! naked! a Human fire fierce glowing, as the wedge
Of iron heated in the furnace; his terrible limbs were fire
With myriads of cloudy terrors banners dark & towers 10
Surrounded; heat but not light went thro' the murky atmosphere.

The King of England looking westward trembles at the vision.

[5] Albion's Angel stood beside the Stone of night, and saw
The terror like a comet, or more like the planet red
That once inclos'd the terrible wandering comets in its sphere.
Then Mars, thou wast our center, & the planets three flew round
Thy crimson disk; so ere the Sun was rent from thy red sphere

The Spectre glow'd, his horrid length staining the temple
long
With beams of blood; & thus a voice came forth, and shook
the temple:

[6] "The morning comes, the night decays, the watchmen leave
their stations;
The grave is burst, the spices shed, the linen wrapped up;
The bones of death, the cov'ring clay, the sinews shrunk &
dry'd.
Reviving shake, inspiring move, breathing! awakening!
Spring like redeemed captives when their bonds & bars are
burst;
Let the slave grinding at the mill run out into the field:
Let him look up into the heavens & laugh in the bright air;
Let the inchained soul shut up in darkness and in sighing,
Whose face has never seen a smile in thirty weary years;
Rise and look out, his chains are loose, his dungeon doors are
open. 10
And let his wife and children return from the oppressor's
scourge;
They look behind at every step & believe it is a dream.
Singing: The Sun has left his blackness, & has found a
fresher morning
And the fair Moon rejoices in the clear & cloudless night!
For Empire is no more, and now the Lion & Wolf shall cease!

[7] In thunders ends the voice. Then Albion's Angel wrathful
burnt
Beside the Stone of Night; and like the Eternal Lion's howl
In famine & war, reply'd: Art thou not Orc; who
serpent-form'd
Stands at the gate of Enitharmon to devour her children?
Blasphemous Demon, Antichrist, hater of Dignities;
Lover of wild rebellion, and transgresser of God's Law;
Why dost thou come to Angels' eyes in this terrific form?

[8] The terror answer'd: I am Orc, wreath'd round the accursed tree:
The times are ended; shadows pass the morning 'gins to break:
The fiery joy, that Urizen perverted to ten commands,
What night he led the starry hosts thro' the wide wilderness:
That stony law I stamp to dust: and scatter religion abroad
To the four winds as a torn book, & none shall gather the leaves.
But they shall rot on desart sands, & consume in bottomless deeps;
To make the desarts blossom, & the deeps shrink to their fountains,
And to renew the fiery joy, and burst the stony roof.
That pale religious letchery, seeking Virginity, 10
May find it in a harlot, and in coarse-clad honesty
The undefil'd, tho' ravish'd in her cradle night and morn:
For every thing that lives is holy, life delights in life;
Because the soul of sweet delight can never be defil'd.
Fires inwrap the earthly globe, yet man is not consum'd;
Amidst the lustful fires he walks: his feet become like brass,
His knees and thighs like silver, & his breast and head like gold.

[9] Sound! sound! my loud war-trumpets & alarm my Thirteen Angels!
Loud howls the eternal Wolf! the eternal Lion lashes his tail!
America is dark'ned; and my punishing Demons terrified
Crouch howling before their caverns deep like skins dry'd in the wind.
They cannot smite the wheat, nor quench the fatness of the earth.
They cannot smite with sorrows, nor subdue the plow and spade.
They cannot wall the city, nor moat round the castle of princes.
They cannot bring the stubbed oak to overgrow the hills.
For terrible men stand on the shores, & in their robes I see
Children take shelter from the lightnings, there stands Washington 10

And Paine and Warren with their foreheads rear'd toward the
east:
But clouds obscure my aged sight. A vision from afar!
Sound! sound! my loud war-trumpets & alarm my thirteen
Angels:
Ah vision from afar! Ah, rebel form that rent the ancient
Heavens; Eternal Viper self-renew'd, rolling in clouds
I see thee in thick clouds and darkness on America's shore.
Writhing in pangs of abhorred birth; red flames the crest
rebellious
And eyes of death; the harlot womb oft opened in vain
Heaves in enormous circles, now the times are return'd upon
thee,
Devourer of thy parent, now thy unutterable torment
renews. 20
Sound! sound! my loud war trumpets & alarm my thirteen
Angels!
Ah terrible birth! a young one bursting! where is the
weeping mouth?
And where the mother's milk? instead those ever-hissing jaws
And parched lips drop with fresh gore: now roll thou in the
clouds!
Thy mother lays her length outstretch'd upon the shore
beneath.
Sound! sound! my loud war-trumpets & alarm my thirteen
Angels!
Loud howls the eternal Wolf: the eternal Lion lashes his tail!

[10] Thus wept the Angel voice & as he wept the terrible blasts
Of trumpets, blew a loud alarm across the Atlantic deep.
No trumpets answer; no reply of clarions or of fifes,
Silent the Colonies remain and refuse the loud alarm.

On those vast shady hills between America & Albion's shore;
Now barr'd out by the Atlantic sea: call'd Atlantean hills:
Because from their bright summits you may pass to the
Golden world
An ancient palace, archetype of mighty Emperies,

Rears its immortal pinnacles, built in the forest of God
By Ariston the king of beauty for his stolen bride, 10

Here on their magic seats the thirteen Angels sat perturb'd
For clouds from the Atlantic hover o'er the solemn roof.

[11] Fiery the Angels rose, & as they rose deep thunder roll'd
Around their shores: indignant burning with the fires of Orc
And Boston's Angel cried aloud as they flew thro' the dark
night.

He cried: Why trembles honesty and like a murderer,
Why seeks he refuge from the frowns of his immortal
station!
Must the generous tremble & leave his joy to the idle, to the
pestilence!
That mock him? who commanded this? what God? what
Angel!
To keep the gen'rous from experience till the ungenerous
Are unrestrain'd performers of the energies of nature;
Till pity is become a trade, and generosity a science, 10
That men get rich by, & the sandy desart is giv'n to the
strong
What God is he, writes laws of peace, & clothes him in a
tempest
What pitying Angel lusts for tears, and fans himself with
sighs
What crawling villain preaches abstinence & wraps himself
In fat of lambs? no more I follow, no more obedience pay.

[12] So cried he, rending off his robe & throwing down his scepter
In sight of Albion's Guardian; and all the thirteen Angels
Rent off their robes to the hungry wind, & threw their
golden scepters
Down on the land of America: indignant they descended
Headlong from out their heav'nly heights, descending swift
as fires
Over the land; naked & flaming are their lineaments seen
In the deep gloom, by Washington & Paine & Warren they
stood

And the flame folded roaring fierce within the pitchy night
Before the Demon red, who burnt towards America,
In black smoke thunders and loud winds rejoicing in its terror 10
Breaking in smoky wreaths from the wild deep, & gath'ring
thick
In flames as of a furnace on the land from North to South

[13] What time the thirteen Governors that England sent
convene
In ⁿBernard's house; the flames cover'd the land, they rouze,
they cry,
Shaking their mental chains they rush in fury to the sea
To quench their anguish; at the feet of Washington down
fall'n
They grovel on the sand and writhing lie, while all
The British soldiers thro' the thirteen states sent up a howl
Of anguish: threw their swords & muskets to the earth & ran
From their encampments and dark castles seeking where to
hide
From the grim flames; and from the visions of Orc: in sight
Of Albion's Angel; who enrag'd, his secret clouds open'd 10
From north to south, and burnt outstretch'd on wings of
wrath, cov'ring
The eastern sky, spreading his awful wings across the
heavens;
Beneath him roll'd his num'rous hosts, all Albion's Angels
camp'd
Darken'd the Atlantic mountains & their trumpets shook the
valleys,
Arm'd with diseases of the earth to cast upon the Abyss,
Their numbers forty millions, must'ring in the eastern sky.

[14] In the flames stood & view'd the armies drawn out in the sky
Washington Franklin Paine & Warren Allen Gates & Lee:
And heard the voice of Albion's Angel give the thunderous
command:
ⁿHis plagues obedient to his voice flew forth out of their
clouds
Falling upon America, as a storm to cut them off

As a blight cuts the tender corn when it begins to appear.
Dark is the heaven above, & cold & hard the earth beneath;
And as a plague wind fill'd with insects cuts off man & beast;
And as a sea o'erwhelms a land in the day of an earthquake:

Fury! rage! madness! in a wind swept through America 10
And the red flames of Orc that folded roaring fierce around
The angry shores, and the fierce rushing of th'inhabitants together:
The citizens of New-York close their books & lock their chests;
The mariners of Boston drop their anchors and unlade;
The scribe of Pensylvania casts his pen upon the earth;
The builder of Virginia throws his hammer down in fear.

Then had America been lost, o'erwhelm'd by the Atlantic,
And Earth had lost another portion of the infinite,
But all rush together in the night in wrath and raging fire
The red fires rag'd! the plagues recoil'd! then roll'd they back with fury 20
[15] On Albion's Angels; then the Pestilence began in streaks of red
Across the limbs of Albion's Guardian, the spotted plague smote Bristol's
And the Leprosy London's Spirit, sickening all their bands:
The millions sent up a howl of anguish and threw off their hammer'd mail,
And cast their swords & spears to earth, & stood a naked multitude.
Albion's Guardian writhed in torment on the eastern sky,
Pale quiv'ring toward the brain his glimmering eyes, teeth chattering,
Howling & shuddering his legs quivering; convuls'd each muscle & sinew.
Sick'ning lay London's Guardian, and the ancient miter'd York
Their heads on snowy hills, their ensigns sick'ning in the sky. 10

The plagues creep on the burning winds driven by flames of
Orc,
And by the fierce Americans rushing together in the night
Driven o'er the Guardians of Ireland and Scotland and Wales.
They, spotted with plagues, forsook the frontiers, & their
banners sear'd
With fires of hell, deform their ancient heavens with shame
& woe.
Hid in his caves the Bard of Albion felt the enormous
plagues,
And a cowl of flesh grew o'er his head & scales on his back &
ribs;
And rough with black scales all his Angels fright their ancient
heavens:
The doors of marriage are open, and the Priests in rustling
scales
Rush into reptile coverts, hiding from the fires of Orc, 20
That play around the golden roofs in wreaths of fierce desire,
Leaving the females naked and glowing with the lusts of
youth.

For the female spirits of the dead, pining in bonds of religion;
Run from their fetters reddening, & in long drawn arches
sitting:
They feel the nerves of youth renew, and desires of ancient
times,
Over their pale limbs as a vine when the tender grape
appears.
[16] Over the hills, the vales, the cities, rage the red flames fierce;
The Heavens melted from north to south: and [n]Urizen who
sat
Above all heavens in thunders wrap'd, emerg'd his leprous
head
From out his holy shrine, his tears in deluge piteous
Falling into the deep sublime! flag'd with grey-brow'd snows
And thunderous visages, his jealous wings wav'd over the
deep;
Weeping in dismal howling woe he dark descended, howling

Around the smitten bands, clothed in tears & trembling
shudd'ring cold.
His stored snows he poured forth, and his icy magazines
He open'd on the deep, and on the Atlantic sea white
shiv'ring. 10
Leprous his limbs, all over white, and hoary was his visage,
Weeping in dismal howlings before the stern Americans
Hiding the Demon red with clouds & cold mists from the
earth;
Till Angels & weak men twelve years should govern o'er the
strong:
And then their end should come, when France reciev'd the
Demon's light.

Stiff shudderings shook the heav'nly thrones! France Spain
& Italy,
In terror view'd the bands of Albion, and the ancient
Guardians
Fainting upon the elements, smitten with their own plagues
They slow advance to shut the five gates of their law-built
heaven
Filled with blasting fancies and with mildews of despair 20
With fierce disease and lust, unable to stem the fires of Orc;
But the five gates were consum'd, & their bolts and hinges
melted
And the fierce flames burnt round the heavens, & round the
abodes of men.

FINIS

Preludium

[2] Of the primeval Priest's assum'd power
When Eternals spurn'd back his religion
And gave him a place in the north,
Obscure, shadowy, void, solitary.

Eternals! I hear your call gladly.
Dictate swift winged words & fear not
To unfold your dark visions of torment.

[3] Chap. I

1. Lo, a shadow of horror is risen
In Eternity! Unknown unprolific,
Self-clos'd, all-repelling: what Demon
Hath form'd this abominable void,
This soul-shudd'ring vacuum? Some said:
'It is Urizen.' But unknown, abstracted,
Brooding secret, the dark power hid.

2. Times on times he divided, & measur'd
Space by space in his ninefold darkness;
Unseen, unknown! changes appear'd 10
Like desolate mountains rifted furious
By the black winds of perturbation:

3. For he strove in battles dire
In unseen conflictions with shapes
Bred from his forsaken wilderness,
Of beast, bird, fish, serpent & element,
Combustion, blast, vapour and cloud,

4. Dark revolving in silent activity:
Unseen in tormenting passions:
An activity unknown and horrible, 20
A self-contemplating shadow,
In enormous labours occupied.

5. But Eternals beheld his vast forests:
Age on ages he lay, clos'd, unknown,
Brooding shut in the deep; all avoid
The petrific abominable chaos.

6. His cold horrors silent, dark Urizen
Prepar'd: his ten thousands of thunders
Rang'd in gloom'd array, stretch out across
The dread world, & the rolling of wheels 30
As of swelling seas, sound in his clouds
In his hills of stor'd snows, in his mountains
Of hail & ice; voices of terror,
Are heard, like thunders of autumn,
When the cloud blazes over the harvests.

Chap. II

1. Earth was not: nor globes of attraction;
The will of the Immortal expanded
Or contracted his all-flexible senses:
Death was not, but eternal life sprung!

2. The sound of a ⁿtrumpet! the heavens 40
Awoke, & vast clouds of blood roll'd
Round the dim rocks of Urizen, so nam'd,
That solitary one in Immensity

3. Shrill the trumpet: & myriads of Eternity
[4] Muster around the bleak desarts
Now fill'd with clouds, darkness & waters
That roll'd perplex'd, lab'ring & utter'd
Words articulate, bursting in thunders
That roll'd on the tops of his mountains:

4. From the depths of dark solitude. From
The eternal abode in my holiness,
Hidden, set apart in my stern counsels
Reserv'd for the days of futurity,
I have sought for a joy without pain, 10
For a solid without fluctuation.

Why will you die O Eternals?
Why live in unquenchable burnings?

5. First I fought with the fire; consum'd
Inwards, into a deep world within:
A void immense, wild dark & deep,
Where nothing was; Nature's wide womb:
And self-balanc'd, stretch'd o'er the void
ⁿI alone, even I! the winds merciless
Bound; but condensing, in torrents 20
They fall & fall; strong I repell'd
The vast waves, & arose on the waters
A wide world of solid obstruction.

6. Here alone I in books form'd of metals
Have written the secrets of wisdom,
The secrets of dark contemplation
By fightings and conflicts dire,
With terrible monsters Sin-bred:
Which the bosoms of all inhabit;
Seven deadly Sins of the soul. 30

7. Lo! I unfold my darkness: and on
This rock, place with strong hand the Book
Of eternal brass, written in my solitude.

8. ⁿLaws of peace, of love, of unity:
Of pity, compassion, forgiveness.
Let each chuse one habitation:
His ancient infinite mansion:
One command, one joy, one desire,
One curse, one weight, one measure
One King, one God, one Law. 40

Chap. III

1. The voice ended, they saw his pale visage
Emerge from the darkness; his hand
On the rock of eternity unclasping
The Book of brass. Rage siez'd the strong!

2. Rage, fury, intense indignation
In cataracts of fire blood & gall
In whirlwinds of sulphurous smoke:
And enormous forms of energy;
All the seven deadly sins of the soul
[5] In living creations appear'd
In the flames of eternal fury.

3. Sund'ring, dark'ning, thund'ring!
Rent away with a terrible crash
Eternity roll'd wide apart,
Wide asunder rolling
Mountainous all around
Departing; departing; departing:
Leaving ruinous fragments of life
Hanging frowning cliffs & all between 10
An ocean of voidness unfathomable.

4. The roaring fires ran o'er the heav'ns
In whirlwinds & cataracts of blood
And o'er the dark desarts of Urizen
Fires pour thro' the void on all sides
On Urizen's self-begotten armies.

5. But no light from the fires! all was darkness
In the flames of Eternal fury.

6. In fierce anguish & quenchless flames
To the desarts and rocks he ran raging 20
To hide, but he could not: combining
He dug mountains & hills in vast strength,
He piled them in incessant labour,
In howlings & pangs & fierce madness,
Long periods in burning fires labouring
Till hoary, and age-broke, and aged,
In despair and the shadows of death.

7. And a roof, vast petrific around,
On all sides he fram'd: like a womb;
Where thousands of rivers in veins 30

Of blood pour down the mountains to cool
The eternal fires beating without
From Eternals; & like a black globe
View'd by sons of Eternity, standing
On the shore of the infinite ocean,
Like a human heart strugling & beating
The vast world of Urizen appear'd.

8. And Los round the dark globe of Urizen,
Kept watch for Eternals, to confine
The obscure separation alone; 40
For Eternity stood wide apart,
[6] As the stars are apart from the earth.

9. Los wept howling around the dark Demon
And cursing his lot; for in anguish,
Urizen was rent from his side;
And a fathomless void for his feet;
And intense fires for his dwelling.

10. But Urizen laid in a stony sleep
Unorganiz'd, rent from Eternity.

11. The Eternals said: What is this? Death:
Urizen is a clod of clay. 10

[7] 12. Los howl'd in a dismal stupor,
Groaning! gnashing! groaning!
Till the wrenching apart was healed.

13. But the wrenching of Urizen heal'd not!
Cold, featureless, flesh or clay,
Rifted with direful changes,
He lay in a dreamless night.

14. Till Los rouz'd his fires, affrighted
At the formless unmeasurable death.

[8] Chap. IV [a]

1. Los smitten with astonishment
Frighten'd at the hurtling bones

2. And at the surging sulphureous
Perturbed Immortal mad raging

3. In whirlwinds & pitch & nitre
Round the furious limbs of Los;

4. And Los formed nets & gins
And threw the nets round about.

5. He watch'd in shudd'ring fear
The dark changes, & bound every change 10
With rivets of iron & brass;

6. And these were the changes of Urizen:

[10]

Chap. IV [b]

1. Ages on ages roll'd over him!
In stony sleep ages roll'd over him!
Like a dark waste stretching chang'able,
By earthquakes riv'n, belching sullen fires:
On ages roll'd ages in ghastly
Sick torment; around him, in whirlwinds
Of darkness the eternal Prophet howl'd
Beating still on his rivets of iron
Pouring solder of iron; dividing
The horrible night into watches. 10

2. And Urizen (so his eternal name)
His prolific delight obscur'd more & more
In dark secresy, hiding in surgeing
Sulphureous fluid his phantasies.
The Eternal Prophet heav'd the dark bellows,
And turn'd restless the tongs; and the hammer
Incessant beat; forging chains new & new
Numb'ring with links, hours, days & years.

3. The eternal mind bounded began to roll
Eddies of wrath ceaseless round & round, 20
And the sulphureous foam surging thick
Settled, a lake, bright, & shining clear:
White as the snow on the mountains cold.

4. Forgetfulness, dumbness, necessity!
In chains of the mind locked up,
Like fetters of ice shrinking together
Disorganiz'd, rent from Eternity,
Los beat on his fetters of iron;
And heated his furnaces & pour'd
Iron solder and solder of brass. 30

5. Restless turnd the immortal inchain'd
Heaving dolorous! anguish'd! unbearable
Till a roof shaggy wild inclos'd
In an orb, his fountain of thought.

6. In a horrible dreamful slumber;
Like the linked infernal chain;
A vast Spine writh'd in torment
Upon the winds; shooting pain'd
Ribs, like a bending cavern
And bones of solidness, froze 40
Over all his nerves of joy.
And [n]a first Age passed over,
And a state of dismal woe.

[11] 7. From the caverns of his jointed Spine,
Down sunk with fright a red
Round globe hot burning, deep
Deep down into the Abyss:
Panting, conglobing, trembling
Shooting out ten thousand branches
Around his solid bones.
And a second Age passed over,
And a state of dismal woe.

8. In harrowing fear rolling round, 10
His nervous brain shot branches
Round the branches of his heart
On high into two little orbs,
And fixed in two little caves
Hiding carefully from the wind.
His Eyes beheld the deep:

And a third Age passed over,
And a state of dismal woe.

9. The pangs of hope began,
In heavy pain striving, struggling. 20
Two Ears in close volutions.
From beneath his orbs of vision
Shot spiring out and petrified
As they grew. And a fourth Age passed
And a state of dismal woe.

10. In ghastly torment sick;
Hanging upon the wind;
[13] Two Nostrils bent down to the deep.
And a fifth Age passed over;
And a state of dismal woe.

11. In ghastly torment sick,
Within his ribs bloated round
A craving Hungry Cavern;
Thence arose his channel'd Throat,
And like a red flame, a Tongue
Of thirst & of hunger appear'd.
And a sixth Age passed over: 10
And a state of dismal woe.

12. Enraged & stifled with torment
He threw his right Arm to the north,
His left Arm to the south
Shooting out in anguish deep;
And his Feet stamp'd the nether Abyss
In trembling & howling & dismay.
And a seventh Age passed over:
And a state of dismal woe.

Chap. V

1. In terrors Los shrunk from his task: 20
His great hammer fell from his hand:
His fires beheld, and sickening
Hid their strong limbs in smoke.

For with noises ruinous loud,
With hurtlings & clashings & groans
The Immortal endur'd his chains,
Tho' bound in a deadly sleep.

2. All the myriads of Eternity,
All the wisdom & joy of life,
Roll like a sea around him, 30
Except what his little orbs
Of sight by degrees unfold.

3. And now his eternal life
Like a dream was obliterated.

4. Shudd'ring, the Eternal Prophet smote
With a stroke, from his north to south region.
The bellows & hammer are silent now
A nerveless silence, his prophetic voice
Siez'd; a cold solitude & dark void
The Eternal Prophet & Urizen clos'd. 40

5. Ages on ages roll'd over them,
Cut off from life & light, frozen
Into horrible forms of deformity,
Los suffer'd his fires to decay:
Then he look'd back with anxious desire
But the space undivided by existence
Struck horror into his soul.

6. Los wept, obscur'd with mourning:
His bosom earthquak'd with sighs;
He saw Urizen deadly black, 50
In his chains bound, & [n]Pity began,

7. In anguish dividing & dividing –
For pity divides the soul –
In pangs, eternity on eternity:
Life in cataracts pour'd down his cliffs,
The void shrunk the lymph into Nerves
Wand'ring wide on the bosom of night,
And left a round globe of blood
Trembling upon the Void.

[15] Thus the Eternal Prophet was divided
Before the death-image of Urizen
For in changeable clouds and darkness
In a winterly night beneath,
The Abyss of Los stretch'd immense:
And now seen, now obscur'd, to the eyes
Of Eternals the visions remote
Of the dark separation appear'd.
As glasses discover Worlds
In the endless Abyss of space, 10
So the expanding eyes of Immortals
Beheld the dark visions of Los,
And the globe of life blood trembling.

[18] 8. The globe of life blood trembled
Branching out into roots;
Fibrous, writhing upon the winds;
Fibres of blood, milk and tears;
In pangs, eternity on eternity.
At length in tears & cries imbodied
A female form trembling and pale
Waves before his deathy face.

9. All Eternity shudder'd at sight
Of the first female now separate: 10
Pale as a cloud of snow
Waving before the face of Los.

10. Wonder, awe, fear, astonishment,
Petrify the eternal myriads;
At the first female form now separate:
[19] They call'd her Pity, and fled.

11. 'Spread a Tent, with strong curtains around them
Let cords & stakes bind in the Void
That Eternals may no more behold them.'

12. They began to weave curtains of darkness;
They erected large pillars round the Void
With golden hooks fasten'd in the pillars.
With infinite labour the Eternals
A woof wove, and called it Science.

Chap. VI

1. But Los saw the Female & pitied: 10
He embrac'd her, she wept, she refus'd,
In perverse and cruel delight
She fled from his arms, yet he follow'd.

2. Eternity shudder'd when they saw,
Man begetting his likeness
On his own divided image.

3. A time passed over, the Eternals
Began to erect the tent;
When Enitharmon, sick,
Felt [n]a Worm within her womb. 20

4. Yet helpless it lay like a Worm
In the trembling womb
To be moulded into existence.

5. All day the worm lay on her bosom;
All night within her womb
The worm lay till it grew to a serpent,
With dolorous hissings & poisons
Round Enitharmon's loins folding,

6. Coil'd within Enitharmon's womb
The serpent grew casting its scales, 30
With sharp pangs the hissings began
To change to a grating cry,
Many sorrows and dismal throes
Many forms of fish, bird & beast,
Brought forth an Infant form
Where was a worm before.

7. The Eternals their tent finished
Alarm'd with these gloomy visions
When Enitharmon groaning
Produc'd a man Child to the light. 40

8. A shriek ran thro' Eternity:
And a paralytic stroke;
At the birth of the Human shadow.

9. Delving earth in his resistless way;
Howling, the Child with fierce flames
Issu'd from Enitharmon.

10. The Eternals closed the tent:
They beat down the stake, the cords
[20] Stretch'd for a work of eternity;
No more Los beheld Eternity.

11. In his hands he siez'd the infant
He bathed him in springs of sorrow
He gave him to Enitharmon.

Chap. VII

1. They named the child Orc; he grew
Fed with milk of Enitharmon.

2. Los awoke her; O sorrow & pain!
A tight'ning girdle grew
Around his bosom. In sobbings 10
He burst the girdle in twain,
But still another girdle
Oppress'd his bosom. In sobbings
Again he burst it. Again
Another girdle succeeds:
The girdle was form'd by day;
By night was burst in twain.

3. These falling down on the rock
Into an iron Chain
In each other link by link lock'd. 20

4. They took Orc to the top of a mountain.
O how Enitharmon wept!
They chain'd his young limbs to the rock
With the Chain of Jealousy
Beneath Urizen's deathful shadow

5. The dead heard the voice of the child,
And began to awake from sleep:
All things heard the voice of the child
And began to awake to life.

6. And [n]Urizen, craving with hunger, 30
Stung with the odours of Nature
Explor'd his dens around.

7. He form'd a line & a plummet
To divide the Abyss beneath.
He form'd a dividing rule:

8. He formed scales to weigh;
He formed massy weights;
He formed a brazen quadrant;
He formed golden compasses,
And began to explore the Abyss 40
And he planted a garden of fruits.

9. But Los encircled Enitharmon
With fires of Prophecy
From the sight of Urizen & Orc.

10. And she bore an enormous race.

Chap. VIII

1. Urizen explor'd his dens
Mountain, moor, & wilderness,
With a globe of fire lighting his journey
A fearful journey, annoy'd
By cruel enormities: forms 50
[23] Of life on his forsaken mountains

2. And his world teem'd vast enormities
Fright'ning; faithless; fawning
Portions of life; similitudes
Of a foot, or a hand, or a head
Or a heart, or an eye, they swam mischevous
Dread terrors! delighting in blood.

3. Most Urizen sicken'd to see
His eternal creations appear;
Sons & daughters of sorrow on mountains, 10
Weeping! wailing! first Thiriel appear'd
Astonish'd at his own existence,
Like a man from a cloud born; & Utha
From the waters emerging, laments!
Grodna rent the deep earth, howling
Amaz'd! his heavens immense cracks
Like the ground parch'd with heat; then Fuzon
Flam'd out! first begotten, last born.
All his eternal sons in like manner,
His daughters from green herbs & cattle 20
From monsters, & worms of the pit.

4. He in darkness clos'd, view'd all his race
And his soul sicken'd! he curs'd
Both sons & daughters; for he saw
That no flesh nor spirit could keep
His iron laws one moment.

5. For he saw that life liv'd upon death;
[25] The Ox in the slaughter house moans,
The Dog at the wintry door,
And he wept, & he called it Pity;
And his tears flowed down on the winds.

6. Cold he wander'd on high, over their cities
In weeping & pain & woe!
And where-ever he wander'd in sorrows
Upon the aged heavens
A cold shadow follow'd behind him,
Like a spider's web, moist, cold, & dim, 10

Drawing out from his sorrowing soul
The dungeon-like heaven dividing
Where-ever the footsteps of Urizen
Walk'd over the cities in sorrow:

7. Till a Web dark & cold, throughout all
The tormented element, stretch'd
From the sorrows of Urizen's soul,
And the Web is a Female in embrio.
None could break the Web, no wings of fire.

8. So twisted the cords, & so knotted 20
The meshes: twisted like to the human brain

9. And all call'd it, The Net of Religion.

Chap. IX

1. Then the Inhabitants of those Cities
Felt their Nerves change into Marrow,
And hardening Bones began
In swift diseases and torments;
In throbbings & shootings & grindings
Thro' all the coasts; till weaken'd
The Senses inward rush'd, shrinking,
Beneath the dark net of infection. 30

2. Till the shrunken eyes, clouded over
Discern'd not the woven hipocrisy;
But the streaky slime in their heavens
Brought together by narrowing perceptions
Appear'd transparent air; for their eyes
Grew small like the eyes of a man,
And in reptile forms shrinking together
Of seven feet stature they remain'd.

3. Six days they shrunk up from existence;
And on the seventh day they rested, 40
And they bless'd the seventh day, in sick hope,
And forgot their eternal life.

4. And their thirty cities divided
In form of a human heart.
No more could they rise at will
In the infinite void, but bound down
To earth by their narrowing perceptions
[28] They lived a period of years;
Then left a noisom body
To the jaws of devouring darkness.

5. And their children wept, & built
Tombs in the desolate places,
And form'd laws of prudence, and call'd them
The eternal laws of God.

6. And the thirty cities remain'd,
Surrounded by salt floods, now call'd
Africa: its name was then Egypt. 10

7. The remaining sons of Urizen
Beheld their brethren shrink together
Beneath the Net of Urizen.
Perswasion was in vain;
For the ears of the inhabitants
Were wither'd & deafen'd & cold,
And their eyes could not discern
Their brethren of other cities.

8. So Fuzon call'd all together
The remaining children of Urizen, 20
And they left the pendulous earth.
They called it Egypt, & left it.

9. And the salt Ocean rolled englob'd.

The End of the first book of Urizen.

from VALA, OR THE FOUR ZOAS

Second Night

[Urizen's Creation]

Mighty was the draught of Voidness to draw Existence in.

Terrific Urizen strode above: in fear & pale dismay.
He saw the indefinite space beneath & his soul shrunk with
horror,
His feet upon the verge of Non Existence; his voice went
forth:

Luvah & Vala trembling & shrinking beheld the great Work
master
And heard his Word: Divide, ye bands, influence by
influence.
Build we a Bower for heaven's darling in the grizly deep:
Build we the Mundane Shell around the Rock of Albion.

The Bands of Heaven flew thro' the air singing & shouting
to Urizen.
Some fix'd the anvil some the loom erected some the plow 10
And harrow form'd & fram'd the harness of silver & ivory,
The golden compasses, the quadrant, & the rule & balance.
They erected the furnaces, they form'd the anvils of gold
beaten in mills
Where winter beats incessant, fixing them firm on their base.
The bellows began to blow, & the Lions of Urizen stood
round the anvil
And the leopards cover'd with skins of beasts tended the
roaring fires
Sublime distinct their lineaments divine of human beauty,
The tygers of wrath called the horses of instruction from
their mangers,
They unloos'd them & put on the harness of gold & silver &
ivory

In human forms distinct they stood round Urizen [n]prince of
Light. 20

*

Rattling the adamantine chains & hooks heave up the ore
In mountainous masses, plung'd in furnaces, & they shut &
seal'd
The furnaces a time & times; all the while blew the North
His cloudy bellows & the South & East & dismal West
And all the while the plow of iron cut the dreadful furrows
In Ulro beneath Beulah where the Dead wail Night & Day.

Luvah was cast into the Furnaces of affliction & sealed
And Vala fed in cruel delight, the furnaces with fire
Stern Urizen beheld urg'd by necessity to keep
The evil day afar, & if perchance with iron power 30
He might avert his own despair . . .

*

Then siez'd the Lions of Urizen their work, & heated in the
forge
Roar the bright masses, thund'ring beat the hammers, many
a pyramid
Is form'd & thrown down thund'ring into the deeps of Non
Entity
Heated red hot they hizzing rend their way down many a
league
Till resting, each his center finds; suspended there they stand
Casting their sparkles dire abroad into the dismal deep
For measur'd out in order'd spaces, the Sons of Urizen
With compasses divide the deep; they the strong scales erect
That Luvah rent from the faint Heart of the Fallen Man 40
And weigh the massy Cubes, then fix them in their awful
stations.

And all the time in Caverns shut, the golden Looms erected
First spun, then wove the Atmospheres, there the Spider &
Worm

Plied the wing'd shuttle piping shrill thro' all the list'ning
threads.
Beneath the Caverns roll the weights of lead & spindles of
iron
The enormous warp & woof rage direful in the affrighted
deep:

While far into the vast unknown, the strong wing'd Eagles
bend
Their venturous flight, in Human forms distinct; thro'
darkness deep
They bear the woven draperies; on golden hooks they hang
abroad
The universal curtains, & spread out from Sun to Sun 50
The vehicles of light, they separate the furious particles
Into mild currents as the water mingles with the wine.

While thus the Spirits of strongest wing enlighten the dark
deep
The threads are spun & the cords twisted & drawn out; then
the weak
Begin their work; & many a net is netted; many a net
Spread & many a Spirit caught, innumerable the nets,
Innumerable the gins & traps; & many a soothing flute
Is form'd & many a corded lyre, outspread over the immense.
In cruel delight they trap the listeners, & in cruel delight
Bind them, condensing the strong energies into little compass 60
Some became seed of every plant that shall be planted; some
The bulbous roots, thrown up together into barns & garners.

Then rose the Builders; First the Architect divine his plan
Unfolds, the wondrous scaffold rear'd all round the infinite
Quadrangular the building rose, the heavens squared by a
line:
Trigon & cubes divide the elements in finite bonds.
Multitudes without number work incessant: the hewn stone
Is plac'd in beds of mortar mingled with the ashes of Vala
Severe the labour, female slaves the mortar trod oppressed.

Twelve halls, after the names of his twelve sons compos'd 70
The wondrous building, & three Central Domes after the
Names
Of his three daughters were encompass'd by the twelve
bright halls:
Every hall surrounded by bright Paradises of Delight
In which are towns & Cities Nations Seas Mountains &
Rivers.
Each Dome open'd toward four halls & the Three Domes
encompass'd
The Golden Hall of Urizen, whose western side glow'd bright
With ever-streaming fires beaming from his awful limbs.

His Shadowy Feminine Semblance here repos'd on a White
Couch
Or hover'd o'er his Starry head, & when he smil'd she
brighten'd
Like a bright Cloud in harvest, but when Urizen frown'd She
wept 80
In mists over his carved throne, & when he turn'd his back
Upon his Golden hall & sought the Labyrinthine porches
Of his wide heaven, trembling, cold in paling fears she sat
A Shadow of Despair; therefore toward the West Urizen
form'd
A recess in the wall for fires to glow upon the pale
Female's limbs in his absence, & her Daughters oft upon
A Golden Altar burnt perfumes with Art Celestial form'd,
Foursquare sculptur'd & sweetly Engrav'd to please their
shadowy mother.
Ascending into her misty garments the blue smoke roll'd to
revive
Her cold limbs in the absence of her Lord. Also her sons 90
With lives of Victims sacrificed upon an altar of brass
On the East side reviv'd her Soul with lives of beasts &
birds
Slain on the Altar up ascending into her cloudy bosom.
Of terrible workmanship the Altar, labour of ten thousand
Slaves,

One thousand Men of wondrous power spent their lives in its formation:
It stood on twelve steps nam'd after the names of her twelve sons
And was erected at the chief entrance of Urizen's hall.

*

[Enion's Second Lament]

Thus Enion wails from the dark deep, the golden heavens tremble:

I am made to sow the thistle for wheat; the nettle for a nourishing dainty:
I have planted a false oath in the earth, it has brought forth a [n]poison tree. 100
I have chosen the serpent for a councellor, & the dog
For a schoolmaster to my children:
I have blotted out from light & living the dove & nightingale,
And I have caused the earth worm to beg from door to door.
I have taught the thief a secret path into the house of the just
I have taught pale artifice to spread his nets upon the morning,
My heavens are brass my earth is iron my moon a clod of clay
My sun a pestilence burning at noon & a vapour of death in night.

What is the price of Experience: do men buy it for a song
Or wisdom for a dance in the street? No it is bought with the price 110
Of all that a man hath, his house his wife his children.
Wisdom is sold in the desolate market where none come to buy
And in the wither'd field where the farmer plows for bread in vain.

It is an easy thing to triumph in the summer's sun
And in the vintage, & to sing on the waggon loaded with corn.

It is an easy thing to talk of patience to the afflicted
To speak the laws of prudence to the houseless wanderer,
To listen to the hungry ravens cry in wintry season
When the red blood is fill'd with wine & with the marrow of lambs.

It is an easy thing to laugh at wrathful elements 120
To hear the dog howl at the wintry door, the ox in the slaughter house moan:
To see a god on every wind & a blessing on every blast,
To hear sounds of love in the thunder storm that destroys our enemies' house,
To rejoice in the blight that covers his field, & the sickness that cuts off his children:
While our olive & vine sing & laugh round our door & our children bring fruits & flowers

Then the groan & the dolor are quite forgotten, & the slave grinding at the mill,
And the captive in chains & the poor in the prison, & the soldier in the field
When the shatter'd bone hath laid him groaning among the happier dead.

It is an easy thing to rejoice in the tents of prosperity:
Thus could I sing & thus rejoice, but it is not so with me! 130

*

Sixth Night

[Urizen journeys through the Abyss]

[n]For Urizen beheld the terrors of the Abyss wand'ring among
The ruin'd spirits once his children & the children of Luvah,
Scar'd at the sound of their own sigh that seems to shake the immense
They wander moping, in their heart a Sun, a dreary moon,
A Universe of fiery constellations in their brain,

An Earth of wintry woe beneath their feet, & round their
loins
Waters or winds or clouds or brooding lightnings &
pestilential plagues.
Beyond the bounds of their own self their senses cannot
penetrate:
As the tree knows not what is outside of its leaves & bark
And yet it drinks the summer joy & fears the winter sorrow, 10
So in the regions of the grave none knows his dark compeer,
Tho' he partakes of his dire woes & mutual returns the pang
The throb the dolor the convulsion in soul sickening woes.

The horrid shapes & sights of torment in burning dungeons
& in
Fetters of red hot iron, some with crowns of serpents & some
With monsters girding round their bosoms. Some lying on
beds of sulphur
On racks & wheels: he beheld women marching o'er burning
wastes
Of Sand in bands of hundreds & of fifties & of thousands,
strucken with
Lightnings which blazed after them upon their shoulders in
their march
In successive vollies with loud thunders: swift flew the King
of Light 20
Over the burning desarts. Then the desarts pass'd, involv'd
in clouds
Of smoke, with myriads moping in the stifling vapours;
Swift
Flew the King tho' flag'd, his powers lab'ring, till over rocks
And Mountains faint weary he wander'd, where multitudes
were shut
Up in the solid mountains & in rocks which heaved with their
torments.
Then came he among fiery cities & castles built of burning
steel,
Then he beheld the forms of tygers & of Lions, dishumaniz'd
men,

Many in serpents & in worms stretch'd out enormous length
Over the sullen mould, & slimy tracks obstruct his way
Drawn out from deep to deep, woven by ribb'd 30
And scaled monsters or arm'd in iron shell or shell of brass
Or gold, a glittering torment shining & hissing in eternal
pain.
Some as columns of fire or of water sometimes stretch'd out
in heighth,
Sometimes in length sometimes englobing, wandering in
vain seeking for ease:
His voice to them was but an inarticulate thunder, for their
Ears
Were heavy & dull & their eyes & nostrils closed up.
Oft he stood by a howling victim, Questioning in words
Soothing or Furious, no one answer'd, every one wrap'd up
In his own sorrow howl'd regardless of his words, nor voice
Of sweet response could he obtain, tho' oft assay'd with tears: 40
He knew they were his Children ruin'd in his ruin'd world.

Oft would he stand & question a fierce scorpion glowing with
gold
In vain the terror heard not, then a lion he would sieze
By the fierce mane, staying his howling course: in vain the
voice
Of Urizen in vain the Eloquent tongue. A Rock a Cloud a
Mountain
Were now not Vocal as in Climes of happy Eternity
Where the lamb replies to the infant voice & the lion to the
man of years,
Giving them sweet instructions; Where the Cloud the River
& the Field
Talk with the husbandman & shepherd. But these attack'd
him sore
Siezing upon his feet & rending the Sinews, that in Caves 50
He hid to recure his obstructed powers with rest & oblivion.

Here he had time enough to repent of his rashly threaten'd
curse

He saw them curs'd beyond his Curse, his soul melted with
fear.

He could not take their fetters off for they grew from the soul
Nor could he quench the fires for they flam'd out from the
heart,
Nor could he calm the Elements because himself was Subject
So he threw his flight in terror & pain & in repentant tears.

When he had pass'd these southern terrors he approach'd the
East
Void pathless beaten with iron sleet & eternal hail & rain.
No form was there no living thing & yet his way lay thro'
This dismal world: he stood a while & look'd back o'er his
former
Terrific voyage: Hills & Vales of torment & despair.
Sighing & wiping a fresh tear, then turning round he threw
Himself into the dismal void, falling he fell & fell
Whirling in unresistible revolutions down & down
In the horrid bottomless vacuity falling falling falling
Into the Eastern vacuity the empty world of Luvah.

The ever pitying one who seeth all things saw his fall
And in the dark vacuity created a bosom of clay.
When wearied dead he fell his limbs repos'd in the bosom of
slime
As the seed falls from the sower's hand so Urizen fell, &
death
Shut up his powers in oblivion: then as the seed shoots forth
In pain & sorrow, so the slimy bed his limbs renew'd.
At first an infant weakness; periods pass'd, he gather'd
strength
But still in solitude he sat, then rising threw his flight
Onward tho' falling thro' the waste of night & ending in
death,
And in another resurrection to sorrow & weary travel.
But still his books he bore in his strong hands & his iron pen,
For when he died they lay beside his grave, & when he rose

He siez'd them with a gloomy smile; for wrap'd in his death
clothes 80
He hid them when he slept in death, when he reviv'd the
clothes
Were rotted by the winds; the books remain'd still
unconsum'd,
Still to be written & interleav'd with brass & iron & gold
Time after time, for such a journey none but iron pens
Can write, and adamantine leaves recieve, nor can the man
who goes
The journey obstinate refuse to write time after time.

*

But Urizen said: Can I not leave this world of Cumbrous
wheels,
Circle o'er Circle, nor on high attain a void
Where self sustaining I may view all things beneath my feet?
Or sinking thro' these Elemental wonders swift to fall, 90
I thought perhaps to find an End, a world beneath of voidness
Whence I might travel round the outside of this dark
confusion.
When I bend downward, bending my head downward into
the deep,
'Tis upward all, which way soever I my course begin;
But when a Vortex form'd on high by labour & sorrow &
care
And weariness begins on all my limbs, then sleep revives
My wearied spirits; waking then 'tis downward all which
way
Soever I my spirits turn, no end I find of all.
O what a world is here, unlike those climes of bliss
Where my sons gather'd round my knees! O, thou poor
ruin'd world, 100
Thou horrible ruin! once like me thou wast all glorious,
And now like me partaking desolate thy master's lot.
Art thou O ruin, the once glorious heaven? are these thy
rocks
Where joy sang in the trees & pleasure sported on the rivers,

And laughter sat beneath the Oaks, & innocence sported round
Upon the green plains, & sweet friendship met in palaces,
And books & instruments of song & pictures of delight?
Where are they, whelmed beneath these ruins in horrible destruction?
And if Eternal falling I repose on the dark bosom
Of winds & waters, or thence fall into a Void where air 110
Is not, down falling thro' immensity ever & ever,
I lose my powers, weaken'd every revolution, till a death
Shuts up my powers; then a seed in the vast womb of darkness
I dwell in dim oblivion: brooding over me the Enormous worlds
Reorganize me, shooting forth in bones & flesh & blood,
I am regenerated, to fall or rise at will or to remain
A labourer of ages, a dire discontent a living woe
Wandering in vain. Here will I fix my foot & here rebuild.

So he began to form of gold silver & iron
And brass, vast instruments to measure out the immense & fix 120
The whole into another world better suited to obey
His will, where none should dare oppose his will, himself being King
Of All & all futurity be bound in his vast chain.

*

Seventh Night

[Urizen's Labourers]

And Urizen Read in his book of brass in sounding tones:

Listen O Daughters to my voice: Listen to the Words of Wisdom!

So shall you govern over all; let Moral Duty tune your tongue,
But be your hearts harder than the nether millstone,
To bring the shadow of Enitharmon beneath our wondrous tree.
That Los may Evaporate like smoke & be no more.
Draw down Enitharmon to the Spectre of Urthona
And let him have dominion over Los the terrible shade.

Compell the poor to live upon a Crust of bread by soft mild arts
Smile when they frown, frown when they smile & when a man looks pale 10
With labour & abstinence, say he looks healthy & happy:
And when his children sicken, let them die there are enough
Born, even too many & our Earth will be overrun
Without these arts. If you would make the poor live with temper,
With pomp give every crust of bread you give, with gracious cunning
Magnify small gifts, reduce the man to want a gift & then give with pomp:
Say he smiles if you hear him sigh, if pale say he is ruddy.
Preach temperance: say he is overgorg'd & drowns his wit
In strong drink tho' you know that bread & water are all
He can afford. Flatter his wife pity his children till we can 20
Reduce all to our will as spaniels are taught with art . . .

*

Then left the sons of Urizen the plow & harrow the loom
The hammer & the chisel & the rule & compasses.
They forg'd the sword the chariot of war the battle ax,
The trumpet fitted to the battle & the flute of summer,
And all the arts of life they chang'd into the arts of death.
The hour glass contemn'd because its simple workmanship
Was as the workmanship of the plowman, & the water wheel

That raises water into Cisterns broken & burn'd in fire,
Because its workmanship was like the workmanship of the shepherd, 30
And in their stead intricate wheels invented; Wheel without wheel,
To perplex youth in their outgoings, & to bind to labours
Of day & night the myriads of Eternity, that they might file
And polish brass & iron hour after hour, laborious workmanship,
Kept ignorant of the use, that they might spend the days of wisdom
In sorrowful drudgery to obtain a scanty pittance of bread;
In ignorance to view a small portion & think that All,
And call it demonstration, blind to all the simple rules of life.

*

[The Labours of Los and Enitharmon]

. . . Los his hands divine inspired began
To modulate his [n]fires: studious the loud roaring flames 40
He vanquish'd with the strength of Art, bending their iron points
And drawing them forth delighted upon the winds of Golgonooza,
From out the ranks of Urizen's war & from the fiery lake
Of Orc binding down as the binder of the Sheaves follows
The reaper in both arms embracing the furious raging flames.
Los drew them forth out of the deeps planting his right foot firm
Upon the iron crag of Urizen, thence springing up aloft
Into the heavens of Enitharmon in a mighty circle.

And first he drew a line upon the walls of shining heaven
And [n]Enitharmon tinctur'd it with beams of blushing love. 50
It remain'd permanent, a lovely form inspir'd divinely human,
Dividing into just proportions. Los unwearied labour'd
The immortal lines upon the heavens till with sighs of love

Sweet Enitharmon, mild entranc'd breath'd forth upon the
wind
The spectrous dead; Weeping the Spectres view'd the
immortal works
Of Los, assimilating to those forms Embodied & Lovely
In youth & beauty in the arms of Enitharmon mild
reposing . . .

*

First his immortal spirit drew Urizen's Shadow away
From out the ranks of war, separating him in sunder,
Leaving his Spectrous form which could not be drawn away, 60
Then he divided Thiriel the Eldest of Urizen's sons:
Urizen became Rintrah, Thiriel became Palamabron,
Thus dividing the powers of every Warrior.
Startled was Los he found his Enemy Urizen now
In his hands: he wonder'd that he felt love & not hate.
His whole soul loved him, he beheld him an infant
Lovely, breath'd from Enitharmon: he trembled within
himself.

*

Eighth Night

Enitharmon wove in tears, singing songs of Lamentations
And pitying comfort as she sigh'd forth on the wind the
spectres
And wove them bodies, calling them her belov'd sons &
daughters,
Employing the daughters in her looms, & Los employ'd the
sons
In Golgonooza's Furnaces among the Anvils of time & space,
Thus forming a vast family, wondrous in beauty & love.

*

[Enion's Last Lament]

. . . Enion replies from the Caverns of the Grave:

Fear not, O poor forsaken one! O land of briars & thorns
Where once the olive flourished & the Cedar spread his
wings!
Once I wail'd desolate like thee; my fallow fields in fear 10
Cried to the Churchyards & the Earthworm came in dismal
state.
I found him in my bosom, & I said the time of love
Appears upon the rocks & hills in silent shades but soon
A voice came in the night a midnight cry upon the mountains
Awake the bridegroom cometh I awoke to sleep no more . . .

*

As the seed waits eagerly watching for its flower & fruit
Anxious its little soul looks out into the clear expanse
To see if hungry winds are abroad with their invisible army
So Man looks out in tree & herb & fish & bird & beast,
Collecting up the scatter'd portions of his immortal body 20
Into the Elemental forms of every thing that grows.
He tries the sullen north wind riding on its angry furrows,
The sultry south when the sun rises, & the angry east
When the sun sets when the clods harden & the cattle stand
Drooping, & the birds hide in their silent nests, he stores his
thoughts
As in a store house in his memory, he regulates the forms
Of all beneath & all above; & in the gentle West
Reposes where the Sun's heat dwells: he rises to the Sun
And to the Planets of the Night & to the stars that gild
The Zodiac & the stars that sullen stand to north & south. 30
He touches the remotest pole & in the Center weeps,
That Man should Labour & sorrow & learn & forget & return
To the dark valley whence he came, to begin his labours
anew.
In pain he sighs, in pain he labours in his universe
Screaming in birds over the deep & howling in the Wolf
Over the slain, & moaning in the cattle & in the winds,

And weeping over Orc & Urizen in clouds & flaming fires,
And in the cries of birth & in the groans of death his voice
Is heard throughout the Universe, whereever a grass grows
Or a leaf buds, the Eternal Man is seen, is heard, is felt, 40
And all his Sorrows, till he reassumes his ancient bliss.

Ninth Night

[Revival of the Eternal Man]

When Morning dawn'd, the Eternals rose to labour at the Vintage.
Beneath they saw their sons & daughters wondering inconcievable
At the dark myriads in Shadows in the worlds beneath.

The morning dawn'd, Urizen rose & in his hand the Flail
Sounds, on the Floor heard terrible by all beneath the heavens,
Dismal loud redounding the nether floor shakes with the sound.
And all Nations were threshed out & the stars thresh'd from their husks.

Then Tharmas took the Winnowing fan, the winnowing wind furious
Above veer'd round by the violent whirlwind driven west & south
Tossed the Nations like Chaff into the seas of Tharmas. 10

O "Mystery Fierce! Tharmas cries: Behold thy end is come!
Art thou she that made the nations drunk with the cup of Religion?
Go down! ye Kings & Councillors & Giant Warriors
Go down! into the depths go down & hide yourselves beneath
Go down with horse & Chariots & Trumpets of hoarse war!

Lo! how the Pomp of Mystery goes down into the Caves
Her great men howl & throw the dust & rend their hoary hair:

Her delicate women & children shriek upon the bitter wind,
Spoil'd of their beauty their hair rent & their skin shrivel'd
  up
Lo! darkness covers the long pomp of banners on the wind 20
And black horses & armed men & miserable bound captives.
Where shall the graves recieve them all & where shall be
  their place
And who shall mourn for Mystery who never loos'd her
  Captives?
Let the slave grinding at the mill run out into the field
Let him look up into the heavens & laugh in the bright air:
Let the inchain'd soul shut up in darkness & in sighing
Whose face has never seen a smile in thirty weary years
Rise & look out! his chains are loose his dungeon doors are
  open,
And let his wife & children return from the oppressor's
  scourge:

They look behind at every step & believe it is a dream. 30
Are these the Slaves that groan'd along the streets of
  Mystery?
Where are your bonds & task masters: are these the
  prisoners?
Where are your chains, where are your tears, why do you
  look around:
If you are thirsty there is the river, go bathe your parched
  limbs.
The good of all the Land is before you for Mystery is no
  more!

Then All the Slaves from every Earth in the wide Universe
Sing a New Song, drowning confusion in its happy notes,
While the flail of Urizen sounded loud & the winnowing
  wind of Tharmas
So loud so clear in the wide heavens: & the song that they
  sung was this,
Composed by an African Black from the little Earth of Sotha: 40

Aha! Aha! how came I here so soon in my sweet native land?
How came I here? Methinks I am as I was in my youth
When in my father's house I sat & heard his chearing voice.
Methinks I see his flocks & herds & feel my limbs renew'd,
And Lo, my Brethren in their tents & their little ones around
them!

The song arose to the Golden feast: the Eternal Man rejoic'd.

LETTERS TO THOMAS BUTTS

[1] *2 October 1800*

To my Friend Butts I write
My first Vision of Light
On the yellow sands sitting:
The Sun was Emitting
His Glorious beams
From Heaven's high Streams
Over Sea over Land
My Eyes did Expand
Into regions of air
Away from all Care, 10
Into regions of fire
Remote from Desire
The Light of the Morning
Heaven's Mountains adorning:
In particles bright
The jewels of Light
Distinct shone & clear, –
Amaz'd & in fear
I each particle gazed,
Astonish'd Amazed 20
For each was a Man
Human-form'd: Swift I ran
For they beckon'd to me
Remote by the Sea
Saying: Each grain of Sand
Every Stone on the Land
Each rock & each hill
Each fountain & rill
Each herb & each tree
Mountain, hill, earth & sea 30
Cloud Meteor & Star
Are Men Seen Afar.
I stood in the Streams

Of Heaven's bright beams
And Saw Felpham sweet
Beneath my bright feet
In soft Female charms,
And in her fair arms
My Shadow I knew
And my wife's shadow too 40
And My Sister & Friend.
We like Infants descend
In our Shadows on Earth,
Like a weak mortal birth:
My Eyes more & more
Like a Sea without shore
Continue Expanding
The Heavens commanding,
Till the Jewels of Light
Heavenly Men beaming bright 50
Appear'd as One Man,
Who Complacent began
My limbs to infold
In his beams of bright gold:
Like dross purg'd away
All my mire & my clay.
Soft consum'd in delight
In his bosom sun bright
I remain'd: Soft he smil'd
And I heard his voice Mild 60
Saying: This is My Fold
O thou [n]Ram horn'd with gold,
Who awakest from Sleep
On the Sides of the Deep.
On the Mountains around
The roarings resound
Of the lion & wolf,
The loud Sea & deep gulf:
These are guards of My Fold
O thou Ram horn'd with gold! 70
And the voice faded mild:

I remain'd as a child
All I ever had known
Before me bright Shone:
I saw you and your Wife
By the fountains of life.
Such the Vision to me
Appear'd on the Sea.

[2] *22 November 1802*

With happiness stretch'd across the hills
In a cloud that dewy sweetness distills,
With a blue sky spread over with wings
And a mild sun that mounts & sings,
With trees & fields full of Fairy elves
And little devils who fight for themselves –
Rememb'ring the Verses that Hayley sung
When my heart knock'd against the root of my tongue
With Angels planted in Hawthorn bowers
And God himself in the passing hours: 10
With Silver Angels across my way
And Golden Demons that none can stay,
With my Father hovering upon the wind
And my Brother "Robert just behind
And my Brother John the evil one
In a black cloud making his mone:
Tho' dead they appear upon my path
Notwithstanding my terrible wrath
They beg, they intreat, they drop their tears
Fill'd full of hopes, fill'd full of fears, 20
With a thousand Angels upon the Wind
Pouring disconsolate from behind,
To drive them off & before my way
A frowning Thistle implores my stay.
What to others a trifle appears
Fills me full of smiles or tears,
For double the vision my Eyes do see

And a double vision is always with me:
With my inward Eye 'tis an old Man grey
With my outward a Thistle across my way. 30
'If thou goest back,' the thistle said
'Thou art to endless woe betray'd,
For here does Theotormon lower
And here is Enitharmon's bower,
And Los the terrible thus hath sworn
Because thou backward dost return
Poverty Envy old age & fear
Shall bring thy Wife upon a bier,
And Butts shall give what Fuseli gave
A dark black Rock & a gloomy Cave.' 40

I struck the Thistle with my foot
And broke him up from his delving root:
'Must the duties of life each other cross
Must every joy be dung & dross?
Must my dear Butts feel cold neglect
Because I give Hayley his due respect?
Must Flaxman look upon me as wild
And all my friends be with doubts beguil'd:
Must my Wife live in my Sisters bane
Or my sister survive on my Love's pain? 50
The curses of Los the terrible shade
And his dismal terrors make me afraid.'

So I spoke & struck in my wrath
The old man weltering upon my path:
Then Los appear'd in all his power,
In the Sun he appear'd descending before
My face in fierce flames: in my double sight
Twas outward a Sun; inward Los in his might.

'My hands are labour'd day & night
And Ease comes never in my sight: 60
My Wife has no indulgence given
Except what comes to her from heaven.
We eat little we drink less,

This Earth breeds not our happiness:
Another Sun feeds our life's streams;
We are not warmed with thy beams.
Thou measurest not the Time to me
Nor yet the Space that I do see.
My Mind is not with thy light array'd
Thy terrors shall not make me afraid.' 70

When I had my Defiance given
The Sun stood trembling in heaven:
The Moon that glow'd remote below
Became leprous & white as snow,
And every Soul of men on the Earth
Felt affliction & sorrow & sickness & dearth.
Los flam'd in my path & the Sun was hot
With the bows of my Mind & the Arrows of Thought.
My bowstring fierce with Ardour breathes
My arrows glow in their golden sheaves, 80
My brothers & father march before
The heavens drop with human gore.

Now I a fourfold vision see
And a fourfold vision is given to me:
Tis fourfold in my supreme delight,
And threefold in soft Beulah's night,
And twofold Always. May God us keep
From Single vision & Newton's sleep.

POEMS FROM THE PICKERING MANUSCRIPT

The Smile

There is a Smile of Love,
And there is a Smile of Deceit,
And there is a Smile of Smiles,
In which these two Smiles meet:

And there is a Frown of Hate,
And there is a Frown of disdain,
And there is a Frown of Frowns
Which you strive to forget in vain,

For it sticks in the Heart's deep Core
And it sticks in the deep Back bone, 10
And no Smile that ever was smil'd
But only one Smile alone

That betwixt the Cradle & Grave
It only once Smil'd can be,
But when it once is Smil'd
There's an end to all Misery.

[n]*The Golden Net*

Three Virgins at the break of day:
Whither young Man whither away?
Alas for woe! alas for woe!
They cry & tears for ever flow.
The one was Cloth'd in flames of fire
The other Cloth'd in iron wire
The other Cloth'd in tears & sighs.
Dazling bright before my Eyes
They bore a Net of Golden twine
To hang upon the Branches fine: 10
Pitying I wept to see the woe
That Love & Beauty undergo

To be consum'd in burning Fires
And in ungratified desires
And in tears cloth'd Night & day,
Melted all my Soul away.
When they saw my Tears, a Smile
That did Heaven itself beguile
Bore the Golden Net aloft
As on downy Pinions soft: 20
Over the Morning of my day
Underneath the Net I stray,
Now intreating Iron Wire
Now intreating Tears & Sighs –
O when will the morning rise?

The Mental Traveller

I travel'd thro' a Land of Men
A Land of Men & Women too,
And heard & saw such dreadful things
As cold Earth wanderers never knew:

For there the Babe is born in joy
That was begotten in dire woe,
Just as we Reap in joy the fruit
Which we in bitter tears did sow.

And if the Babe is born a Boy
He's given to a Woman Old 10
Who nails him down upon a rock,
Catches his shrieks in cups of gold;

She binds iron thorns around his head
She pierces both his hands & feet,
She cuts his heart out at his side
To make it feel both cold & heat.

Her fingers number every Nerve
Just as a Miser counts his gold:
She lives upon his shrieks & cries
And she grows young as he grows old, 20

Till he becomes a bleeding youth
And she becomes a Virgin bright;
Then he rends up his Manacles
And binds her down for his delight.

He plants himself in all her Nerves
Just as a Husbandman his mould,
And she becomes his dwelling place
And Garden fruitful seventy fold.

An aged Shadow soon he fades,
Wand'ring round an Earthly Cot, 30
Full filled all with gems & gold
Which he by industry had got.

And these are the gems of the Human Soul,
The rubies & pearls of a lovesick eye,
The countless gold of the akeing heart
The martyr's groan & the lover's sigh;

They are his meat, they are his drink;
He feeds the Beggar & the Poor
And the wayfaring Traveller,
For ever open is his door. 40

His grief is their eternal joy
They make the roofs & walls to ring
Till from the fire on the hearth
A little Female Babe does spring.

And she is all of solid fire
And gems & gold, that none his hand
Dares stretch to touch her Baby form
Or wrap her in his swaddling-band.

But She comes to the Man she loves
If young or old or rich or poor 50
They soon drive out the aged Host,
A Beggar at another's door.

He wanders weeping far away
Until some other take him in,
Oft blind & age-bent sore distrest
Untill he can a Maiden win;

And to allay his freezing Age
The Poor Man takes her in his arms:
The Cottage fades before his sight,
The Garden & its lovely Charms. 60

The Guests are scatter'd thro' the land,
For the Eye altering alters all;
The Senses roll themselves in fear
And the flat Earth becomes a Ball.

The Stars Sun Moon, all shrink away
A desart vast without a bound
And nothing left to eat or drink
And a dark desart all around.

The honey of her Infant lips
The bread & wine of her sweet smile, 70
The wild game of her roving Eye
Does him to Infancy beguile;

For as he eats & drinks he grows
Younger & younger every day
And on the desart wild they both
Wander in terror & dismay.

Like the wild Stag she flees away
Her fear plants many a thicket wild,
While he pursues her night & day
By various arts of Love beguil'd, 80

By various arts of Love & Hate,
Till the wide desart planted o'er
With Labyrinths of wayward Love
Where roams the Lion Wolf & Boar:

Till he becomes a wayward Babe
And she a weeping Woman Old.
Then many a Lover wanders here
The Sun & Stars are nearer roll'd,

The trees bring forth sweet Extacy
To all who in the desart roam, 90
Till many a City there is Built
And many a pleasant Shepherd's home.

But when they find the frowning Babe
Terror strikes thro' the region wide
They cry: the Babe, the Babe is Born!
And flee away on Every side.

For who dare touch the frowning form
His arm is wither'd to its root
Lions Boars Wolves, all howling flee
And every Tree does shed its fruit. 100

And none can touch that frowning form,
Except it be a Woman Old:
She nails him down upon the Rock
And all is done as I have told.

Mary

Sweet Mary the first time she ever was there,
Came into the Ball room among the Fair;
The young Men & Maidens around her throng,
And these are the words upon every tongue:

'An Angel is here from the heavenly Climes,
Or again does return the Golden times;
Her eyes outshine every brilliant ray,
She opens her lips, 'tis the Month of May.'

Mary moves in soft beauty & conscious delight
To augment with sweet smiles all the joys of the Night, 10
Nor once blushes to own to the rest of the Fair
That sweet Love & Beauty are worthy our care.

In the Morning the Villagers rose with delight
And repeated with pleasure the joys of the night,
And Mary arose among Friends to be free,
But no Friend from henceforward thou, Mary, shalt see.

Some said she was proud, some call'd her a whore,
And some when she passed by shut to the door:
A damp cold came o'er her, her blushes all fled,
Her lillies & roses are blighted & shed. 20

'O, why was I born with a different Face?
Why was I not born like this Envious Race?
Why did Heaven adorn me with bountiful hand,
And then set me down in an envious Land?

'To be weak as a Lamb & smooth as a dove,
And not to raise Envy is call'd Christian Love:
But if you raise Envy your Merit's to blame
For planting such spite in the weak & the tame.

'I will humble my Beauty, I will not dress fine, 30
I will keep from the Ball & my Eyes shall not shine;
And if any Girl's Lover forsakes her for me,
I'll refuse him my hand & from Envy be free.'

She went out in Morning attir'd plain & neat:
'Proud Mary's gone Mad,' said the Child in the Street.
She went out in Morning in plain neat attire,
And came home in Evening bespatter'd with mire.

She trembled & wept sitting on the Bed side;
She forgot it was Night & she trembled & cried; 40
She forgot it was Night she forgot it was Morn,
Her soft Memory imprinted with Faces of Scorn,

With Faces of Scorn & with Eyes of disdain
Like foul Fiends inhabiting Mary's mild Brain;
She remembers no Face like the Human Divine.
All Faces have Envy, sweet Mary, but thine;

And thine is a Face of sweet Love in despair,
And thine is a Face of mild sorrow & care,
And thine is a Face of wild terror & fear
That shall never be quiet till laid on its bier.

[n] *The Crystal Cabinet*

The Maiden caught me in the Wild,
Where I was dancing merrily;
She put me into her Cabinet
And Lock'd me up with a golden Key.

This Cabinet is form'd of Gold
And Pearl & Crystal shining bright,
And within it opens into a World
And a little lovely Moony Night.

Another England there I saw,
Another London with its Tower, 10
Another Thames & other Hills,
And another pleasant Surrey Bower,

Another Maiden like herself,
Translucent, lovely, shining clear,
Threefold each in the other clos'd:
O, what a pleasant trembling fear!

O, what a smile! a threefold Smile
Fill'd me that like a flame I burn'd;
I bent to Kiss the lovely Maid
And found a Threefold Kiss return'd: 20

I strove to sieze the inmost Form
With ardor fierce & hands of flame,
But burst the Crystal Cabinet
And like a Weeping Babe became:

A weeping Babe upon the wild
And Weeping Woman pale reclin'd
And in the outward air again
I fill'd with woes the passing Wind.

[n]*The Grey Monk*

I die I die the Mother said
My Children die for lack of Bread
What more has the merciless Tyrant said?
The Monk sat down on the Stony Bed

The blood red ran from the Grey Monk's side
His hands & feet were wounded wide
His Body bent his arms & knees
Like to the roots of ancient trees.

His eye was dry no tear could flow
A hollow groan first spoke his woe 10
He trembled & shudder'd upon the Bed:
At length with a feeble cry he said:

When God commanded this hand to write
In the studious hours of deep midnight
He told me the writing I wrote should prove
The Bane of all that on Earth I lov'd.

My Brother starv'd between two Walls
His Children's Cry my Soul appalls.
I mock'd at the wrack & griding chain
My bent body mocks their torturing pain. 20

Thy Father drew his sword in the North
With his thousands strong he marched forth:
Thy Brother has arm'd himself in Steel
To avenge the wrongs thy Children feel:

But vain the Sword & vain the Bow
They never can work War's overthrow.
The Hermit's Prayer & the Widow's tear
Alone can free the World from fear.

For a Tear is an Intellectual Thing
And a Sigh is the Sword of an Angel King 30
And the bitter groan of the Martyr's woe
Is an Arrow from the Almightie's Bow.

The hand of Vengeance found the Bed
To which the Purple Tyrant fled
The iron hand crush'd the Tyrant's head
And became a Tyrant in his stead.

[n]*Auguries of Innocence*

To see a World in a Grain of Sand
And a Heaven in a Wild Flower,
Hold Infinity in the palm of your hand
And Eternity in an hour.

A Robin Red breast in a Cage
Puts all Heaven in a Rage.
A dove house fill'd with doves & Pigeons
Shudders Hell thro' all its regions.
A dog starv'd at his Master's Gate
Predicts the ruin of the State. 10
A Horse misus'd upon the Road
Calls to Heaven for Human blood.
Each outcry of the hunted Hare
A fibre from the Brain does tear.
A Skylark wounded in the wing,
A Cherubim does cease to sing.
The Game Cock clip'd & arm'd for fight
Does the Rising Sun affright.
Every Wolf's & Lion's howl
Raises from Hell a Human Soul. 20
The wild deer wand'ring here & there
Keeps the Human Soul from Care.
The Lamb misus'd breeds Public strife
And yet forgives the Butcher's Knife.
The Bat that flits at close of Eve
Has left the Brain that won't Believe.
The Owl that calls upon the Night
Speaks the Unbeliever's fright.
He who shall hurt the little Wren
Shall never be belov'd by Men. 30

He who the Ox to wrath has mov'd
Shall never be by Woman lov'd.
The wanton Boy that kills the Fly
Shall feel the Spider's enmity.
He who torments the Chafer's sprite
Weaves a Bower in endless Night.
The Catterpiller on the Leaf
Repeats to thee thy Mother's grief.
Kill not the Moth nor Butterfly,
For the Last Judgment draweth nigh. 40
He who shall train the Horse to War
Shall never pass the Polar Bar.
The Beggar's Dog & Widow's Cat,
Feed them & thou wilt grow fat.
The Gnat that sings his Summer's song
Poison gets from Slander's tongue.
The poison of the Snake & Newt
Is the sweat of Envy's Foot.
The Poison of the Honey Bee
Is the Artist's Jealousy. 50
The Prince's Robes & Beggar's Rags
Are Toadstools on the Miser's Bags.
A truth that's told with bad intent
Beats all the Lies you can invent.
It is right it should be so;
Man was made for Joy & Woe,
And when this we rightly know
Thro' the World we safely go.
Joy & Woe are woven fine
A Clothing for the Soul divine: 60
Under every grief & pine
Runs a joy with silken twine.
The Babe is more than swadling Bands:
Throughout all these Human Lands
Tools were made, & Born were hands,
Every Farmer Understands.
Every Tear in Every Eye
Becomes a Babe in Eternity;

This is caught by Females bright
And return'd to its own delight. 70
The Bleat, the Bark, Bellow & Roar
Are Waves that Beat on Heaven's Shore.
The Babe that weeps the Rod beneath
Writes Revenge in realms of death.
The Beggar's Rags, fluttering in Air,
Does to Rags the Heavens tear.
The Soldier arm'd with Sword & Gun
Palsied strikes the Summer's Sun.
The poor Man's Farthing is worth more
Than all the Gold on Afric's Shore. 80
One Mite wrung from the Lab'rer's hands
Shall buy & sell the Miser's Lands:
Or, if protected from on high,
Does that whole Nation sell & buy.
He who mocks the Infant's Faith
Shall be mock'd in Age & Death.
He who shall teach the Child to Doubt
The rotting Grave shall ne'er get out.
He who respects the Infant's faith
Triumphs over Hell & Death. 90
The Child's Toys & the Old Man's Reasons
Are the Fruits of the Two seasons.
The Questioner who sits so sly,
Shall never know how to Reply.
He who replies to words of Doubt
Doth put the Light of Knowledge out.
The Strongest Poison ever known
Came from Caesar's Laurel Crown.
Nought can deform the Human Race
Like to the Armour's iron brace. 100
When Gold & Gems adorn the Plow
To peaceful Arts shall Envy Bow.
A Riddle or the Cricket's Cry
Is to Doubt a fit Reply.
The Emmet's Inch & Eagle's Mile
Make Lame Philosophy to smile.

He who Doubts from what he sees
Will ne'er Believe, do what you Please.
If the Sun & Moon should doubt,
They'd immediately Go out. 110
To be in a Passion you Good may do,
But no Good if a Passion is in you.
The Whore & Gambler by the State
Licenc'd build that Nation's Fate.
The Harlot's cry from Street to Street
Shall weave Old England's winding Sheet.
The Winner's Shout the Loser's Curse
Dance before dead England's Hearse.
Every night & every Morn
Some to Misery are Born. 120
Every Morn & every Night
Some are Born to sweet delight.
Some are Born to sweet delight,
Some are Born to Endless Night.
We are led to Believe a Lie
When we see not Thro' the Eye,
Which was Born in a Night to perish in a Night,
When the Soul Slept in Beams of Light.
God Appears & God is Light
To those poor Souls who dwell in Night, 130
But does a Human Form Display
To those who Dwell in Realms of day.

NOTEBOOK POEMS: FELPHAM AND AFTER

[n]My Spectre around me night & day
Like a Wild beast guards my way,
My Emanation far within
Weeps incessantly for my Sin.

A Fathomless & boundless deep
There we wander there we weep:
On the hungry craving wind
My Spectre follows thee behind.

He scents thy footsteps in the snow
Wheresoever thou dost go 10
Thro' the wintry hail & rain:
When wilt thou return again?

Dost thou not in Pride & Scorn
Fill with tempests all my morn,
And with jealousies & fears
Fill my pleasant nights with tears?

Seven of my sweet loves thy knife
Has bereaved of their life:
Their marble tombs I built with tears
And with cold & shuddering fears. 20

Seven more loves weep night & day
Round the tombs where my loves lay,
And seven more loves attend each night
Around my couch with torches bright:

And seven more Loves in my bed
Crown with wine my mournful head
Pitying & forgiving all
Thy transgressions great & small.

When wilt thou return & view
My loves & them to life renew, 30
When wilt thou return & live,
When wilt thou pity as I forgive?

Never Never I return
Still for Victory I burn.
Living thee alone I'll have
And when dead I'll be thy Grave:

Thro' the Heaven & Earth & Hell
Thou shalt never never quell
I will fly & thou pursue
Night & Morn the flight renew 40

Till I turn from Female Love
And root up the Infernal Grove
I shall never worthy be
To Step into Eternity:

And to end thy cruel mocks
Annihilate thee on the rocks
And another form create
To be subservient to my Fate.

Let us agree to give up Love
And root up the infernal grove: 50
Then shall we return & see
The worlds of happy Eternity.

& Throughout all Eternity
I forgive you, you forgive me,
As our Dear Redeemer said:
This the Wine & this the Bread.

O'er my Sins Thou sit & moan
Hast thou no sins of thy own?
O'er my Sins thou sit & weep
And lull thy own Sins fast asleep.

What transgressions I commit
Are for thy Transgressions fit,
They thy Harlots thou their Slave
And my Bed becomes their Grave.

Poor pale pitiable form
That I follow in a Storm, 10
Iron tears & groans of lead
Bind around my akeing head:

And let us go to the highest downs
With many pleasing wiles
The Woman that does not love your Frowns
Will never embrace your smiles.

---

[n]Mock on, Mock on Voltaire, Rousseau:
Mock on, Mock on: 'tis all in vain!
You throw the sand against the wind
And the wind blows it back again.

And every sand becomes a Gem
Reflected in the beams divine;
Blown back they blind the mocking Eye
But still in Israel's paths they shine.

The Atoms of Democritus
And Newton's Particles of light 10
Are sands upon the Red sea shore
Where Israel's tents do shine so bright.

You don't believe I won't attempt to make ye
You are asleep I won't attempt to wake ye:
Sleep on, Sleep on: while in your pleasant dreams
Of Reason you may drink of Life's clear streams.
Reason and Newton they are quite two things
For so the Swallow & the Sparrow sings.

Reason says Miracle, Newton says Doubt –
Aye that's the way to make all Nature out –
Doubt, Doubt & don't believe without experiment:
That is the very thing that Jesus meant 10
When he said, Only Believe Believe & try
Try Try & never mind the Reason why.

The Angel that presided o'er my birth
Said, Little creature form'd of Joy & Mirth
Go love without the help of any King on Earth.

[n]From Cratetos

Me Time has Crook'd. No good Workman
Is he: Infirm is all that he does.

Anger & Wrath my bosom rends
I thought them the Errors of friends
But all my limbs with warmth glow
I find them the Errors of the foe.

Was I angry with Hayley who us'd me so ill
Or can I be angry with Felpham's old Mill
Or angry with [n]Flaxman or Cromek or Stothard,
Or poor Schiavonetti whom they to death bother'd
Or angry with Macklin or Boydel or Bowyer
Because they did not say O what a Beau ye are
At a Friend's Errors Anger shew
Mirth at the Errors of a Foe.

My title as a Genius thus is prov'd
Not Prais'd by Hayley nor by Flaxman lov'd.

To H[ayley]

You think Fuseli is not a Great Painter: I'm Glad
This is one of the best compliments he ever had.

To forgive Enemies H[ayley] does pretend
Who never in his Life forgave a friend.

On H[ayle]y's Friendship

When H[ayle]y finds out what you cannot do
That is the very thing he'll set you to
If you break not your Neck 'tis not his fault
But pecks of poison are not pecks of salt:
And when he could not act upon my wife
Hired a Villain to bereave my Life.

To H[ayley]

Thy Friendship oft has made my heart to ake
Do be my Enemy for Friendship's sake.

On H[ayley] the Pick thank

I write the Rascal Thanks till he & I
With Thanks & Compliments are quite drawn dry.

[n]*William Cowper Esq[re]*

For this is being a Friend just in the nick
Not when he's well but waiting till he's sick
He calls you to his help be you not mov'd
Untill by being Sick his wants are prov'd

You see him spend his Soul in Prophecy
Do you believe it a confounded lie
Till some Bookseller & the Public Fame
Proves there is truth in his extravagant claim

For 'tis atrocious in a Friend you love
To tell you any thing that he can't prove 10
And 'tis most wicked in a Christian Nation
For any Man to pretend to Inspiration.

The only Man that e'er I knew
Who did not make me almost spew
Was Fuseli: he was both Turk & Jew –
And so dear Christian Friends how do you do?

Madman I have been call'd, Fool they call thee –
I wonder which they Envy Thee or Me?

He's a Blockhead who wants a proof of what he can't
Percieve
And he's a Fool who tries to make such a Blockhead believe.

He has observ'd the Golden Rule
Till he's become the Golden Fool.

To S[tothar]d

You all your Youth observ'd the Golden Rule
Till you're at last become the golden fool.
I sport with Fortune, Merry Blithe & gay

Like to the Lion Sporting with his Prey.
Take you the hide & horns which you may wear,
Mine is the flesh: the bones may be your Share.

Cr[omek] loves artists as he loves his Meat
He loves the Art: but 'tis the Art to Cheat.

A Petty sneaking Knave I knew:
O Mr. Cr[omek] how do ye do?

---

[n]You say their Pictures well Painted be
And yet they are Blockheads you all agree:
Thank God I never was sent to school
To be flog'd into following the Style of a Fool.

The Errors of a Wise Man make your Rule
Rather than the Perfections of a Fool.

Great things are done when Men & Mountains meet
This is not done by Jostling in the Street.

[n]*Florentine Ingratitude*

Sir Joshua sent his own Portrait to
The birth Place of Michael Angelo
And in the hand of the simpering fool
He put a dirty paper scroll
And on the paper to be polite

Did 'Sketches by Michael Angelo' write.
The Florentines said, 'Tis a Dutch-English bore,
Michael Angelo's name writ on Rembrandt's door.
The Florentines call it an English Fetch
For Michael Angelo did never Sketch: 10
Every line of his has Meaning
And needs neither Suckling nor Weaning.
'Tis the trading English-Venetian Cant
To speak Michael Angelo & Act Rembrandt.
It will set his Dutch friends all in a roar
To write Mch. Ang. on Rembrandt's Door:
But you must not bring in your hand a Lie
If you mean that the Florentines should buy.
[n]Ghiotto's Circle or Apelles' Line
Were not the Work of Sketchers drunk with Wine 20
Nor of the City Clarks' merry hearted Fashion
Nor of Sir Isaac Newton's Calculation
Nor of the City Clarks' Idle Facilities
Which sprang from Sir Isaac Newton's great Abilities.

These Verses were written by a very Envious Man
Who whatever likeness he may have to Michael Angelo
Never can have any to Sir Jehoshuan.

I Rubens am a Statesman & a Saint.
Deceptions? O no – so I'll learn to Paint.

These are the Idiot's chiefest arts
To blend & not define the Parts.
The Swallow sings in Courts of Kings
That Fools have their high finishings,
And this the Prince's golden rule
The Laborious stumble of a Fool.
To make out the parts is the wise man's aim
But to lose them the Fool makes his foolish Game.

O dear Mother Outline of Knowledge most sage
What's the First Part of Painting? she said Patronage.
And what is the second to please & Engage?
She frown'd like a Fury & said Patronage.
And what is the Third? she put off Old Age
And smil'd like a Syren & said Patronage.

Her whole Life is an Epigram, smack-smooth & nobly pen'd,
Platted quite neat to catch applause with a sliding noose at the end.

When a Man has Married a Wife he finds out whether
Her knees & elbows are only glued together.

Grown old in Love from Seven till Seven times Seven
I oft have wish'd for Hell for Ease from Heaven.

To God

If you have form'd a Circle to go into
Go into it yourself & see how you would do.

I rose up at the dawn of day –
Get thee away! get thee away!
Pray'st thou for Riches? away! away!
This is the Throne of Mammon grey.

Said I, This sure is very odd.
I took it to be the Throne of God.
For every Thing besides I have:
It is only for Riches that I can crave.

I have Mental Joy & Mental Health
And Mental Friends & Mental wealth; 10
I've a Wife I love & that loves me;
I've all but Riches Bodily.

I am in God's presence night & day,
And he never turns his face away.
The Accuser of Sins by my side does stand
And he holds my money bag in his hand.

For my worldly things God makes him pay,
And he'd pay more if to him I would pray;
And so you may do the worst you can do:
Be assur'd Mr devil I won't pray to you. 20

Then If for Riches I must not Pray,
God knows I little of Prayers need say.
So as a Church is known by its Steeple,
If I pray it must be for other People.

He says, if I do not worship him for a God,
I shall eat coarser food & go worse shod;
So as I don't value such things as these,
You must do, Mr devil, just as God please.

from MILTON

a Poem in 2 Books

TO JUSTIFY THE WAYS OF GOD TO MEN

[1] [n]And did those feet in ancient time
Walk upon England's mountains green?
And was the holy Lamb of God
On England's pleasant pastures seen?

And did the Countenance Divine
Shine forth upon our clouded hills?
And was Jerusalem builded here
Among these dark Satanic Mills?

Bring me my Bow of burning gold:
Bring me my Arrows of desire: 10
Bring me my Spear: O clouds unfold!
Bring me my Chariot of fire.

I will not cease from Mental Fight,
Nor shall my Sword sleep in my hand
Till we have built Jerusalem
In England's green & pleasant Land.

'Would to God that all the Lord's people were Prophets.'

Numbers, xi. ch., 29 v.

Book the First

[Invocation]

[2] Daughters of Beulah! Muses who inspire the Poet's Song
Record the journey of immortal Milton thro' your Realms
Of terror & mild moony lustre in soft sexual delusions
Of varied beauty to delight the wanderer and repose
His burning thirst & freezing hunger! Come into my hand
By your mild power; descending down the Nerves of my
right arm
From out the Portals of my brain, where by your ministry

The Eternal Great Humanity Divine planted his Paradise,
And in it caus'd the [n]Spectres of the Dead to take sweet forms
In likeness of himself. Tell also of the [n]False Tongue!
  vegetated 10
Beneath your land of shadows: of its sacrifices and
Its offerings; even till Jesus, the image of the Invisible God,
Became its prey: a curse, an offering and an atonement
For Death Eternal in the heavens of Albion, & before the
  Gates
Of Jerusalem his Emanation, in the heavens beneath Beulah.

Say first! what mov'd Milton, who walk'd about in Eternity
One hundred years, pond'ring the intricate mazes of
  Providence –
Unhappy tho' in heav'n, he obey'd, he murmur'd not, he
  was silent
Viewing his [n]Sixfold Emanation scatter'd thro' the deep
In torment! To go into the deep her to redeem & himself
  perish? 20
What cause at length mov'd Milton to this unexampled deed?
A Bard's prophetic Song! for sitting at eternal tables,
Terrific among the Sons of Albion in chorus solemn & loud
A Bard broke forth! all sat attentive to the awful man.

*

[The Bard's Song: Palamabron's Dispute with Los]

[6] [n]Loud sounds the Hammer of Los, loud turn the Wheels of
  Enitharmon
Her Looms vibrate with soft affections, weaving the Web of
  Life
Out from the ashes of the Dead; Los lifts his iron Ladles
With molten ore: he heaves the iron cliffs in his rattling
  chains
From Hyde Park to the Alms-houses of Mile-end & old Bow.
Here the [n]Three Classes of Mortal Men take their fix'd
  destinations

And hence they overspread the Nations of the whole Earth & hence
The Web of Life is woven: & the tender sinews of life created
And the Three Classes of Men regulated by Los's Hammer . . .

[7] The first, The [n]Elect from before the foundation of the World:
The second, The Redeem'd. The Third, The Reprobate & form'd
To destruction from the mothers womb: follow with me my plow!

Of the first class was [n]Satan: with incomparable mildness;
His primitive tyrannical attempts on Los: with most endearing love
He soft intreated Los to give to him Palamabron's station;
For Palamabron return'd with labour wearied every evening.
Palamabron oft refus'd; and as often Satan offer'd
His service till by repeated offers and repeated intreaties
Los gave to him the Harrow of the Almighty; alas blamable. 10
Palamabron fear'd to be angry, lest Satan should accuse him of
Ingratitude, & Los believe the accusation thro' Satan's extreme
Mildness. Satan labour'd all day; it was a thousand years;
In the evening returning terrified, overlabour'd & astonish'd,
Embrac'd soft with a brother's tears Palamabron, who also wept.

Mark well my words! they are of your eternal salvation.

Next morning Palamabron rose: the horses of the Harrow
Were madden'd with tormenting fury, & the servants of the Harrow,
The Gnomes, accus'd Satan with indignation fury and fire.
Then Palamabron reddening like the Moon in an eclipse, 20
Spoke saying; You know Satan's mildness and his self-imposition,
Seeming a brother, being a tyrant, even thinking himself a brother

While he is murdering the just; prophetic I behold
His future course thro' darkness and despair to eternal death.
But we must not be tyrants also! he hath assum'd my place
For one whole day, under pretence of pity and love to me:
My horses hath he madden'd! and my fellow servants injur'd:
How should he, he, know the duties of another? O foolish forbearance!
Would I had told Los all my heart! but patience O my friends,
All may be well: silent remain, while I call Los and
Satan . . .[n] 30

*

[Satan Speaks]

[9] I am God alone
There is no other! let all obey my principles of moral individuality.
I have brought them from the uppermost innermost recesses
Of my Eternal Mind, transgressors I will rend off for ever,
As now I rend this accursed Family from my covering.

Thus Satan rag'd amidst the Assembly! and his bosom grew
Opake against the Divine Vision: the paved terraces of
His bosom inwards shone with fires, but the stones becoming opake!
Hid him from sight, in an extreme blackness and darkness,
And there a World of deeper [n]Ulro was open'd, in the midst 10
Of the Assembly. In Satan's bosom a vast unfathomable Abyss.

Astonishment held the Assembly in an awful silence: and tears
Fell down as dews of night, & a loud solemn universal groan
Was utter'd from the east & from the west & from the south
And from the north: and Satan stood opake, immeasurable,

Covering the east with solid blackness, round his hidden heart,
With thunders utter'd from his hidden wheels: accusing loud
The Divine Mercy, for protecting Palamabron in his tent . . .

*

And Satan, not having the Science of Wrath, but only of Pity,
Rent them asunder, and wrath was left to wrath, & pity to pity. 20
He sunk down a dreadful Death, unlike the slumbers of Beulah.

The Separation was terrible: the Dead was repos'd on his Couch
Beneath the Couch of Albion, on the seven mountains of Rome
In the whole place of the [n]Covering Cherub, Rome Babylon & Tyre.
His Spectre raging furious descended into its Space . . .

*

[13] The Bard ceas'd. All consider'd and a loud resounding murmur
Continu'd round the Halls; and much they question'd the immortal
Loud voic'd Bard and many condemn'd the high toned Song
Saying, Pity and Love are too venerable for the imputation
Of Guilt. Others said, If it is true, if the acts have been perform'd,
Let the Bard himself witness. Where hadst thou this terrible Song?

The Bard replied, I am Inspired! I know it is Truth! for I Sing
[14] According to the inspiration of the Poetic Genius
Who is the eternal all-protecting Divine Humanity
To whom be Glory & Power & Dominion Evermore. Amen.

*

[Milton begins his Journey]

Then Milton rose up from the heavens of Albion ardorous!
The whole Assembly wept prophetic seeing in Milton's face
And in his lineaments divine the Shades of Death & Ulro.
He took off the robe of the promise & ungirded himself from
the oath of God.

And Milton said: I go to Eternal Death! The Nations still
Follow after the detestable Gods of Priam; in pomp
Of warlike selfhood contradicting and blaspheming. 10
When will the Resurrection come? to deliver the sleeping
body
From corruptibility. O when Lord Jesus wilt thou come?
Tarry no longer; for my soul lies at the gates of death.
I will arise and look forth for the morning of the grave,
I will go down to the sepulcher to see if morning breaks!
I will go down to self annihilation and eternal death,
Lest the Last Judgment come & find me unannihilate
And I be siez'd & giv'n into the hands of my own Selfhood.
The Lamb of God is seen thro' mists & shadows, hov'ring
Over the sepulchers in clouds of Jehovah & winds of Elohim, 20
A disk of blood, distant; & heav'ns & earths roll dark
between.
What do I here before the Judgment? without my
Emanation?
With the daughters of memory, & not with the daughters of
Inspiration!
I in my Selfhood am that Satan: I am that Evil One!
He is my Spectre! in my obedience to loose him from my
Hells
To [n]claim the Hells, my Furnaces, I go to Eternal Death.

And Milton said: I go to Eternal Death! Eternity shudder'd,
For he took the outside course, among the graves of the dead,
A mournful shade. Eternity shudder'd at the image of eternal
death.

Then on the verge of Beulah he beheld his own Shadow; 30
A mournful form double, hermaphroditic: male & female

In one wonderful body, and he enter'd into it
In direful pain for the dread shadow, twenty-seven-fold
Reach'd to the depths of direst Hell, & thence to Albion's
land:
Which is this earth of vegetation on which now I write.

The Seven Angels of the Presence wept over Milton's
Shadow!

[15] As when a man dreams, he reflects not that his body sleeps,
Else he would wake; so seem'd he entering his Shadow: but
With him the Spirits of the Seven Angels of the Presence
Entering, they gave him still perceptions of his Sleeping
Body,
Which now arose and walk'd with them in Eden, as an Eighth
Image Divine tho' darken'd; and tho' walking as one walks
In sleep: and the Seven comforted and supported him.

Like as a [n]Polypus that vegetates beneath the deep
They saw his Shadow vegetated underneath the Couch
Of death: for when he enter'd into his Shadow, Himself, 10
His real and immortal Self, was as appear'd to those
Who dwell in immortality, as One sleeping on a couch
Of gold; and those in immortality gave forth their
Emanations
[n]Like Females of sweet beauty, to guard round him & to feed
His lips with food of Eden in his cold and dim repose!
But to himself he seem'd a wanderer lost in dreary night.

[n]Onwards his Shadow kept its course among the Spectres; call'd
Satan, but swift as lightning passing them, startled, the
shades
Of Hell beheld him in a trail of light as of a comet
That travels into Chaos: so Milton went guarded within. 20

The nature of infinity is this: That every thing has its
Own Vortex; and when once a traveller thro' Eternity
Has pass'd that Vortex, he percieves it roll backward behind
His path, into a globe itself infolding, like a sun:

Or like a moon, or like a universe of starry majesty,
While he keeps onwards in his wondrous journey on the
earth
Or like a human form, a friend with whom he liv'd
benevolent.
As the eye of man views both the east & west encompassing
Its vortex; and the north & south, with all their starry host;
Also the rising sun & setting moon he views surrounding 30
His corn-fields and his valleys of five hundred acres square.
Thus is the earth one infinite plane, and not as apparent
To the weak traveller confin'd beneath the moony shade.
Thus is the heaven a vortex pass'd already, and the earth
A vortex not yet pass'd by the traveller thro' Eternity.

First Milton saw Albion upon the Rock of Ages,
Deadly pale outstretch'd and snowy cold, storm cover'd,
A Giant form of perfect beauty outstretch'd on the rock
In solemn death: the Sea of Time & Space thunder'd aloud
Against the rock, which was inwrapped with the weeds of
death 40
Hovering over the cold bosom; in its vortex Milton bent
down
To the bosom of death: what was underneath soon seem'd
above,
A cloudy heaven mingled with stormy seas in loudest ruin;
But as a wintry globe descends precipitant thro' Beulah
bursting,
With thunders loud, and terrible: so Milton's shadow fell,
Precipitant loud thund'ring into the Sea of Time & Space.

Then first I saw him in the Zenith as a falling star,
Descending perpendicular, swift as the swallow or swift;
And on my left foot falling on the tarsus, enter'd there;
But from my left foot a black cloud redounding spread over
Europe. 50

*

[17] Los the Vehicular terror beheld him, & divine Enitharmon
Call'd all her daughters, Saying, "[n]Surely to unloose my bond
Is this Man come! Satan shall be unloos'd upon Albion!

Los heard in terror Enitharmon's words: in fibrous strength
His limbs shot forth like roots of trees against the forward path
Of Milton's journey. Urizen beheld the immortal Man,
[18] And Tharmas, Demon of the Waters, & Orc, who is Luvah.

The [n]Shadowy Female seeing Milton howl'd in her lamentation
Over the Deeps, outstretching her Twenty seven Heavens over Albion,

And thus the Shadowy Female howls in articulate howlings:

I will lament over Milton in the lamentations of the afflicted
My Garments shall be woven of sighs & heart broken lamentations
The misery of unhappy Families shall be drawn out into its border
Wrought with the needle with dire sufferings, poverty pain & woe
Along the rocky Island & thence throughout the whole Earth:
There shall be the sick Father & his starving Family! there 10
The Prisoner in the stone Dungeon & the Slave at the Mill.
I will have writings written all over it in Human Words
That every Infant that is born upon the Earth shall read
And get by rote as a hard task of a life of sixty years.
I will have Kings inwoven upon it & Councellors & Mighty Men.
The Famine shall clasp it together with buckles & Clasps
And the Pestilence shall be its fringe & the War its girdle
To divide into Rahab & Tirzah that Milton may come to our tents,
For I will put on the Human Form & take the Image of God
Even Pity & Humanity, but my Clothing shall be Cruelty. 20
And I will put on Holiness as a breastplate & as a helmet
And all my ornaments shall be of the gold of broken hearts
And the precious stones of anxiety & care & desperation & death

And repentance for sin & sorrow & punishment & fear,
To defend me from thy terrors! O Orc, my only beloved!

*

Urizen emerged from his Rocky Form & from his Snows,
[19] And he also darken'd his brows: freezing dark rocks between
The footsteps, and infixing deep the feet in marble beds,
That Milton labour'd with his journey, & his feet bled sore
Upon the clay now chang'd to marble; also Urizen rose,
And met him on the shores of [n]Arnon; & by the streams of
the brooks.

Silent they met, and silent strove among the streams of
Arnon
Even to Mahanaim, when with cold hand Urizen stoop'd
down
And took up water from the river Jordan: pouring on
To Milton's brain the icy fluid from his broad cold palm.
But Milton took of the red clay of Succoth, moulding it with
care 10
Between his palms; and filling up the furrows of many years
Beginning at the feet of Urizen, and on the bones
Creating new flesh on the Demon cold, and building him,
As with new clay a Human form in the Valley of Beth Peor.

*

[20] Silent Milton stood before
The darken'd Urizen, as the sculptor silent stands before
His forming image; he walks round it patient labouring.
Thus Milton stood forming bright Urizen, while his Mortal
part
Sat frozen in the rock of Horeb, and his Redeemed portion
Thus form'd the Clay of Urizen; but within that portion
His real Human walk'd above in power and majesty
Tho' darken'd, and the Seven Angels of the Presence
attended him.

O how can I with my gross tongue that cleaveth to the dust
Tell of the Four-fold Man in starry numbers fitly order'd; 10

Or how can I with my cold hand of clay! But thou, O Lord,
Do with me as thou wilt! for I am nothing, and vanity.
If thou chuse to elect a worm, it shall remove the mountains.
For that portion nam'd the Elect, the Spectrous body of Milton,
Redounding from my left foot into Los's Mundane ⁿSpace
Brooded over his Body in Horeb against the Resurrection,
Preparing it for the Great Consummation; red the Cherub on Sinai
Glow'd, but in terrors folded round his clouds of blood.

Now Albion's sleeping Humanity began to turn upon his Couch
Feeling the electric flame of Milton's awful precipitate descent. 20
Seest thou the little winged fly, smaller than a grain of sand?
It has a heart like thee, a brain open to heaven & hell,
Withinside wondrous & expansive: its gates are not clos'd;
I hope thine are not: hence it clothes itself in rich array:
Hence thou art cloth'd with human beauty, O thou mortal man.
Seek not thy heavenly father then beyond the skies,
There Chaos dwells & ancient Night & ⁿOg & Anak old.
For every human heart has gates of brass & bars of adamant
Which few dare unbar because dread Og & Anak guard the gates
Terrific: and each mortal brain is wall'd and moated round 30
Within, and Og & Anak watch here: here is the Seat
Of Satan in its Webs, for in brain and heart and loins
Gates open behind Satan's Seat to the City of Golgonooza,
Which is the spiritual fourfold London in the loins of Albion.

Thus Milton fell thro' Albion's heart, travelling outside of Humanity
Beyond the Stars in Chaos, in Caverns of the Mundane Shell.

But many of the Eternals rose up from eternal tables
Drunk with the Spirit: burning round the Couch of death they stood

Looking down into Beulah, wrathful, fill'd with rage!
They rend the heavens round the Watchers in a fiery circle 40
And round the Shadowy Eighth: the Eight close up the
Couch
Into a tabernacle, and flee with cries down to the Deeps:
Where Los opens his three wide gates, surrounded by raging
fires!
They soon find their own place & join the Watchers of the
Ulro.

*

[21] But Milton entering my Foot, I saw in the nether
Regions of the Imagination; also all men on Earth,
And all in Heaven, saw in the nether regions of the
Imagination,
In Ulro beneath Beulah, the vast breach of Milton's descent:
But I knew not that it was Milton, for man cannot know
What passes in his members till periods of Space & Time
Reveal the secrets of Eternity; for more extensive
Than any other earthly things are Man's earthly lineaments.

And all this Vegetable World appear'd on my left Foot,
As a bright sandal form'd immortal of precious stones &
gold: 10
I stooped down & bound it on to walk forward thro' Eternity.

[Ololon]

There is in Eden a sweet River, of milk & liquid pearl,
Nam'd Ololon, on whose mild banks dwelt "those who
Milton drove
Down into Ulro: and they wept in long resounding song
For seven days of eternity, and the rivers' living banks,
The mountains wail'd! & every plant that grew, in solemn
sighs lamented . . .

*

And Ololon said: Let us descend also, and let us give
Ourselves to death in Ulro among the Transgressors.
Is Virtue a Punisher? O no! how is this wondrous thing:

This World beneath, unseen before: this refuge from the
wars 20
Of Great Eternity! unnatural refuge! unknown by us till
now?
Or are these the pangs of repentance? let us enter into them.

Then the Divine Family said: Six Thousand Years are now
Accomplish'd in this World of Sorrow; Milton's Angel knew
The Universal Dictate; and you also feel this Dictate,
And now you know this World of Sorrow, and feel Pity.
Obey
The Dictate! Watch over this World, and with your brooding
wings,
Renew it to Eternal Life: Lo! I am with you alway
But you cannot renew Milton; he goes to Eternal Death!

So spake the Family Divine as One Man, even Jesus, 30
Uniting in One with Ololon & the appearance of One Man.
Jesus the Saviour appear'd coming in the Clouds of Ololon!

[22] Tho' driven away with the Seven Starry Ones into the Ulro
Yet the Divine Vision remains Every-where For-ever. Amen.
And Ololon lamented for Milton with a great lamentation.

[Los]

While Los heard indistinct in fear, what time I bound my
sandals
On to walk forward thro' Eternity, Los descended to me:
And Los behind me stood: a terrible flaming Sun just close
Behind my back; I turned round in terror, and behold!
Los stood in that fierce glowing fire; & he also stoop'd down
And bound my sandals on in Udan-Adan; trembling I stood
Exceedingly with fear & terror, standing in the Vale 10
Of Lambeth: but he kissed me, and wish'd me health,
And I became One Man with him arising in my strength:
'Twas too late now to recede. Los had enter'd into my soul:
His terrors now possess'd me whole! I arose in fury &
strength.

'I am that Shadowy Prophet who Six Thousand Years ago
Fell from my station in the Eternal bosom. Six Thousand
Years
Are finish'd; I return! both Time & Space obey my will.
I in Six Thousand Years walk up and down; for not one
Moment
Of Time is lost, nor one Event of Space unpermanent,
But all remain: every fabric of Six Thousand Years 20
Remains permanent: tho' on the Earth where Satan
Fell and was cut off all things vanish & are seen no more.
They vanish not from me & mine, we guard them first &
last.
The generations of men run on in the tide of Time
But leave their destin'd lineaments permanent for ever &
ever.'

So spoke Los as we went along to his supreme abode.

*

[24] Los is by mortals nam'd Time, Enitharmon is nam'd Space.
But they depict him bald & aged who is in eternal youth
All powerful and his locks flourish like the brows of morning.
He is the Spirit of Prophecy, the ever apparent Elias.
Time is the mercy of Eternity; without Time's swiftness,
Which is the swiftest of all things, all were eternal torment.
All the Gods of the Kingdoms of Earth labour in Los's Halls:
Every one is a fallen Son of the Spirit of Prophecy.
He is the Fourth Zoa that stood around the Throne Divine.

*

[The Works of Los]

Thou seest the Constellations in the deep & wondrous Night; 10
They rise in order and continue their immortal courses
Upon the mountain & in vales with harp & heavenly song
With flute & clarion, with cups & measures fill'd with
foaming wine.

Glitt'ring the streams reflect the Vision of beatitude,
And the calm Ocean joys beneath & smooths his awful
waves!

[n][26(27)] These are the Sons of Los, & these the Labourers of the
Vintage:
Thou seest the gorgeous clothed Flies that dance & sport in
summer
Upon the sunny brooks & meadows: every one the dance
Knows in its intricate mazes of delight artful to weave;
Each one to sound his instruments of music in the dance,
To touch each other & recede; to cross & change and return.
These are the Children of Los: thou seest the Trees on
mountains
The wind blows heavy, loud they thunder thro' the darksom
sky
Uttering prophecies & speaking instructive words to the sons
Of men: These are the Sons of Los! These the Visions of
Eternity 10
But we see only as it were the hem of their garments
When with our vegetable eyes we view these wond'rous
Visions.

*

[27(25)] But the [n]Wine-press of Los is eastward of Golgonooza before
the Seat
Of Satan. Luvah laid the foundation & Urizen finish'd it
in howling woe.
How red the sons & daughters of Luvah! here they tread the
grapes,
Laughing & shouting drunk with odours many fall
o'erwearied
Drown'd in the wine is many a youth & maiden: those
around
Lay them on skins of Tygers & of the spotted Leopard & the
Wild Ass
Till they revive, or bury them in cool grots, making
lamentation.

This Wine-press is call'd War on Earth, it is the Printing-Press
Of Los; and here he lays his words in order above the mortal brain
As cogs are form'd in a wheel to turn the cogs of the adverse wheel. 10

Timbrels & violins sport round the Wine-presses; the little Seed,
The sportive Root, the Earth-worm, the gold Beetle, the wise Emmet,
Dance round the Wine-presses of Luvah: the Centipede is there;
The ground Spider with many eyes; the Mole clothed in velvet;
The ambitious Spider in his sullen web; the lucky golden Spinner;
The Earwig arm'd; the tender Maggot emblem of immortality;
The Flea; Louse; Bug; the Tape-Worm; all the Armies of Disease
Visible or invisible to the slothful vegetating Man.
The slow Slug; the Grasshopper that sings & laughs & drinks;
Winter comes, he folds his slender bones without a murmur. 20
The cruel Scorpion is there; the Gnat; Wasp; Hornet & the Honey Bee;
The Toad & venomous Newt; the Serpent cloth'd in gems & gold:
They throw off their gorgeous raiment: they rejoice with loud jubilee
Around the Wine-presses of Luvah, naked & drunk with wine.

There is the Nettle that stings with soft down; and there
The indignant Thistle, whose bitterness is bred in his milk,
Who feeds on contempt of his neighbour: there all the idle Weeds

That creep around the obscure places shew their various
limbs,
Naked in all their beauty dancing round the Wine-presses.

But in the Wine-presses the Human grapes sing not, nor
dance: 30
They howl & writhe in shoals of torment, in fierce flames
consuming,
In chains of iron & in dungeons circled with ceaseless fires,
In pits & dens & shades of death; in shapes of torment &
woe.
The plates & screws & wracks & saws & cords & fires &
cisterns
The cruel joys of Luvah's Daughters lacerating with knives
And whips their Victims & the deadly sport of Luvah's Sons.
They dance around the dying, & they drink the howl &
groan,
They catch the shrieks in cups of gold, they hand them to one
another:
These are the sports of love, & these the sweet delights of
amorous play;
Tears of the grape, the death sweat of the cluster, the last sigh 40
Of the mild youth who listens to the lureing songs of Luvah.

*

But in Eternity the Four Arts: Poetry, Painting, Music,
And Architecture, which is Science; are the Four Faces of
Man.
Not so in Time & Space: there Three are shut out, and only
Science remains thro' Mercy; & by means of Science, the
Three
Become apparent in Time & Space, in the Three Professions.
Poetry in Religion: Music, Law: Painting, in Physic &
Surgery:
That Man may live upon Earth till the time of his awaking,
And from these Three, Science derives every Occupation of
Men.
And Science is divided into Bowlahoola & Allamanda. 50

[28] Some Sons of Los surround the Passions with porches of iron & silver
Creating form & beauty around the dark regions of sorrow,
Giving to airy nothing a name and a habitation
Delightful! with bounds to the Infinite putting off the Indefinite
Into most holy forms of Thought: (such is the power of inspiration).
They labour incessant; with many tears & afflictions:
Creating the beautiful House for the piteous sufferer.

Others, Cabinets richly fabricate of gold & ivory;
For Doubts & fears unform'd & wretched & melancholy
The little weeping Spectre stands on the threshold of Death 10
Eternal; and sometimes two Spectres like lamps quivering
And often malignant they combat (heart-breaking sorrowful & piteous);
Antamon takes them into his beautiful flexible hands,
As the Sower takes the seed, or as the Artist his clay
Or fine wax, to mould artful a model for golden ornaments.
The soft hands of Antamon draw the indelible line,
Form immortal with golden pen; such as the Spectre admiring
Puts on the sweet form; then smiles Antamon bright thro' his windows.
The Daughters of beauty look up from their Loom & prepare
The integument soft for its clothing with joy & delight. 20

*

The Sons of Ozoth within the Optic Nerve stand fiery glowing
And the number of his Sons is eight millions & eight.
They give delights to the man unknown; artificial riches
They give to scorn, & their possessors to trouble & sorrow & care,
Shutting the sun & moon, & stars, & trees, & clouds, & waters,

And hills, out from the Optic Nerve & hardening it into a bone
Opake and like the black pebble on the enraged beach.
While the poor indigent is like the diamond which tho' cloth'd
In rugged covering in the mine, is open all within,
And in his hallow'd center holds the heavens of bright eternity. 30
Ozoth here builds walls of rocks against the surging sea;
And timbers crampt with iron cramps bar in the joys of life
From fell destruction in the Spectrous cunning or rage. He Creates
The speckled Newt, the Spider & Beetle, the Rat & Mouse,
The Badger & Fox: they worship before his feet in trembling fear.

But others of the Sons of Los build Moments & Minutes & Hours
And Days & Months & Years & Ages & Periods; wondrous buildings:
And every Moment has a Couch of gold for soft repose
(A Moment equals a pulsation of the artery),
And between every two Moments stands a Daughter of Beulah 40
To feed the Sleepers on their Couches with maternal care,
And every Minute has an azure Tent with silken Veils,
And every Hour has a bright golden Gate carved with skill,
And every Day & Night, has Walls of brass & Gates of adamant,
Shining like precious stones & ornamented with appropriate signs:
And every Month, a silver paved Terrace builded high:
And every Year, invulnerable Barriers with high Towers,
And every Age is Moated deep with Bridges of silver & gold:
And every Seven Ages is Incircled with a Flaming Fire.
Now Seven Ages is amounting to Two Hundred Years 50
Each has its Guard, each Moment Minute Hour Day Month & Year.

All are the work of Fairy hands of the Four Elements;
The Guard are Angels of Providence on duty evermore.
Every Time less than a pulsation of the artery
Is equal in its period & value to Six Thousand Years,
[29] For in this Period the Poet's Work is Done: and all the Great
Events of Time start forth & are conciev'd in such a Period,
Within a Moment: a Pulsation of the Artery.

The Sky is an immortal Tent built by the Sons of Los
And every Space that a Man views around his
dwelling-place:
Standing on his own roof, or in his garden on a mount
Of twenty-five cubits in height, such space is his Universe;
And on its verge the Sun rises & sets, the Clouds bow
To meet the flat Earth & the Sea in such an order'd Space:
The Starry heavens reach no further, but here bend and set 10
On all sides, & the two Poles turn on their valves of gold:
And if he move his dwelling-place, his heavens also move
Where'er he goes, & all his neighbourhood bewail his loss:
Such are the Spaces called Earth & such its dimension:
As to that false appearance which appears to the reasoner,
As of a Globe rolling thro' Voidness, it is a delusion of Ulro.
The Microscope knows not of this nor the Telescope; they
alter
The ratio of the Spectator's Organs but leave Objects
untouch'd,
For every Space larger than a red Globule of Man's blood.
Is visionary: and is created by the Hammer of Los 20
And every Space smaller than a Globule of Man's blood opens
Into Eternity, of which this vegetable Earth is but a shadow:
The red Globule is the unwearied Sun by Los created
To measure Time and Space to mortal Men every morning.

*

Such is the World of Los the labour of six thousand years.
Thus Nature is a Vision of the Science of the Elohim.

End of the First Book.

Book the Second

[30] *[Beulah]*

There is a place where Contrarieties are equally True:
This place is called Beulah. It is a pleasant lovely Shadow
Where no dispute can come, because of those who Sleep.
Into this place the Sons & Daughters of Ololon descended
With solemn mourning, into Beulah's moony shades & hills
Weeping for Milton: mute wonder held the Daughters of Beulah
Enraptur'd with affection sweet and mild benevolence.

Beulah is evermore Created around Eternity; appearing
To the Inhabitants of Eden, around them on all sides.
But Beulah to its Inhabitants appears within each district 10
As the beloved infant in his mother's bosom round incircled
With arms of love & pity & sweet compassion. But to
The Sons of Eden the moony habitations of Beulah,
Are from Great Eternity a mild & pleasant Rest.

And it is thus Created: Lo the Eternal Great Humanity
To whom be Glory & Dominion Evermore, Amen!
Walks among all his awful Family seen in every face
As the breath of the Almighty: such are the words of man to
man
In the great Wars of Eternity, in fury of Poetic Inspiration,
To build the Universe stupendous: Mental forms Creating. 20

But the Emanations trembled exceedingly, nor could they
Live, because the life of Man was too exceeding unbounded
His joy became terrible to them, they trembled & wept
Crying with one voice. Give us a habitation & a place
In which we may be hidden under the shadow of wings
For if we who are but for a time, & who pass away in winter
Behold these wonders of Eternity we shall consume,
But you, O our Fathers & Brothers, remain in Eternity:
But grant us a Temporal Habitation, do you speak
To us; we will obey your words as you obey Jesus 30
The Eternal who is blessed for ever & ever. Amen.

So spake the lovely Emanations; & there appear'd a pleasant

Mild Shadow above: beneath: & on all sides round.
[31] Into this pleasant Shadow all the weak & weary
Like Women & Children were taken away as on wings
Of dovelike softness, & shadowy habitations prepared for them.
But every Man return'd & went still going forward thro'
The Bosom of the Father in Eternity on Eternity,
Neither did any lack or fall into Error without
A Shadow to repose in all the Days of happy Eternity.

Into this pleasant Shadow Beulah, all Ololon descended;
And when the Daughters of Beulah heard the lamentation
All Beulah wept, for they saw the Lord coming in the Clouds. 10
And the Shadows of Beulah terminate in rocky Albion.

*

Thou hearest the Nightingale begin the Song of Spring;
The Lark sitting upon his earthy bed: just as the morn
Appears; listens silent; then springing from the waving
Corn-field! loud
He leads the Choir of Day! trill, trill, trill, trill,
Mounting upon the wings of light into the Great Expanse:
Reecchoing against the lovely blue & shining heavenly Shell:
His little throat labours with inspiration; every feather
On throat & breast & wings vibrates with the effluence
Divine.
All Nature listens silent to him & the awful Sun 20
Stands still upon the Mountain looking on this little Bird
With eyes of soft humility & wonder, love & awe.
Then loud from their green covert all the Birds begin their Song:
The Thrush, the Linnet & the Goldfinch, Robin & the Wren
Awake the Sun from his sweet reverie upon the Mountain.
The Nightingale again assays his song, & thro' the day
And thro' the night warbles luxuriant, every Bird of Song
Attending his loud harmony with admiration & love.
This is a Vision of the lamentation of Beulah over Ololon.

Thou percievest the Flowers put forth their precious Odours, 30
And none can tell how from so small a center comes such
sweets,

Forgetting that within that Center Eternity expands
Its ever during doors, that Og & Anak fiercely guard.
First, e'er the morning breaks, joy opens in the flowery
  bosoms,
Joy even to tears, which the Sun rising dries; first the Wild
  Thyme
And Meadow-sweet, downy & soft waving among the reeds,
Light springing on the air, lead the sweet Dance: they wake
The Honeysuckle sleeping on the Oak; the flaunting beauty
Revels along upon the wind; the White-thorn, lovely May,
Opens her many lovely eyes listening; the Rose still sleeps, 40
None dare to wake her; soon she bursts her crimson curtain'd
  bed
And comes forth in the majesty of beauty; every Flower,
The Pink, the Jessamine, the Wall-flower, the Carnation,
The Jonquil, the mild Lilly, opes her heavens; every Tree
And Flower & Herb soon fill the air with an innumerable
  Dance,
Yet all in order sweet & lovely. Men are sick with Love.
Such is a Vision of the lamentation of Beulah over Ololon.

*

[Ololon comes to Beulah]

[34] Here in these Chaoses the Sons of Ololon took their abode,
In Chasms of the Mundane Shell which open on all sides
  round,
Southward & by the East within the Breach of Milton's
  descent,
To watch the time, pitying, & gentle to awaken Urizen.
They stood in a dark land of death, of fiery corroding waters,
Where lie in evil death the Four Immortals, pale and cold:
And the Eternal Man, even Albion, upon the Rock of Ages.
Seeing Milton's Shadow, some Daughters of Beulah
  trembling
Return'd, but Ololon remain'd before the Gates of the Dead.

*

[35] O! how the Starry Eight rejoic'd to see Ololon descended!
And now that a wide road was open to Eternity,
By Ololon's descent thro Beulah to Los & Enitharmon.
For mighty were the multitudes of Ololon, vast the extent
Of their great sway, reaching from Ulro to Eternity
Surrounding the Mundane Shell outside in its Caverns
And through Beulah, and all silent forbore to contend
With Ololon, for they saw the Lord in the Clouds of Ololon.

[Ololon comes to Blake]

There is a Moment in each Day that Satan cannot find
Nor can his Watch Fiends find it, but the Industrious find 10
This Moment & it multiply, & when it once is found
It renovates every Moment of the Day if rightly placed:
In this Moment Ololon descended to Los & Enitharmon
Unseen beyond the Mundane Shell Southward in Milton's
track.

Just in this Moment when the morning odours rise abroad
And first from the Wild Thyme, stands a Fountain in a rock
Of crystal flowing into two Streams, one flows thro'
Golgonooza
And thro' Beulah to Eden beneath Los's western Wall;
The other flows thro' the Aerial Void & all the Churches,
Meeting again in Golgonooza beyond Satan's Seat. 20

The Wild Thyme is Los's Messenger to Eden, a mighty
Demon
Terrible deadly & poisonous his presence in Ulro dark;
Therefore he appears only a small Root creeping in grass,
Covering over the Rock of Odours his bright purple mantle
Beside the Fount above the Lark's nest in Golgonooza.
Luvah slept here in death & here is Luvah's empty Tomb.
Ololon sat beside this Fountain on the Rock of Odours.

Just at the place to where the Lark mounts, is a Crystal Gate
It is the entrance of the [n]First Heaven named Luther: for
The Lark is Los's Messenger thro' the [n]Twenty-seven
Churches, 30

That the Seven Eyes of God who walk even to Satan's Seat
Thro' all the Twenty-seven Heavens may not slumber nor
sleep:
But the Lark's Nest is at the Gate of Los, at the eastern
Gate of wide Golgonooza & the Lark is Los's Messenger.

[36] When on the highest lift of his light pinions he arrives
At that bright Gate, another Lark meets him & back to back
They touch their pinions, tip tip: and each descend
To their respective Earths & there all night consult with
Angels
Of Providence & with the Eyes of God, all night in slumbers
Inspired: & at the dawn of day send out another Lark
Into another Heaven to carry news upon his wings.
Thus are the Messengers dispatch'd till they reach the Earth
again.
In the East Gate of Golgonooza, & the Twenty-eighth bright
Lark met the Female Ololon descending into my Garden; 10
Thus it appears to Mortal eyes & those of the Ulro Heavens
But not thus to Immortals, the Lark is a mighty Angel.

*

And as One Female, Ololon and all its mighty Hosts
Appear'd: a Virgin of twelve years; nor time nor space was
To the perception of the Virgin Ololon, but as the
Flash of lightning but more quick the Virgin in my Garden
Before my Cottage stood, for the Satanic Space is delusion.

For when Los join'd with me he took me in his fiery
whirlwind;
My Vegetated portion was hurried from Lambeth's shades.
He set me down in Felpham's Vale & prepared a beautiful 20
Cottage for me, that in three years I might write all these
Visions,
To display Nature's cruel holiness: the deceits of Natural
Religion.
Walking in my Cottage Garden, sudden I beheld
The Virgin Ololon & address'd her as a Daughter of Beulah:

Virgin of Providence, fear not to enter into my Cottage:
What is thy message to thy friend? What am I now to do?
Is it again to plunge into deeper affliction? behold me
Ready to obey, but pity thou my Shadow of Delight:
Enter my Cottage, comfort her, for she is sick with fatigue.

[37] The Virgin answer'd: Knowest thou of Milton who
descended
Driven from Eternity; him I seek! terrified at my Act
In Great Eternity which thou knowest! I come him to seek.

[Milton comes to Blake]

So Ololon utter'd in words distinct the anxious thought:
Mild was the voice, but more distinct than any earthly,
That Milton's Shadow heard & condensing all his Fibres
Into a strength impregnable of majesty & beauty infinite
I saw he was the [n]Covering Cherub & within him Satan
And [n]Rahab, in an outside which is fallacious! within
Beyond the outline of Identity, in the Selfhood deadly; 10
And he appear'd the Wicker Man of Scandinavia in whom
Jerusalem's children consume in flames among the Stars.

Descending down into my Garden, a Human Wonder of God
Reaching from heaven to earth a Cloud & Human Form
I beheld Milton with astonishment & in him beheld
The Monstrous Churches of Beulah, the Gods of Ulro dark:
Twelve monstrous dishumaniz'd terrors, Synagogues of
Satan,
A Double Twelve & Thrice Nine: such their divisions.

And these their Names & their Places within the Mundane
Shell:

In Tyre & Sidon I saw Baal & Ashtaroth. In Moab Chemosh 20
In Ammon, Molech: loud his Furnaces rage among the
Wheels
Of Og, & pealing loud the cries of the Victims of Fire!
And pale his Priestesses infolded in Veils of Pestilence,
border'd

With War; Woven in Looms of Tyre & Sidon by beautiful
Ashtaroth.
In Palestine Dagon, Sea Monster! worship'd o'er the Sea.
Thammuz in Lebanon & Rimmon in Damascus curtain'd:
Osiris; Isis; Orus; in Egypt: dark their Tabernacles on Nile
Floating with solemn songs, & on the Lakes of Egypt nightly
With pomp, even till morning break & Osiris appear in the
sky.
But Belial of Sodom & Gomorrha, obscure Demon of Bribes 30
And secret Assassinations, not worship'd nor ador'd; but
With the finger on the lips & the back turn'd to the light:
And Saturn Jove & Rhea of the Isles of the Sea remote.
These Twelve Gods are the Twelve Spectre Sons of the Druid
Albion.

And these the names of the Twenty-seven Heavens & their
Churches
[n]Adam, Seth, Enos, Cainan, Mahalaleel, Jared, Enoch,
Methuselah, Lamech: these are Giants mighty
Hermaphroditic.
Noah, Shem, Arphaxad, Cainan the second, Salah, Heber,
Peleg, Reu, Serug, Nahor, Terah, these are the Female-Males
A Male within a Female hid as in an Ark & Curtains, 40
Abraham, Moses, Solomon, Paul, Constantine, Charlemaine
Luther, these seven are the Male-Females, the Dragon Forms
Religion hid in War, a Dragon red & hidden Harlot.

All these are seen in Milton's Shadow who is the Covering
Cherub.

*

[38] And Milton collecting all his fibres into impregnable strength
Descended down a Paved work of all kinds of precious stones
Out from the eastern sky; descending down into my Cottage
Garden, clothed in black: severe & silent he descended.

The Spectre of Satan stood upon the roaring sea & beheld
Milton within his sleeping Humanity! trembling &
shudd'ring

He stood upon the waves, a Twenty-seven-fold mighty
 Demon
Gorgeous & beautiful: loud roll his thunders against Milton
Loud Satan thunder'd, loud & dark upon mild Felpham
 shore;
Not daring to touch one fibre he howl'd round upon the Sea. 10

I also stood in Satan's bosom & beheld its desolations!
A ruin'd Man: a ruin'd building of God not made with hands;
Its plains of burning sand, its mountains of marble terrible:
Its pits & declivities flowing with molten ore & fountains
Of pitch & nitre: its ruin'd palaces & cities & mighty works;
Its furnaces of affliction in which his Angels & Emanations
Labour with blacken'd visages among its stupendous ruins,
Arches & pyramids & porches colonades & domes:
In which dwells Mystery, Babylon; here is her secret place,
From hence she comes forth on the Churches in delight. 20
Here is her Cup fill'd with its poisons, in these horrid vales
And here her scarlet Veil woven in pestilence & war:
Here is Jerusalem bound in chains, in the Dens of Babylon.

[Milton rejects Satan]

In the Eastern porch of Satan's Universe Milton stood & said:

Satan! my Spectre! I know my power thee to annihilate
And be a greater in thy place, & be thy Tabernacle,
A covering for thee to do thy will, till one greater comes
And smites me as I smote thee & becomes my covering.
Such are the Laws of thy false Heav'ns! but Laws of Eternity
Are not such: know thou, I come to Self Annihilation! 30
Such are the Laws of Eternity that each shall mutually
Annihilate himself for others' good, as I for thee.
Thy purpose & the purpose of thy Priests & of thy Churches
Is to impress on men the fear of death; to teach
Trembling & fear, terror, constriction; abject selfishness.
Mine is to teach Men to despise death & to go on
In fearless majesty annihilating Self, laughing to scorn

Thy Laws & terrors, shaking down thy Synagogues as webs.
I come to discover before Heav'n & Hell the
Self-righteousness
In all its Hypocritic turpitude, opening to every eye 40
These wonders of Satan's holiness, shewing to the Earth
The Idol Virtues of the Natural Heart, & Satan's Seat
Explore in all its Selfish Natural Virtue, & put off
In Self-annihilation all that is not of God alone:
To put off Self & all I have ever & ever, Amen.

Satan heard! Coming in a cloud, with trumpets & flaming
fire,
Saying I am God the judge of all, the living & the dead,
Fall therefore down & worship me, submit thy supreme
Dictate, to my eternal Will & to my dictate bow.
I hold the Balances of Right & Just & mine the Sword: 50
Seven Angels bear my Name & in those Seven I appear
But I alone am God & I alone in Heav'n & Earth
Of all that live dare utter this, others tremble & bow
[39] Till All Things become One Great Satan, in Holiness
Oppos'd to Mercy, and the Divine Delusion Jesus be no
more.

Suddenly around Milton on my Path, the Starry Seven
Burn'd terrible! my Path became a solid fire, as bright
As the clear Sun & Milton silent came down on my Path.
And there went forth from the Starry limbs of the Seven:
Forms
Human; with Trumpets innumerable, sounding articulate
As the Seven spake; and they stood in a mighty Column of
Fire
Surrounding Felpham's Vale, reaching to the Mundane
Shell, Saying:

Awake Albion awake! reclaim thy Reasoning Spectre!
Subdue 10
Him to the Divine Mercy, Cast him down into the Lake
Of Los, that ever burneth with fire, ever & ever Amen!

Let the Four Zoas awake from Slumbers of [n]Six Thousand
Years!

Then loud the Furnaces of Los were heard! & seen as Seven
Heavens
Stretching from south to north over the mountains of
Albion.

Satan heard; trembling round his Body, he incircled it
He trembled with exceeding great trembling & astonishment
Howling in his Spectre round his Body hung'ring to devour,
But fearing for the pain; for if he touches a Vital,
His torment is unendurable: therefore he cannot devour: 20
But howls round it as a lion round his prey continually.
Loud Satan thunder'd, loud & dark upon mild Felpham's
Shore,
Coming in a Cloud with Trumpets & with Fiery Flame
An awful Form eastward from midst of a bright Paved-work
Of precious stones by Cherubim surrounded: so permitted
(Lest he should fall apart in his Eternal Death) to imitate
The Eternal Great Humanity Divine surrounded by
His Cherubim & Seraphim in ever happy Eternity.
Beneath sat Chaos: Sin on his right hand Death on his left
And Ancient Night spread over all the heav'n his Mantle of
Laws. 30
He trembled with exceeding great trembling &
astonishment.

[Albion stirs in his Sleep]

Then Albion rose up in the Night of Beulah on his Couch
Of dread repose seen by the visionary eye; his face is toward
The east, toward Jerusalem's Gates: groaning he sat above
His rocks; London & Bath & Legions & Edinburgh
Are the four pillars of his Throne; his left foot near London
Covers the shades of Tyburn: his instep from Windsor
To Primrose Hill stretching to Highgate & Holloway
London is between his knees: its basements fourfold.
His right foot stretches to the sea on Dover cliffs, his heel 40

On Canterbury's ruins; his right hand covers lofty Wales
His left Scotland; his bosom girt with gold involves
York, Edinburgh, Durham & Carlisle & on the front
Bath, Oxford, Cambridge, Norwich; his right elbow
Leans on the Rocks of Erin's Land, Ireland ancient nation:
His head bends over London: he sees his embodied Spectre
Trembling before him with exceeding great trembling & fear.
He views Jerusalem & Babylon, his tears flow down.
He mov'd his right foot to Cornwall, his left to the Rocks of
  Bognor;
He strove to rise to walk into the Deep, but strength failing 50
Forbad, & down with dreadful groans he sunk upon his
  Couch
In moony Beulah. Los his strong Guard walks round beneath
  the Moon.

Urizen faints in terror striving among the Brooks of Arnon
With Milton's Spirit: as the Plowman or Artificer or
  Shepherd
While in the labours of his Calling sends his Thought abroad
To labour in the ocean or in the starry heaven, so Milton
Labour'd in Chasms of the Mundane Shell, tho' here before
My Cottage midst the Starry Seven, where the Virgin Ololon
Stood trembling in the Porch: loud Satan thunder'd on the
  stormy Sea
Circling Albion's Cliffs in which the Four-fold World resides 60
Tho' seen in fallacy outside: a fallacy of Satan's Churches.

[The Reunion of Milton and Ololon]

[40] Before Ololon Milton stood & perciev'd the Eternal Form
Of that mild Vision; wondrous were their acts by me
  unknown
Except remotely; and I heard Ololon say to Milton:

I see thee strive upon the Brooks of Arnon; there a dread
And awful Man I see, o'ercover'd with the mantle of years.
I behold Los & Urizen, I behold Orc & Tharmas;

The Four Zoas of Albion, & thy Spirit with them striving
In Self-annihilation giving thy life to thy enemies.
Are those who contemn Religion & seek to annihilate it
Become in their Feminine portions the causes & promoters 10
Of these Religions; how is this thing? this "Newtonian
Phantasm
This Voltaire & Rousseau: this Hume & Gibbon &
Bolingbroke,
This Natural Religion! this impossible absurdity!
Is Ololon the cause of this? O where shall I hide my face?
These tears fall for the little-ones: the Children of Jerusalem
Lest they be annihilated in thy annihilation.

No sooner she had spoke but Rahab Babylon appear'd
Eastward upon the Paved work across Europe & Asia,
Glorious as the midday Sun in Satan's bosom glowing,
A Female hidden in a Male, Religion hidden in War 20
Nam'd Moral Virtue; cruel two-fold Monster shining bright
A Dragon red & hidden Harlot which John in Patmos saw.

*

But turning toward Ololon in terrible majesty Milton
Replied: Obey thou the Words of the Inspired Man!
All that can be annihilated must be annihilated
That the Children of Jerusalem may be saved from slavery.
There is a Negation, & there is a Contrary
The Negation must be destroy'd to redeem the Contraries.
The Negation is the Spectre; the Reasoning Power in Man
This is a false Body: an Incrustation over my Immortal 30
Spirit; a Selfhood, which must be put off & annihilated
alway.
To cleanse the Face of my Spirit by Self-examination,
[41] To bathe in the Waters of Life; to wash off the Not Human
I come in Self-annihilation & the grandeur of Inspiration
To cast off Rational Demonstration by Faith in the Saviour
To cast off the rotten rags of Memory by Inspiration
To cast off Bacon, Locke & Newton from Albion's covering
To take off his filthy garments, & clothe him with
Imagination;

To cast aside from Poetry, all that is not Inspiration
That it no longer shall dare to mock with the aspersion of
Madness
Cast on the Inspired, by the tame high finisher of paltry
Blots,
Indefinite, or paltry Rhymes; or paltry Harmonies. 10
Who creeps into State Government like a catterpiller to
destroy
To cast off the idiot Questioner who is always questioning,
But never capable of answering; who sits with a sly grin
Silent plotting when to question, like a thief in a cave;
Who publishes doubt & calls it knowledge; whose Science is
Despair,
Whose pretence to knowledge is Envy, whose whole Science
is
To destroy the wisdom of ages to gratify ravenous Envy;
That rages round him like a Wolf day & night without rest.
He smiles with condescension; he talks of Benevolence &
Virtue
And those who act with Benevolence & Virtue, they murder
time on time. 20
These are the destroyers of Jerusalem, these are the
murderers
Of Jesus, who deny the Faith & mock at Eternal Life!
Who pretend to Poetry that they may destroy Imagination;
By imitation of Nature's Images drawn from Remembrance:
These are the Sexual Garments, the Abomination of
Desolation
Hiding the Human Lineaments as with an Ark & Curtains
Which Jesus rent: & now shall wholly purge away with Fire
Till Generation is swallow'd up in Regeneration.

Then trembled the Virgin Ololon & reply'd in clouds of
despair:

Is this our Feminine Portion, the Six-fold Miltonic Female? 30
Terribly this Portion trembles before thee O awful Man:
Although our Human Power can sustain the severe
contentions

Of Friendship, our Sexual cannot; but flies into the Ulro.
Hence arose all our terrors in Eternity! & now remembrance
Returns upon us! are we Contraries, O Milton, Thou & I?
O Immortal! how were we led to War the Wars of Death?
Is this the Void Outside of Existence, which if enter'd into
[42] Becomes a Womb? & is this the Death Couch of Albion?
Thou goest to Eternal Death & all must go with thee.

So saying, the Virgin divided Six-fold & with a shriek
Dolorous that ran thro' all Creation, a Double Six-fold
Wonder!
Away from Ololon she divided & fled into the depths
Of Milton's Shadow as a Dove upon the stormy Sea.

Then as a Moony Ark Ololon descended to Felpham's Vale
In clouds of blood, in streams of gore, with dreadful
thunderings
Into the Fires of Intellect that rejoic'd in Felpham's Vale
Around the Starry Eight: with one accord the Starry Eight
became 10
One Man, Jesus the Saviour, wonderful! round his limbs
The Clouds of Ololon folded as a Garment dipped in blood,
Written within & without in woven letters; & the Writing
Is the Divine Revelation in the Litteral expression:
A Garment of War, I heard it nam'd the Woof of Six
Thousand Years.

And I beheld the Twenty-four Cities of Albion
Arise upon their Thrones to Judge the Nations of the Earth
And the Immortal Four in whom the Twenty-four appear
Four-fold
Arose around Albion's body: Jesus wept & walked forth
From Felpham's Vale clothed in Clouds of blood, to enter into 20
Albion's Bosom, the bosom of death, & the Four surrounded
him
In the Column of Fire in Felpham's Vale; then to their
mouths the Four
Applied their Four Trumpets & them sounded to the Four
winds.

Terror struck in the Vale! I stood at that immortal sound,
My bones trembled, I fell outstretch'd upon the path
A moment, & my Soul return'd into its mortal state
To Resurrection & Judgment in the Vegetable Body
And my sweet Shadow of Delight stood trembling by my side.

Immediately the Lark mounted with a loud trill from Felpham's Vale
And the Wild Thyme from Wimbleton's green & impurpled Hills 30
And Los & Enitharmon rose over the Hills of Surrey:
Their clouds roll over London with a south wind, soft Oothoon
Pants in the Vales of Lambeth weeping o'er her Human Harvest.
Los listens to the Cry of the Poor Man: his Cloud
Over London in volume terrific, low bended in anger.

Rintrah & Palamabron view the Human Harvest beneath,
Their Wine-presses & Barns stand open; the Ovens are prepar'd,
The Waggons ready: terrific Lions & Tygers sport & play.
All Animals upon the Earth are prepar'd in all their strength
[43] To go forth to the Great Harvest & Vintage of the Nations.

from JERUSALEM

The Emanation of the Giant Albion

[4] Μονος ὁ Ιεςους

[The Theme: Albion's Disease]

CHAP. 1

Of the Sleep of [n]Ulro! and of the passage through
Eternal Death! and of the awaking to Eternal Life.

This theme calls me in sleep night after night, & ev'ry morn
Awakes me at sun-rise, then I see the Saviour over me
Spreading his beams of love, & dictating the words of this
mild song.

Awake! awake O sleeper of the land of shadows, wake!
expand!
I am in you and you in me, mutual in love divine:
Fibres of love from man to man thro Albion's pleasant land.
In all the dark Atlantic vale down from the hills of Surrey
A black water accumulates, return Albion! return! 10
Thy brethren call thee, and thy fathers, and thy sons,
Thy nurses and thy mothers, thy sisters and thy daughters
Weep at thy soul's disease, and the Divine Vision is
darken'd:
Thy Emanation that was wont to play before thy face,
Beaming forth with her daughters into the Divine bosom –
Where hast thou hidden thy Emanation, lovely Jerusalem
From the vision and fruition of the Holy-one?
I am not a God afar off, I am a brother and friend;
Within your bosoms I reside, and you reside in me:
Lo! we are One; forgiving all Evil, Not seeking recompense! 20
Ye are my members O ye sleepers of Beulah, land of shades!

But the perturbed Man away turns down the valleys dark:

*

Phantom of the over-heated brain! shadow of immortality!
Seeking to keep my soul a victim to thy Love! which binds
Man the enemy of man into deceitful friendships:
Jerusalem is not! her daughters are indefinite:
By demonstration man alone can live, and not by faith.
My mountains are my own, and I will keep them to myself:
The Malvern and the Cheviot, the Wolds Plinlimmon & Snowdon
Are mine. Here will I build my Laws of Moral Virtue! 30
Humanity shall be no more: but war & princedom & victory!

So spoke Albion in jealous fears, hiding his Emanation
Upon the Thames and Medway, rivers of Beulah: dissembling
His jealousy before the throne divine, darkening, cold!

*

[5] Trembling I sit day and night, my friends are astonish'd at me,
Yet they forgive my wanderings. I rest not from my great task!
To open the Eternal Worlds, to open the immortal Eyes
Of Man inwards into the Worlds of Thought: into Eternity
Ever expanding in the Bosom of God: the Human Imagination!
O Saviour pour upon me thy Spirit of meekness & love:
Annihilate the Selfhood in me, be thou all my life!
Guide thou my hand which trembles exceedingly upon the rock of ages,
While I write of the building of Golgonooza, & of the terrors of Entuthon:
Of [n]Hand & Hyle & Coban, of Kwantok, Peachey, Brereton, Slayd & Hutton: 10
Of the terrible sons & daughters of Albion, and their Generations.

*

O what avail the loves & tears of Beulah's lovely Daughters?
They hold the Immortal Form in gentle bands & tender tears:
But all within is open'd into the deeps of ⁿEntuthon
Benython,
A dark and unknown night, indefinite, unmeasurable,
without end,
Abstract Philosophy warring in enmity against Imagination
(Which is the Divine Body of the Lord Jesus, blessed for
ever).
And there Jerusalem wanders with Vala upon the mountains,
Attracted by the revolutions of those Wheels the Cloud of
smoke
Immense; and ⁿJerusalem & Vala weeping in the Cloud 20
Wander away into the Chaotic Void, lamenting with her
Shadow
Among the Daughters of Albion, among the Starry Wheels;
Lamenting for her children, for the sons & daughters of
Albion.

[Los and his Spectre]

Los heard her lamentations in the deeps afar! his tears fall
Incessant before the Furnaces, and his Emanation divided in
pain,
Eastward toward the Starry Wheels. But Westward, a black
Horror,
[6] His spectre driv'n by the Starry Wheels of Albion's sons,
black and
Opake divided from his back; he labours and he mourns!

For as his Emanation divided, his Spectre also divided
In terror of those starry wheels: and the Spectre stood over
Los
Howling in pain: a black'ning Shadow, black'ning dark &
opake
Cursing the terrible Los: bitterly cursing him for his
friendship
To Albion, suggesting murderous thoughts against Albion.

Los rag'd and stamp'd the earth in his might & terrible wrath!
He stood and stamp'd the earth! then he threw down his hammer in rage &
In fury: then he sat down and wept, terrified! Then arose 10
And chaunted his song, labouring with the tongs and hammer:
But still the Spectre divided, and still his pain increas'd!

In pain the Spectre divided: in pain of hunger and thirst:
To devour Los's Human Perfection, but when he saw that Los
[7] Was living; panting like a frighted wolf, and howling
He stood over the Immortal, in the solitude and darkness:
Upon the dark'ning Thames, across the whole Island westward,
A horrible Shadow of Death, among the Furnaces, beneath
The pillar of folding smoke; and he sought by other means,
To lure Los: by tears, by arguments of science & by terrors:
Terrors in every Nerve, by spasms & extended pains:
While Los answer'd unterrified to the opake blackening Fiend.

And thus the Spectre spoke: Wilt thou still go on to destruction?
Till thy life is all taken away by this deceitful Friendship? 10
He drinks thee up like water! like wine he pours thee
Into his tuns: thy Daughters are trodden in his vintage,
He makes thy Sons the trampling of his bulls, they are plow'd
And harrow'd for his profit, lo! thy stolen Emanation
Is his garden of pleasure! all the Spectres of his Sons mock thee
Look how they scorn thy once admired palaces! now in ruins
Because of Albion! because of deceit and friendship! . . .

*

Los answer'd: Altho' I know not this! I know far worse than this:
I know that Albion hath divided me, and that thou O my Spectre,

Hast just cause to be irritated; but look stedfastly upon me: 20
Comfort thyself in my strength the time will arrive,
When all Albion's injuries shall cease, and when we shall
Embrace him tenfold bright, rising from his tomb in
immortality.
They have divided themselves by Wrath, they must be
united by
Pity: let us therefore take example & warning, O my Spectre,
O that I could abstain from wrath! O that the Lamb
Of God would look upon me and pity me in my fury! . . .

*

Hand sits before his furnace: scorn of others & furious pride
Freeze round him to bars of steel & to iron rocks beneath
His feet! indignant self-righteousness like whirlwinds of the
north! 30
[8] Rose up against me thundering from the Brook of Albion's
River
From Ranelagh & Strumbolo, from Cromwell's gardens &
Chelsea
The place of wounded Soldiers: but when he saw my Mace
Whirl'd round from heaven to earth, trembling he sat: his
cold
Poisons rose up: & his sweet deceits cover'd them all over
With a tender cloud. As thou art now; such was he O
Spectre!
I know thy deceit & thy revenges, and unless thou desist
I will certainly create an eternal Hell for thee. Listen!
Be attentive! be obedient! Lo, the Furnaces are ready to
recieve thee!
I will break thee into shivers! & melt thee in the furnaces of
death; 10
I will cast thee into forms of abhorrence & torment if thou
Desist not from thine own will, & obey not my stern
command!
I am clos'd up from my children: my Emanation is dividing
And thou my Spectre art divided against me. But mark:

I will compell thee to assist me in my terrible labours. To beat
These hypocritic Selfhoods on the Anvils of bitter Death
I am inspired: I act not for myself: for Albion's sake
I now am what I am: a horror and an astonishment,
Shudd'ring the heavens to look upon me: Behold what cruelties
Are practised in ⁿBabel & Shinar, & have approach'd to Zion's Hill! 20

While Los spoke, the terrible Spectre fell shudd'ring before him
Watching his time with glowing eyes to leap upon his prey.
Los open'd the Furnaces in fear; the Spectre saw to Babel & Shinar
Across all Europe & Asia, he saw the tortures of the Victims.
He saw now from the outside what he before saw & felt from within,
He saw that Los was the sole, uncontroll'd Lord of the Furnaces
Groaning he kneel'd before Los's iron-shod feet on ⁿLondon Stone,
Hung'ring & thirsting for Los's life yet pretending obedience.
While Los pursu'd his speech in threat'nings loud & fierce:

Thou art my Pride & Self-righteousness: I have found thee out: 30
Thou art reveal'd before me in all thy magnitude & power
The Uncircumcised pretences to Chastity must be cut in sunder!
Thy holy wrath & deep deceit cannot avail against me
Nor shalt thou ever assume the triple-form of Albion's Spectre
For I am one of the living: dare not to mock my inspired fury
If thou wast cast forth from my life! if I was dead upon the mountains
Thou mightest be pitied & lov'd: but now I am living; unless
Thou abstain ravening I will create an eternal Hell for thee.

Take thou this Hammer & in patience heave the thundering
Bellows
Take thou these Tongs: strike thou alternate with me: labour
obedient. 40

*

[9] Loud roar my Furnaces and loud my hammer is heard:
I labour day and night, I behold the soft affections
Condense beneath my hammer into forms of cruelty,
But still I labour in hope, tho' still my tears flow down:
That he who will not defend Truth may be compell'd to
defend
A Lie: that he may be snared and caught and snared and
taken:
That Enthusiasm and Life may not cease; arise Spectre,
arise!

Thus they contended among the Furnaces with groans &
tears.
Groaning the Spectre heav'd the bellows, obeying Los's
frowns,
Till the [n]Spaces of Erin were perfected in the furnaces 10
Of affliction, and Los drew them forth, compelling the harsh
Spectre
[10] Into the Furnaces & into the valleys of the Anvils of Death
And into the mountains of the Anvils & of the heavy
Hammers,
Till he should bring the Sons & Daughters of Jerusalem to be
The Sons & daughters of Los, that he might protect them
from
Albion's dread Spectres: storming, loud, thunderous &
mighty
The Bellows & the Hammers move compell'd by Los's hand.

*

Therefore Los stands in London building Golgonooza,
Compelling his Spectre to labours mighty; trembling in fear

The Spectre weeps, but Los unmov'd by tears or threats remains:

I must Create a System or be enslav'd by another Man's. 10
I will not Reason & Compare: my business is to Create.

*

[Golgonooza]

[12] And they builded Golgonooza: terrible eternal labour!

What are those golden builders doing? where was the burying-place
Of soft Ethinthus? near Tyburn's fatal Tree? is that
Mild Zion's hill's most ancient promontory, near mournful
Ever weeping Paddington? is that Calvary and Golgotha
Becoming a building of pity and compassion? Lo!
The stones are pity, and the bricks, well wrought affections
Enamel'd with love & kindness, & the tiles engraven gold,
Labour of merciful hands: the beams & rafters are forgiveness:
The mortar & cement of the work, tears of honesty: the nails 10
And the screws & iron braces are well wrought blandishments
And well contrived words, firm fixing, never forgotten,
Always comforting the remembrance: the floors, humility:
The cielings, devotion: the hearths, thanksgiving.
Prepare the furniture, O Lambeth, in thy pitying looms,
The curtains, woven tears & sighs wrought into lovely forms
For comfort; there the secret furniture of Jerusalem's chamber
Is wrought. Lambeth! the Bride, the Lamb's Wife, loveth thee.
Thou art one with her & knowest not of self in thy supreme joy.
Go on, builders in hope, tho' Jerusalem wanders far away 20
Without the gate of Los, among the dark Satanic wheels.

Fourfold the Sons of Los in their divisions, and fourfold

The great City of Golgonooza: fourfold toward the north,
And toward the south fourfold, & fourfold toward the east & west,
Each within other toward the four points: that toward
Eden, and that toward the World of Generation,
And that toward Beulah, and that toward Ulro.
Ulro is the space of the terrible starry wheels of Albion's sons,
But that toward Eden is walled up till time of renovation;
Yet it is perfect in its building, ornaments & perfection. 30

And the Four Points are thus beheld in Great Eternity:
West, the Circumference: South, the Zenith: North,
The Nadir: East, the Center, unapproachable for ever.
These are the four Faces towards the Four Worlds of Humanity
In every Man. Ezekiel saw them by Chebar's flood.
And the Eyes are the South, and the Nostrils are the East,
And the Tongue is the West, and the Ear is the North.

And the North Gate of Golgonooza, toward Generation
Has four sculptur'd Bulls, terrible, before the Gate of iron,
And iron the Bulls; and that which looks toward Ulro, 40
Clay bak'd & enamel'd, eternal glowing as four furnaces,
Turning upon the Wheels of Albion's sons with enormous power:
And that toward Beulah four, gold, silver, brass & iron;
[13] And that toward Eden, four, form'd of gold, silver, brass & iron.

The South, a golden Gate, has four Lions terrible, living:
That toward Generation, four, of iron carv'd wondrous:
That toward Ulro, four, clay bak'd, laborious workmanship:
That toward Eden, four, immortal gold, silver, brass & iron.

The Western Gate fourfold is clos'd, having four Cherubim
Its guards, living, the work of elemental hands, laborious task,
Like Men hermaphroditic, each winged with eight wings.
That towards Generation, iron: that toward Beulah, stone:

That toward Ulro, clay: that toward Eden, metals: 10
But all clos'd up till the last day, when the graves shall yield
their dead.

The Eastern Gate fourfold, terrible & deadly its ornaments,
Taking their forms from the Wheels of Albion's sons, as cogs
Are form'd in a wheel to fit the cogs of the adverse wheel.

That toward Eden, eternal ice frozen in seven folds
Of forms of death: and that toward Beulah, stone,
The seven diseases of the earth are carved terrible:
And that toward Ulro, forms of war, seven enormities:
And that toward Generation, seven generative forms.

And every part of the City is fourfold; & every inhabitant,
fourfold. 20
And every pot & vessel & garment & utensil of the houses,
And every house, fourfold; but the third Gate in every one
Is clos'd as with a threefold curtain of ivory & fine linen &
ermine.
And Luban stands in middle of the City; a moat of fire
Surrounds Luban, Los's Palace & the golden Looms of
Cathedron.

And sixty-four thousand Genii guard the Eastern Gate,
And sixty-four thousand Gnomes guard the Northern Gate,
And sixty-four thousand Nymphs guard the Western Gate,
And sixty-four thousand Fairies guard the Southern Gate.

Around Golgonooza lies the land of death eternal, a Land 30
Of pain and misery and despair and ever brooding
melancholy
In all the Twenty-seven Heavens, number'd from Adam to
Luther,
From the blue Mundane Shell, reaching to the Vegetative
Earth.

The Vegetative Universe opens like a flower from the Earth's
center
In which is Eternity. It expands in Stars to the Mundane
Shell

And there it meets Eternity again, both within and without,
And the abstract Voids between the Stars are the Satanic
  Wheels.

There is the Cave; the Rock; the Tree; the Lake of Udan
  Adan;
The Forest, and the Marsh, and the Pits of bitumen deadly:
The Rocks of solid fire: the Ice valleys: the Plains 40
Of burning sand: the rivers, cataract & Lakes of Fire:
The Islands of the fiery Lakes: the Trees of Malice: Revenge:
And black Anxiety; and the Cities of the Salamandrine men:
(But whatever is visible to the Generated Man,
Is a Creation of mercy & love, from the Satanic Void.)
The land of darkness flamed but no light, & no repose:
The land of snows of trembling, & of iron hail incessant:
The land of earthquakes: and the land of woven labyrinths:
The land of snares & traps & wheels & pit-falls & dire mills:
The Voids, the Solids, & the land of clouds & regions of
  waters: 50
With their inhabitants, in the Twenty-seven Heavens
  beneath Beulah:
Self-righteousnesses conglomerating against the Divine
  Vision:
A Concave Earth wondrous, Chasmal, Abyssal, Incoherent!
Forming the Mundane Shell: above; beneath: on all sides
  surrounding
Golgonooza: Los walks round the walls night and day.

He views the City of Golgonooza, & its smaller Cities:
The Looms & Mills & Prisons & Work-houses of Og &
  Anak:
The Amalekite: the Canaanite: the Moabite: the Egyptian:
And all that has existed in the space of six thousand years,
Permanent, & not lost, not lost nor vanish'd; & every little
  act, 60
Word, work, & wish, that has existed, all remaining still
In those Churches, ever consuming & ever building by the
  Spectres
Of all the inhabitants of Earth wailing to be Created:

Shadowy to those who dwell not in them, meer possibilities:
But to those who enter into them they seem the only substances
For every thing exists & not one sigh nor smile nor tear,
[14] One hair nor particle of dust, not one can pass away.

*

And Los beheld his Sons, and he beheld his Daughters:
Every one a translucent Wonder: a Universe within,
Increasing inwards, into length and breadth, and heighth:
Starry & glorious: and they every one in their bright loins
Have a beautiful golden gate which opens into the vegetative world:
And every one a gate of rubies & all sorts of precious stones
In their translucent hearts, which opens into the vegetative world:
And every one a gate of iron, dreadful and wonderful,
In their translucent heads, which opens into the vegetative world: 10
And every one has the three regions Childhood, Manhood, & Age:
But the gate of the tongue, the western gate in them is clos'd,
Having a wall builded against it: and thereby the gates
Eastward & Southward & Northward, are incircled with flaming fires.
And the North is Breadth, the South is Heighth & Depth:
The East is Inwards: & the West is Outwards every way.

And Los beheld the mild Emanation Jerusalem eastward bending
Her revolutions toward the Starry Wheels in maternal anguish
Like a pale cloud arising from the arms of Beulah's Daughters:
In Entuthon Benython's deep Vales beneath Golgonooza. 20

*

[Blake's Vision]

[15] I see the Four-fold Man. The Humanity in deadly sleep
And its fallen Emanation. The Spectre & its cruel Shadow.
I see the Past, Present & Future, existing all at once
Before me; O Divine Spirit sustain me on thy wings!
That I may awake Albion from his long & cold repose.
For Bacon & Newton, sheath'd in dismal steel, their terrors
hang
Like iron scourges over Albion, Reasonings like vast Serpents
Infold around my limbs, bruising my minute articulations.

I turn my eyes to the Schools & Universities of Europe
And there behold the [n]Loom of Locke whose Woof rages dire 10
Wash'd by the Water-wheels of Newton; black the cloth
In heavy wreathes folds over every Nation; cruel Works
Of many Wheels I view, wheel without wheel, with cogs
tyrannic
Moving by compulsion each other: not as those in Eden,
which
Wheel within Wheel in freedom revolve in harmony &
peace.

*

I see Albion sitting upon his Rock in the first Winter,
And thence I see the Chaos of Satan & the World of Adam
When the Divine Hand went forth on Albion in the mid
Winter
And at the place of Death, when Albion sat in Eternal Death
Among the Furnaces of Los in the [n]Valley of the Son of
Hinnom. 20

*

[16] All things acted on Earth are seen in the bright Sculptures of
Los's Halls, & every Age renews its powers from these
Works
With every pathetic story possible to happen from Hate or
Wayward Love; & every sorrow & distress is carved here,
Every Affinity of Parents, Marriages & Friendships are here

In all their various combinations wrought with wondrous Art,
All that can happen to Man in his pilgrimage of seventy years.
Such is the Divine Written Law of Horeb & Sinai,
And such the Holy Gospel of Mount Olivet & Calvary.

*

[Albion, Jerusalem and Vala]

[18] Hoarse turn'd the Starry Wheels rending a way in Albion's Loins:
Beyond the Night of Beulah, in a dark & unknown Night:
Outstretch'd his Giant beauty on the ground in pain & tears:
[19] His Children exil'd from his breast pass to and fro before him,
His birds are silent on his hills, flocks die beneath his branches,
His tents are fall'n; his trumpets and the sweet sound of his harp
Are silent on his clouded hills that belch forth storms & fire.
His milk of Cows & honey of Bees & fruit of golden harvest
Is gather'd in the scorching heat & in the driving rain.
Where once he sat, he weary walks in misery and pain,
His Giant beauty and perfection fallen into dust,
Till, from within his wither'd breast, grown narrow with his woes,
The corn is turn'd to thistles & the apples into poison, 10
The birds of song to murderous crows, his joys to bitter groans,
The voices of children in his tents to cries of helpless infants,
And self-exiled from the face of light & shine of morning,
In the dark world, a narrow house! he wanders up and down
Seeking for rest and finding none! and hidden far within,
His Eon weeping in the cold and desolated Earth.

*

[20] Then thus Jerusalem spoke, while Vala wove the veil of tears:
Weeping in pleadings of Love, in the web of despair.

Wherefore hast thou shut me into the winter of human life
And clos'd up the sweet regions of youth and virgin
innocence:
Where we live, forgetting error, not pondering on evil:
Among my lambs & brooks of water, among my warbling
birds:
Where we delight in innocence before the face of the Lamb,
Going in and out before him in his love and sweet affection?

Vala replied weeping & trembling, hiding in her veil:

When winter rends the hungry family and the snow falls 10
Upon the ways of men hiding the paths of man and beast,
Then mourns the wanderer: then he repents his wanderings
& eyes
The distant forest: then the slave groans in the dungeon of
stone,
The captive in the mill of the stranger, sold for scanty hire.
They view their former life; they number moments over and
over,
Stringing them on their remembrance as on a thread of
sorrow.
Thou art my sister and my daughter! thy shame is mine also!
Ask me not of my griefs! thou knowest all my griefs.

Jerusalem answer'd with soft tears over the valleys:

O Vala, what is Sin? that thou shudderest and weepest 20
At sight of thy once lov'd Jerusalem! What is Sin but a little
Error & fault that is soon forgiven; but mercy is not a Sin,
Nor pity nor love nor kind forgiveness! O! if I have Sinned
Forgive & pity me! O! unfold thy [n]Veil in mercy & love!
Slay not my little ones, beloved Virgin daughter of Babylon
Slay not my infant loves & graces, beautiful daughter of
Moab
I cannot put off the human form; I strive but strive in vain.
When Albion rent thy beautiful net of gold and silver twine,

Thou hadst woven it with art, thou hadst caught me in the bands
Of love; thou refusedst to let me go: Albion beheld thy beauty 30
Beautiful thro' our Love's comeliness, beautiful thro' pity.
The Veil shone with thy brightness in the eyes of Albion,
Because it inclos'd pity & love; because we lov'd one-another!
Albion lov'd thee! he rent thy Veil! he embrac'd thee! he lov'd thee!
Astonish'd at his beauty & perfection, thou forgavest his furious love:
I redounded from Albion's bosom in my virgin loveliness.
The Lamb of God reciev'd me in his arms he smil'd upon us:
He made me his Bride & Wife: he gave thee to Albion.
Then was a time of love: O why is it passed away!

Then Albion broke silence and with groans reply'd: 40

[21] O Vala! O Jerusalem! do you delight in my groans
You, O lovely forms, you have prepared my death-cup:
The disease of Shame covers me from head to feet: I have no hope.
Every boil upon my body is a separate & deadly Sin.
Doubt first assail'd me, then Shame took possession of me;
Shame divides Families, Shame hath divided Albion in sunder!
First fled my Sons, & then my Daughters, then my Wild Animations.
My Cattle next, last ev'n the Dog of my Gate; the Forests fled
The Corn-fields, & the breathing Gardens outside separated
The Sea; the Stars: the Sun: the Moon: driv'n forth by my disease. 10
All is Eternal Death unless you can weave a chaste
Body over an unchaste Mind! Vala! O that thou wert pure!
That the deep wound of Sin might be clos'd up with the Needle,

And with the Loom: to cover [n]Gwendolen & Ragan with costly Robes
Of Natural Virtue, for their Spiritual forms without a Veil
Wither in Luvah's Sepulcher. I thrust him from my presence,
And all my Children follow'd his loud howlings into the Deep.
Jerusalem! dissembler Jerusalem! I look into thy bosom:
I discover thy secret places: Cordella! I behold
Thee whom I thought pure as the heavens in innocence & fear: 20
Thy [n]Tabernacle taken down, thy secret Cherubim disclosed
Art thou broken? Ah me [n]Sabrina, running by my side:
In childhood what wert thou? unutterable anguish! Conwenna
Thy cradled infancy is most piteous. O hide, O hide!
Their secret gardens were made paths to the traveller:
I knew not of their secret loves with those I hated most,
Nor that their every thought was Sin & secret appetite . . .

*

I hear my Children's voices,
I see their piteous faces gleam out upon the cruel winds
From Lincoln & Norwich, from Edinburgh & Monmouth: 30
I see them distant from my bosom scourg'd along the roads
Then lost in clouds; I hear their tender voices! clouds divide
I see them die beneath the whips of the Captains! they are taken
In solemn pomp into Chaldea across the bredths of Europe.
Six months they lie embalm'd in silent death: worshipped,
Carried in Arks of Oak before the armies in the spring:
Bursting their Arks they rise again to life: they play before
The Armies: I hear their loud cymbals & their deadly cries.
Are the Dead cruel? are those who are infolded in moral Law
Revengeful? O that Death & Annihilation were the same! 40

*

[22] Jerusalem then stretch'd her hand toward the Moon and spoke:

Why should Punishment Weave the Veil with Iron Wheels of War
When Forgiveness might it Weave with Wings of Cherubim?

*

[25] And there was heard a great lamenting in Beulah; all the Regions
Of Beulah were moved as the tender bowels are moved, & they said:

Why did you take Vengeance, O ye Sons of the mighty Albion,
Planting these Oaken Groves, Erecting these Dragon Temples?
Injury the Lord heals, but Vengeance cannot be healed.
As the Sons of Albion have done to Luvah, so they have in him
Done to the Divine Lord & Saviour, who suffers with those that suffer;
For not one sparrow can suffer & the whole Universe not suffer also
In all its Regions, & its Father & Saviour not pity and weep.
But Vengeance is the destroyer of Grace & Repentance in the bosom 10
Of the Injurer, in which the Divine Lamb is cruelly slain.
Descend, O Lamb of God, & take away the imputation of Sin
By the Creation of States & the deliverance of Individuals Evermore! Amen.

Thus wept they in Beulah over the Four Regions of Albion;
But many doubted & despair'd & imputed Sin & Righteousness
To Individuals & not to States; and these Slept in Ulro.

[from the Preface to Chap. 2]

[27] *[n]To the Jews*

The fields from Islington to Marybone,
To Primrose Hill and Saint John's Wood
Were builded over with pillars of gold,
And there Jerusalem's pillars stood.

Her Little-ones ran on the fields,
The Lamb of God among them seen,
And fair Jerusalem his Bride
Among the little meadows green.

Pancrass & Kentish-town repose
Among her golden pillars high, 10
Among her golden arches which
Shine upon the starry sky.

The Jew's-harp-house & the Green Man;
The Ponds where Boys to bathe delight:
The fields of Cows by Willan's farm
Shine in Jerusalem's pleasant sight.

She walks upon our meadows green:
The Lamb of God walks by her side:
And every English Child is seen,
Children of Jesus & his Bride, 20

Forgiving trespasses and sins
Lest Babylon with cruel Og,
With Moral & Self-righteous Law
Should Crucify in Satan's Synagogue!

What are those golden Builders doing
Near mournful ever-weeping Paddington
Standing above that mighty Ruin
Where Satan the first victory won?

Where Albion slept beneath the Fatal Tree
And the Druids' golden Knife, 30
Rioted in human gore,
In Offerings of Human Life:

They groan'd aloud on London Stone
They groan'd aloud on Tyburn's Brook;
Albion gave his deadly groan,
And all the Atlantic Mountains shook

Albion's Spectre from his Loins
Tore forth in all the pomp of War!
Satan his name: in flames of fire
He stretch'd his Druid Pillars far. 40

Jerusalem fell from Lambeth's Vale,
Down thro' Poplar & Old Bow;
Thro' Malden & across the Sea,
In War & howling, death & woe.

The Rhine was red with human blood:
The Danube roll'd a purple tide:
On the Euphrates Satan stood:
And over Asia stretch'd his pride.

He wither'd up sweet Zion's Hill,
From every Nation of the Earth: 50
He wither'd up Jerusalem's Gates,
And in a dark Land gave her birth.

He wither'd up the Human Form,
By laws of sacrifice for sin:
Till it became a Mortal Worm:
But O! translucent all within.

The Divine Vision still was seen
Still was the Human Form Divine,
Weeping in weak & mortal clay:
O Jesus! still the Form was thine. 60

And thine the Human Face, & thine
The Human Hands & Feet & Breath:
Entering thro' the Gates of Birth
And passing thro' the Gates of Death;

And O thou Lamb of God, whom I
Slew in my dark self-righteous pride:
Art thou return'd to Albion's Land!
And is Jerusalem thy Bride?

Come to my arms & never more
Depart; but dwell for ever here: 70
Create my Spirit to thy Love:
Subdue my Spectre to thy Fear.

Spectre of Albion! warlike Fiend!
In clouds of blood & ruin roll'd:
I here reclaim thee as my own
My Selfhood! Satan! arm'd in gold.

Is this thy soft Family-Love,
Thy cruel Patriarchal pride
Planting thy Family alone,
Destroying all the World beside? 80

A man's worst enemies are those
Of his own house & family;
And he who makes his law a curse,
By his own law shall surely die.

In my Exchanges every Land
Shall walk, & mine in every Land,
Mutual shall build Jerusalem:
Both heart in heart & hand in hand.

If Humility is Christianity, you, O Jews are the true Christians: If your tradition that Man contained in his Limbs, 90 all Animals, is True, & they were separated from him by cruel Sacrifices: and when compulsory cruel Sacrifices had brought Humanity into a Feminine Tabernacle, in the loins of Abraham & David: the Lamb of God, the Saviour became apparent on Earth as the Prophets had foretold? The Return of Israel is a Return to Mental Sacrifice & War. Take up the Cross, O Israel & follow Jesus.

CHAP. 2

[Albion in Despair]

[28] Every ornament of perfection, and every labour of love,
In all the Garden of Eden, & in all the golden mountains
Was become an envied horror, and a remembrance of
jealousy:
And every Act a Crime, and Albion the punisher & judge.

And Albion spoke from his secret seat and said:

All these ornaments are crimes, they are made by the labours
Of loves: of unnatural consanguinities and friendships
Horrid to think of when enquired deeply into; and all
These hills & valleys are accursed witnesses of Sin
I therefore condense them into solid rocks, stedfast! 10
A foundation and certainty and demonstrative truth:
That Man be separate from Man, & here I plant my seat.

Cold snows drifted around him: ice cover'd his loins around.
He sat by Tyburn's brook, and underneath his heel, shot up!
A deadly Tree, he nam'd it Moral Virtue, and the Law
Of God who dwells in Chaos hidden from the human sight.
The Tree spread over him its cold shadows, (Albion groan'd)
They bent down, they felt the earth and again enrooting
Shot into many a Tree! an endless labyrinth of woe!

From willing sacrifice of Self, to sacrifice of (miscall'd)
Enemies 20
For Atonement: Albion began to erect twelve Altars,
Of rough unhewn rocks, before the Potter's Furnace.
He nam'd them Justice, and Truth: and Albion's Sons
Must have become the first Victims, being the first
transgressors,
But they fled to the mountains to seek ransom: building a
Strong
Fortification against the Divine Humanity and Mercy,
In Shame & Jealousy to annihilate Jerusalem!

*

[n][34(38)] Turning from Universal Love petrific as he went,
His cold against the warmth of Eden rag'd with loud
Thunders of deadly war (the fever of the human soul)
Fires and clouds of rolling smoke! But mild the Saviour
follow'd him,
Displaying the Eternal Vision! the Divine Similitude!
In loves and tears of brothers, sisters, sons, fathers, and
friends
Which if Man ceases to behold, he ceases to exist:

Saying: Albion! Our wars are wars of life, & wounds of love,
With intellectual spears, & long winged arrows of thought:
Mutual in one another's love and wrath all renewing 10
We live as One Man; for contracting our infinite senses
We behold multitude; or expanding, we behold as one,
As One Man all the Universal Family; and that One Man
We call Jesus the Christ: and he in us, and we in him,
Live in perfect harmony in Eden the land of life,
Giving, recieving, and forgiving each other's trespasses.
He is the Good shepherd, he is the Lord and master;
He is the Shepherd of Albion, he is all in all,
In Eden: in the garden of God: and in heavenly Jerusalem.
If we have offended, forgive us, take not vengeance against
us. 20

Thus speaking; the Divine Family follow Albion:
I see them in the Vision of God upon my pleasant valleys.

I behold London; a Human awful wonder of God!
He says: Return, Albion, return! I give myself for thee:
My Streets are my Ideas of Imagination.
Awake Albion, awake! and let us awake up together.
My Houses are Thoughts: my Inhabitants, Affections,
The children of my thoughts, walking within my
blood-vessels,
Shut from my nervous form which sleeps upon the verge of
Beulah
In dreams of darkness, while my vegetating blood in veiny
pipes, 30

Rolls dreadful thro' the Furnaces of Los, and the Mills of
Satan.
For Albion's sake, and for Jerusalem thy Emanation
I give myself, and these my brethren give themselves for
Albion.

So spoke London, immortal Guardian! I heard in Lambeth's
shades:
In Felpham I heard and saw the Visions of Albion.
I write in South Molton Street, what I both see and hear
In regions of Humanity, in London's opening streets.

I see thee awful Parent Land in light, behold I see!
Verulam! Canterbury! venerable parent of men,
Generous immortal Guardian golden clad! for Cities 40
Are Men, fathers of multitudes, and Rivers & Mountains
Are also Men; every thing is Human, mighty! sublime!
In every bosom a Universe expands as wings,
Let down at will around, and call'd the Universal Tent.

*

There is in Albion a Gate of Precious stones and gold
Seen only by Emanations, by vegetations viewless,
Bending across the road of Oxford Street; it from Hyde Park
To Tyburn's deathful shades, admits the wandering souls
Of multitudes who die from Earth: this Gate cannot be found
[35(39)] By Satan's Watch-fiends tho' they search numbering every
grain
Of sand on Earth every night, they never find this Gate.
It is the Gate of Los. Withoutside is the Mill, intricate,
dreadful
And fill'd with cruel tortures; but no mortal man can find the
Mill
Of Satan, in his mortal pilgrimage of seventy years,

For Human beauty knows it not: nor can Mercy find it!

*

[37(41)] There is a Grain of Sand in Lambeth that Satan cannot find,
Nor can his Watch Fiends find it; 'tis translucent & has many Angles,
But he who finds it will find Oothoon's palace; for within
Opening into Beulah, every angle is a lovely heaven.
But should the Watch Fiends find it, they would call it Sin,
And lay its Heavens & their inhabitants in blood of punishment.
Here Jerusalem & Vala were hid in soft slumberous repose,
Hid from the terrible East, shut up in the South & West.

*

[Los and Albion]

[42] Albion spoke in his dismal dreams: O thou deceitful friend,
Worshipping mercy & beholding thy friend in such affliction!
Los! thou now discoverest thy turpitude to the heavens.
I demand righteousness & justice, O thou ingratitude!
Give me my Emanations back, food for my dying soul.
My daughters are harlots: my sons are accursed before me,
Enitharmon is my daughter, accursed with a father's curse.
O! I have utterly been wasted. I have given my daughters to devils.

So spoke Albion in gloomy majesty, and deepest night
Of Ulro roll'd round his skirts from Dover to Cornwall. 10

Los answer'd: Righteousness & justice I give thee in return
For thy righteousness, but I add mercy also and bind
Thee from destroying these little ones: am I to be only
Merciful to thee and cruel to all that thou hatest?
Thou wast the Image of God surrounded by the Four Zoas.
Three thou hast slain, I am the Fourth: thou canst not destroy me.
Thou art in Error; trouble me not with thy righteousness.
I have innocence to defend and ignorance to instruct:

I have no time for seeming and little arts of compliment
In morality and virtue, in self-glorying and pride. 20
There is a limit of Opakeness and a limit of Contraction
In every Individual Man, and the limit of Opakeness
Is named Satan, and the limit of Contraction is named Adam.
But when Man sleeps in Beulah, the Saviour in Mercy takes
Contraction's Limit, and of the Limit he forms Woman, that
Himself may in process of time be born Man to redeem.
But there is no Limit of Expansion; there is no Limit of
  Translucence
In the bosom of Man for ever from eternity to eternity.
Therefore I break thy bonds of righteousness: I crush thy
  messengers,
That they may not crush me and mine; do thou be righteous 30
And I will return it; otherwise I defy thy worst revenge.
Consider me as thine enemy: on me turn all thy fury;
But destroy not these little ones, nor mock the Lord's
  anointed!
Destroy not by Moral Virtue the little ones whom he hath
  chosen,
The little ones whom he hath chosen in preference to thee.
He hath cast thee off for ever: the little ones he hath
  anointed!
Thy Selfhood is for ever accursed from the Divine presence.

So Los spoke, then turn'd his face & wept for Albion.

*

[43(29)] Then the Divine Vision like a silent Sun appear'd above
Albion's dark rocks: setting behind the Gardens of
  Kensington
On Tyburn's River in clouds of blood, where was mild Zion
  Hill's
Most ancient promontory, and in the Sun a Human Form
  appear'd,
And thus the Voice Divine went forth upon the rocks of
  Albion

I elected Albion for my glory: I gave to him the Nations
Of the whole Earth. He was the Angel of my Presence; and all
The Sons of God were Albion's Sons; and Jerusalem was my joy.
The ⁿReactor hath hid himself thro' envy. I behold him,
But you cannot behold him till he be reveal'd in his System. 10
Albion's Reactor must have a Place prepar'd: Albion must Sleep
The Sleep of Death till the Man of Sin & Repentance be reveal'd.
Hidden in Albion's Forests he lurks: he admits of no Reply
From Albion: but hath founded his Reaction into a Law
Of Action, for Obedience to destroy the Contraries of Man.
He hath compell'd Albion to become a Punisher & hath possess'd
Himself of Albion's Forests & Wilds, and Jerusalem is taken!
The City of the Woods in the Forest of Ephratah is taken!
London is a stone of her ruins, Oxford is the dust of her walls!
Sussex & Kent are her scatter'd garments, Ireland her holy place; 20
And the murder'd bodies of her little ones are Scotland and Wales.
The Cities of the Nations are the smoke of her consummation.
The Nations are her dust, ground by the chariot wheels
Of her lordly conquerors, her palaces levell'd with the dust.
I come that I may find a way for my banished ones to return.
Fear not O little Flock, I come! Albion shall rise again.

So saying, the mild Sun inclos'd the Human Family.

*

[44(30)] And Los prayed and said, O Divine Saviour, arise
Upon the Mountains of Albion as in ancient time! Behold!
The Cities of Albion seek thy face. London groans in pain
From Hill to Hill, & the Thames laments along the Valleys

The little Villages of Middlesex & Surrey hunger & thirst:
The Twenty-eight Cities of Albion stretch their hands to thee
Because of the Oppressors of Albion in every City & Village:
They mock at the Labourer's limbs: they mock at his starv'd
Children:
They buy his Daughters that they may have power to sell his
Sons:
They compell the Poor to live upon a crust of bread by soft
mild arts: 10
They reduce the Man to want: then give with pomp &
ceremony:
The praise of Jehovah is chaunted from lips of hunger &
thirst!
Humanity knows not of Sex: wherefore are Sexes in Beulah?
In Beulah the Female lets down her beautiful Tabernacle
Which the Male enters magnificent between her Cherubim:
And becomes One with her, mingling condensing in
Self-love
The Rocky Law of Condemnation & double Generation &
Death.
Albion hath enter'd the Loins, the place of the Last
Judgment:
And Luvah hath drawn the Curtains around Albion in Vala's
bosom
The Dead awake to Generation! Arise O Lord, & rend the
Veil! 20

So Los in lamentations follow'd Albion. Albion cover'd
[45(31)] His western heaven with rocky clouds of death & despair.

Fearing that Albion should turn his back against the Divine
Vision,
[n]Los took his globe of fire to search the interiors of Albion's
Bosom, in all the terrors of friendship; entering the caves
Of despair & death, to search the tempters out, walking
among
Albion's rocks & precipices! caves of solitude & dark despair,
And saw every Minute Particular of Albion degraded &
murder'd

But saw not by whom; they were hidden within in the minute particulars
Of which they had possess'd themselves: and there they take up
The articulations of a man's soul, and laughing throw it down 10
Into the frame, then knock it out upon the plank, & souls are bak'd
In bricks to build the pyramids of Heber & Terah. But Los
Search'd in vain: clos'd from the minutia he walk'd difficult.
He came down from Highgate thro' Hackney & Holloway towards London
Till he came to old Stratford, & thence to Stepney & the Isle
Of Leutha's Dogs, thence thro' the narrows of the River's side:
And saw every minute particular, the jewels of Albion, running down
The kennels of the streets & lanes as if they were abhorr'd.
Every Universal Form was become barren mountains of Moral
Virtue: and every Minute Particular harden'd into grains of sand: 20
And all the tendernesses of the soul cast forth as filth & mire,
Among the winding places of deep contemplation intricate;
To where the Tower of London frown'd dreadful over Jerusalem:
A building of Luvah builded in Jerusalem's eastern gate to be
His secluded Court: thence to ⁿBethlehem where was builded
Dens of despair in the house of bread: enquiring in vain
Of stones and rocks he took his way, for human form was none:
And thus he spoke, looking on Albion's City with many tears.

What shall I do! what could I do, if I could find these Criminals?
I could not dare to take vengeance; for all things are so constructed 30

And builded by the Divine hand, that the sinner shall always
escape,
And he who takes vengeance alone is the criminal of
Providence;
If I should dare to lay my finger on a grain of sand
In way of vengeance, I punish the already punish'd: O whom
Should I pity if I pity not the sinner who is gone astray!
O Albion, if thou takest vengeance, if thou revengest thy
wrongs
Thou art for ever lost! What can I do to hinder the Sons
Of Albion from taking vengeance? or how shall I them
perswade?

So spoke Los, travelling thro' darkness & horrid solitude;
And he beheld Jerusalem in Westminster & Marybone, 40
Among the ruins of the Temple: and Vala who is her
Shadow,
Jerusalem's Shadow bent northward over the Island white.
At length he sat on London Stone, & heard Jerusalem's
voice:

Albion, I cannot be thy Wife: thine own Minute Particulars,
Belong to God alone, and all thy little ones are holy
They are of Faith & not of Demonstration: wherefore is Vala
Cloth'd in black mourning upon my river's currents? Vala
awake!
I hear thy shuttles sing in the sky, and round my limbs
I feel the iron threads of love & jealousy & despair.

Vala reply'd: Albion is mine! Luvah gave me to Albion 50
And now recieves reproach & hate. Was it not said of old,
Set your Son before a man & he shall take you & your sons
For slaves: but set your Daughter before a man & She
Shall make him & his sons & daughters your slaves for ever!
And is this Faith? Behold the strife of Albion & Luvah
Is great in the east, their spears of blood rage in the eastern
heaven.
Urizen is the champion of Albion, they will slay my Luvah:
And thou, O harlot daughter! daughter of despair, art all

This cause of these shakings of my towers on Euphrates.
Here is the House of Albion, & here is thy secluded place 60
And here we have found thy sins: & hence we turn thee forth,
For all to avoid thee: to be astonish'd at thee for thy sins:
Because thou art the impurity & the harlot: & thy children
Children of whoredoms: born for Sacrifice: for the meat & drink
Offering, to sustain the glorious combat & the battle & war,
That Man may be purified by the death of thy delusions.

So saying she her dark threads cast over the trembling River:
And over the valleys; from the hills of Hertfordshire to the hills
Of Surrey across Middlesex, & across Albion's House
Of Eternity! pale stood Albion at his eastern gate, 70
[46(32)] Leaning against the pillars, & his disease rose from his skirts:
Upon the Precipice he stood! ready to fall into Non-Entity.

*

[50] Expanding on wing, the Daughters of Beulah replied in sweet response

Come O thou Lamb of God and take away the remembrance of Sin.
To Sin & to hide the Sin in sweet deceit is lovely!!
To Sin in the open face of day is cruel & pitiless! But
To record the Sin for a reproach: to let the Sun go down
In a remembrance of the Sin is a Woe & a Horror!
A brooder of an Evil Day, and a Sun rising in blood
Come then O Lamb of God and take away the remembrance of Sin!

End of Chap. 2^d.

[Preface to Chap. 3]

[52]

Rahab is an Eternal State	To the Deists.	The spiritual States of the Soul are all Eternal Distinguish between the Man, & his present State

He never can be a Friend to the Human Race who is the Preacher of Natural Morality or Natural Religion. He is a flatterer who means to betray, to perpetuate Tyrant Pride & the Laws of that Babylon which he forsees shall shortly be destroyed, with the Spiritual and not the Natural Sword: He is in the State named Rahab, which State must be put off before he can be the Friend of Man.

You, O Deists profess yourselves the Enemies of Christianity: and you are so: you are also the Enemies of the Human Race & of Universal Nature. Man is born a Spectre or Satan & 10
is altogether an Evil, & requires a New Selfhood continually & must continually be changed into his direct Contrary. But your Greek Philosophy (which is a [n]remnant of Druidism) teaches that Man is Righteous in his Vegetated Spectre: an Opinion of fatal & accursed consequence to Man, as the Ancients saw plainly by Revelation to the intire abrogation of Experimental Theory: and many believed what they saw, and Prophecied of Jesus.

Man must & will have Some Religion; if he has not the Religion of Jesus, he will have the Religion of Satan, & will 20
erect the Synagogue of Satan, calling the Prince of this World, God; and destroying all who do not worship Satan under the Name of God. Will any one say: Where are those who worship Satan under the Name of God! Where are they? Listen! Every Religion that Preaches Vengeance for Sin is the Religion of the Enemy & Avenger, and not of the Forgiver of Sin: and their God is Satan, Named by the Divine Name. Your Religion, O Deists, Deism, is the Worship of the God of this World by the means of what you call Natural Religion and Natural Philosophy, and of Natural Morality or Self- 30
Righteousness, the Selfish Virtues of the Natural Heart. This

was the Religion of the Pharisees who murder'd Jesus. Deism is the same & ends in the same.

Voltaire, Rousseau, Gibbon, Hume, charge the Spiritually Religious with Hypocrisy! but how a Monk or a Methodist either, can be a Hypocrite: I cannot concieve. We are Men of like passions with others & pretend not to be holier than others: therefore, when a Religious Man falls into Sin, he ought not to be call'd a Hypocrite: this title is more properly to be given to a Player who falls into Sin; whose profession 40 is Virtue & Morality & the making Men Self-Righteous. Foote in calling Whitefield, Hypocrite: was himself one: for Whitefield pretended not to be holier than others: but confessed his Sins before all the World; Voltaire! Rousseau! You cannot escape my charge that you are Pharisees & Hypocrites, for you are constantly talking of the Virtues of the Human Heart, and particularly of your own, that you may accuse others & especially the Religious, whose errors, you by this display of pretended Virtue, chiefly design to expose. Rousseau thought Men Good by Nature; he found them Evil & 50 found no friend. Friendship cannot exist without Forgiveness of Sins continually. The Book written by Rousseau call'd his Confessions is an apology & cloke for his sin & not a confession.

But you also charge the poor Monks & Religious with being the causes of War: while you acquit & flatter the Alexanders & Caesars, the Lewis's & Fredericks: who alone are its causes & its actors. But the Religion of Jesus, Forgiveness of Sin, can never be the cause of a War nor of a single Martyrdom.

Those who Martyr others or who cause War are Deists, but 60 never can be Forgivers of Sin. The Glory of Christianity is, To Conquer by Forgiveness. All the Destruction therefore, in Christian Europe has arisen from Deism, which is Natural Religion.

  I saw a Monk of Charlemaine
Arise before my sight;
  I talk'd with the Grey Monk as we stood
In beams of infernal light.

Gibbon arose with a lash of steel
And Voltaire with a racking wheel,
The Schools in clouds of learning roll'd
Arose with War in iron & gold.

Thou lazy Monk! they sound afar
In vain condemning glorious War! 10
And in your Cell you shall ever dwell;
Rise, War & bind him in his Cell.

The blood red ran from the Grey Monk's side,
His hands & feet were wounded wide;
His body bent, his arms & knees
Like to the roots of ancient trees.

When Satan first the black bow bent
And the Moral Law from the Gospel rent
He forg'd the Law into a Sword
And spill'd the blood of mercy's Lord. 20

Titus! Constantine! Charlemaine!
O Voltaire! Rousseau! Gibbon! Vain
Your Grecian Mocks & Roman Sword
Against this image of his Lord!

For a Tear is an Intellectual thing;
And a Sigh is the Sword of an Angel King
And the bitter groan of a Martyr's woe
Is an Arrow from the Almightie's Bow!

CHAP. 3

[Los's Children at Work]

[53] But Los, who is the Vehicular Form of strong Urthona
Wept vehemently over Albion where Thames currents spring
From the rivers of Beulah; pleasant river! soft, mild, parent stream
And the roots of Albion's Tree enter'd the Soul of Los
As he sat before his Furnaces clothed in sackcloth of hair,

In gnawing pain dividing him from his Emanation;
Inclosing all the children of Los time after time.

*

[59] And one [n]Daughter of Los sat at the fiery Reel, & another
Sat at the shining Loom with her Sisters attending round;
Terrible their distress & their sorrow cannot be utter'd.
And another Daughter of Los sat at the Spinning Wheel
Endless their labour, with bitter food, void of sleep;
Tho' hungry they labour: they rouze themselves anxious
Hour after hour labouring at the whirling Wheel;
Many Wheels & as many lovely Daughters sit weeping.
Yet the intoxicating delight that they take in their work
Obliterates every other evil; none pities their tears; 10
Yet they regard not pity & they expect no one to pity,
For they labour for life & love, regardless of any one
But the poor Spectres that they work for, always incessantly.
They are mock'd by every one that passes by, they regard not
They labour; & when their Wheels are broken by scorn & malice
They mend them sorrowing with many tears & afflictions.

Other Daughters Weave on the Cushion & Pillow, Network fine
That [n]Rahab & Tirzah may exist & live & breathe & love
Ah, that it could be as the Daughters of Beulah wish!

Other Daughters of Los, labouring at Looms less fine 20
Create the Silk-worm & the Spider & the Catterpiller
To assist in their most grievous work of pity & compassion:
And others Create the wooly Lamb & the downy Fowl
To assist in the work: the Lamb bleats; the Sea-fowl cries.
Men understand not the distress & the labour & sorrow
That in the Interior Worlds is carried on in fear & trembling,
Weaving the shudd'ring fears & loves of Albion's Families.
Thunderous rage the Spindles of iron, & the iron Distaff
Maddens in the fury of their hands, weaving in bitter tears
The Veil of [n]Goats'-hair & Purple & Scarlet & fine twined Linen. 30

[Jerusalem Imprisoned]

[60] But [n]Jerusalem faintly saw him, clos'd in the Dungeons of
Babylon.
Her Form was held by Beulah's Daughters, but all within
unseen
She sat at the Mills, her hair unbound, her feet naked,
Cut with the flints: her tears run down, her reason grows like
The Wheel of Hand, incessant turning day & night without
rest.
Insane she raves upon the winds hoarse, inarticulate:
All night Vala hears, she triumphs in pride of holiness
To see Jerusalem deface her lineaments with bitter blows
Of despair, while the Satanic Holiness triumph'd in Vala,
In a Religion of Chastity & Uncircumcised Selfishness, 10
Both of the Head & Heart & Loins, clos'd up in Moral Pride.

But the Divine Lamb stood beside Jerusalem; oft she saw
The lineaments Divine, & oft the Voice heard, & oft she said:

O Lord & Saviour, have the Gods of the Heathen pierced
thee?
Or hast thou been pierced in the House of thy Friends?
Art thou alive! & livest thou for-evermore? or art thou
Not; but a delusive shadow, a thought that liveth not.
Babel mocks saying, there is no God nor Son of God;
That thou O Human Imagination, O Divine Body art all
A delusion, but I know thee O Lord, when thou arisest upon 20
My weary eyes even in this dungeon & this iron mill.
The Stars of Albion cruel rise; [n]thou bindest to sweet
influences:
For thou also sufferest with me altho' I behold thee not;
And altho' I sin & blaspheme thy holy name, thou pitiest
me;
Because thou knowest I am deluded by the turning mills.
And by these visions of pity & love because of Albion's
death.

Thus spake Jerusalem, & thus the Divine Voice replied:

Mild Shade of Man, pitiest thou these Visions of terror & woe!
Give forth thy pity & love. Fear not! lo I am with thee always.
Only believe in me that I have power to raise from death 30
Thy Brother who Sleepeth in Albion: fear not trembling Shade,
[61] Behold: in the Visions of Elohim Jehovah, behold Joseph & Mary
And be comforted O Jerusalem in the Visions of Jehovah Elohim.

[Joseph and Mary]

She looked & saw Joseph the Carpenter in Nazareth & Mary
His espoused Wife. And Mary said, If thou put me away from thee
Dost thou not murder me? Joseph spoke in anger & fury. Should I
Marry a Harlot & an Adulteress? Mary answer'd, Art thou more pure
Than thy Maker who forgiveth Sins & calls again Her that is Lost:
Tho' She hates, he calls her again in love. I love my dear Joseph,
But he driveth me away from his presence; yet I hear the voice of God
In the voice of my Husband: tho' he is angry for a moment, he will not 10
Utterly cast me away: if I were pure, never could I taste the sweets
Of the Forgiveness of Sins! if I were holy I never could behold the tears
Of love! of him who loves me in the midst of his anger in furnace of fire.

Ah my Mary! said Joseph, weeping over & embracing her closely in

His arms: Doth he forgive Jerusalem & not exact Purity from
her who is
Polluted? I heard his voice in my sleep & his Angel in my
dream:

Saying, Doth Jehovah Forgive a Debt only on condition that
it shall
Be Payed? Doth he Forgive Pollution only on conditions of
Purity?
That Debt is not Forgiven! That Pollution is not Forgiven!
Such is the Forgiveness of the Gods, the Moral Virtues of the 20
Heathen, whose tender Mercies are Cruelty. But Jehovah's
Salvation
Is without Money & without Price, in the Continual
Forgiveness of Sins
In the Perpetual Mutual Sacrifice in Great Eternity! for
behold!
There is none that liveth & Sinneth not! And this is the
Covenant
Of Jehovah: If you Forgive one-another, so shall Jehovah
Forgive You:
That He Himself may Dwell among You. Fear not then to
take
To thee Mary thy Wife, for she is with Child by the Holy
Ghost.

Then Mary burst forth into a Song! she flowed like a River of
Many Streams in the arms of Joseph, & gave forth her tears
of joy
Like many waters, and Emanating into gardens & palaces
upon 30
[n]Euphrates, & to forests & floods & animals wild & tame
from
Gihon to Hiddekel, & to corn-fields & villages & inhabitants
Upon Pison & Arnon & Jordan. And I heard the voice among
The Reapers Saying, Am I Jerusalem the lost Adulteress? or
am I
Babylon come up to Jerusalem? And another voice answer'd,
Saying,

Does the voice of my Lord call me again? am I pure thro' his Mercy
And Pity: Am I become lovely as a Virgin in his sight who am
Indeed a Harlot drunken with the Sacrifice of Idols! does he
Call her pure as he did in the days of her Infancy when She
Was cast out to the loathing of her person? The Chaldean took 40
Me from my Cradle. The Amalekite stole me away upon his Camels
Before I had ever beheld with love the Face of Jehovah, or known
That there was a God of Mercy: O Mercy! O Divine Humanity!
O Forgiveness & Pity & Compassion! If I were Pure I should never
Have known Thee; If I were Unpolluted I should never have
Glorified thy Holiness, or rejoiced in thy great Salvation.

Mary leaned her side against Jerusalem, Jerusalem recieved
The Infant into her hands in the Visions of Jehovah. Times passed on:
Jerusalem fainted over the Cross & Sepulcher; She heard the voice:
Wilt thou make Rome thy Patriarch Druid, & the Kings of Europe his 50
Horsemen? Man in the Resurrection changes his Sexual Garments at will:
Every Harlot was once a Virgin: every Criminal an Infant Love!
[62] Repose on me till the morning of the Grave. I am thy life.

Jerusalem replied, I am an outcast: Albion is dead!
I am left to the trampling foot & the spurning heel!
A Harlot I am call'd, I am sold from street to street!
I am defaced with blows & with the dirt of the Prison!
And wilt thou become my Husband O my Lord & Saviour?
Shall Vala bring thee forth? shall the Chaste be ashamed also?

*

But I thy Magdalen behold thy Spiritual Risen Body:
Shall Albion arise? [n]I know he shall arise at the Last Day!
I know that in my flesh I shall see God: but Emanations 10
Are weak; they know not whence they are, nor whither tend.

Jesus replied, I am the Resurrection & the Life.
I Die & pass the limits of possibility, as it appears
To individual perception. Luvah must be Created
And Vala; for I cannot leave them in the gnawing Grave.
But will prepare a way for my banished-ones to return.
Come now with me into the villages, walk thro' all the cities:
Tho' thou art taken to prison & judgment, starved in the streets,
I will command the cloud to give thee food, & the hard rock
To flow with milk & wine; tho' thou seest me not a season, 20
Even a long season & a hard journey & a howling wilderness!
Tho' Vala's cloud hide thee & Luvah's fires follow thee!
Only believe & trust in me; Lo, I am always with thee!

So spoke the Lamb of God while Luvah's Cloud reddening above
Burst forth in streams of blood upon the heavens, & dark night
Involv'd Jerusalem; & the Wheels of Albion's Sons turn'd hoarse
Over the Mountains & the fires blaz'd on Druid Altars
And the Sun set in Tyburn's Brook where Victims howl & cry.

But Los beheld the Divine Vision among the flames of the Furnaces,
Therefore he lived & breathed in hope; but his tears fell incessant 30
Because his Children were clos'd from him apart: & Enitharmon
Dividing in fierce pain: also the Vision of God was clos'd in clouds
Of Albion's Spectres, that Los in despair oft sat, & often ponder'd

On Death Eternal in fierce shudders upon the mountains of
Albion
Walking: & in the vales in howlings fierce; then to his Anvils
Turning, anew began his labours, tho' in terrible pains!

*

[Rahab and Tirzah]

[64] Then All the Daughters of Albion became One before Los,
even Vala
And she put forth her hand upon the Looms in dreadful
howlings
Till she vegetated into a hungry Stomach & a devouring
Tongue.
Her Hand is a Court of Justice: her Feet two Armies in
Battle:
Storms & Pestilence in her Locks, & in her Loins Earthquake
And Fire & the Ruin of Cities & Nations & Families &
Tongues.

She cries: The Human is but a Worm, & thou, O Male! Thou
art
Thyself Female, a Male, a breeder of Seed; a Son & Husband:
& Lo,
The Human Divine is Woman's Shadow, a Vapor in the
summer's heat.
Go assume Papal dignity, thou Spectre, thou Male Harlot!
Arthur, 10
Divide into the Kings of Europe in times remote, O
Woman-born
And Woman-nourish'd & Woman-educated &
Woman-scorn'd!

Wherefore art thou living, said Los, & Man cannot live in thy
presence:
Art thou Vala the Wife of Albion, O thou lovely Daughter of
Luvah?
All Quarrels arise from Reasoning, the secret Murder and

The violent Man-slaughter, these are the Spectre's double
Cave;
The Sexual Death living on accusation of Sin & Judgment
To freeze Love & Innocence into the gold & silver of the
Merchant;
Without Forgiveness of Sin Love is Itself Eternal Death.

Then the Spectre drew Vala into his bosom magnificent
terrific, 20
Glittering with precious stones & gold, with Garments of
blood & fire.
He wept in deadly wrath of the Spectre, in self-contradicting
agony
Crimson with Wrath & green with Jealousy, dazling with
Love
And Jealousy immingled & the purple of the violet darken'd
deep
Over the Plow of Nations thund'ring in the hand of Albion's
Spectre.

A dark Hermaphrodite they stood frowning upon London's
River,
And the Distaff & Spindle in the hands of Vala, with the Flax
of
Human Miseries turn'd fierce with the Lives of Men along
the Valley.

*

[66] Los behold in terror: he pour'd his loud storms on the
Furnaces:
The Daughters of Albion clothed in garments of needle work
Strip them off from their shoulders and bosoms, they lay
aside
Their garments; they sit naked upon the Stone of trial.
The Knife of flint passes over the howling ⁿVictim: his blood
Gushes & stains the fair side of the fair Daughters of Albion.
They put aside his curls; they divide his seven locks upon
His forehead: they bind his forehead with thorns of iron,
They put into his hand a reed, they mock, Saying: Behold

The [n]King of Canaan whose are seven hundred chariots of iron! 10
They take off his vesture whole with their Knives of flint:

But they cut asunder his inner garments: searching with
Their cruel fingers for his heart, & there they enter in pomp,
In many tears; & there they erect a temple & an altar:
They pour cold water on his brain in front, to cause
Lids to grow over his eyes in veils of tears: and caverns
To freeze over his nostrils, while they feed his tongue from cups
And dishes of painted clay. Glowing with beauty & cruelty:
They obscure the sun & the moon; no eye can look upon them.

Ah! alas! at the sight of the Victim, & at sight of those who are smitten, 20
All who see become what they behold; their eyes are cover'd
With veils of tears and their nostrils & tongues shrunk up,
Their ear bent outwards; as their Victim, so are they in the pangs
Of unconquerable fear! amidst delights of revenge Earth-shaking!
And as their eye & ear shrunk, the heavens shrunk away
The Divine Vision became first [n]a burning flame, then a column
Of fire, then an awful fiery wheel surrounding earth & heaven:
And then a globe of blood wandering distant in an unknown night:
Afar into the unknown night the mountains fled away:
Six months of mortality, a summer: & six months of mortality, a winter: 30
The Human form began to be alter'd by the Daughters of Albion
And the perceptions to be dissipated into the Indefinite, becoming
A mighty Polypus nam'd Albion's Tree: they tie the Veins
And Nerves into two knots: & the Seed into a double knot:

They look forth: the Sun is shrunk; the Heavens are shrunk
Away into the far remote, and the Trees & Mountains
  wither'd
Into indefinite cloudy shadows in darkness & separation.
By Invisible Hatreds adjoin'd, [n]they seem remote and
  separate
From each other; and yet are a Mighty Polypus in the Deep!
As the Mistletoe grows on the Oak, so Albion's Tree on
  Eternity: Lo! 40
He who will not comingle in Love must be adjoin'd by Hate.

*

[67] Tirzah sits weeping to hear the shrieks of the dying: her
  Knife
Of flint is in her hand: she passes it over the howling Victim.
The Daughters Weave their Work in loud cries over the Rock
Of Horeb! still eyeing Albion's Cliffs eagerly siezing &
  twisting
The threads of Vala & Jerusalem running from mountain to
  mountain
Over the whole Earth: loud the Warriors rage in Beth Peor
Beneath the iron whips of their Captains & consecrated
  banners:
Loud the Sun & Moon rage in the conflict; loud the Stars
Shout in the night of battle & their spears grow to their
  hands
With blood, weaving the deaths of the Mighty into a
  Tabernacle 10
For Rahab & Tirzah; till the Great Polypus of Generation
  covered the Earth.

*

[The Forms of Male Evil]

[69] Then all the Males combined into One Male & every one
Became a ravening eating Cancer growing in the Female
A Polypus of Roots of Reasoning Doubt Despair & Death.
Going forth & returning from Albion's Rocks to Canaan:
Devouring Jerusalem from every Nation of the Earth.

Envying stood the enormous Form at variance with Itself
In all its Members, in eternal torment of love & jealousy:
Driv'n forth by Los time after time from Albion's cliffy
shore,
Drawing the free loves of Jerusalem into infernal bondage;
That they might be born in contentions of Chastity & in 10
Deadly Hate between "Leah & Rachel, Daughters of Deceit &
Fraud,
Bearing the Images of various Species of Contention
And Jealousy & Abhorrence & Revenge & deadly
Murder . . .

*

And now the Spectres of the Dead awake in Beulah: all
The Jealousies become Murderous: uniting together in
Rahab
A Religion of Chastity, forming a Commerce to sell Loves,
With Moral Law, an Equal Balance, not going down with
decision
Therefore the Male severe & cruel fill'd with stern Revenge:
Mutual Hate returns & mutual Deceit & mutual Fear.

Hence the Infernal Veil grows in the disobedient Female: 20
Which Jesus rends & the whole Druid Law removes away
From the Inner Sanctuary: a False Holiness hid within the
Center.
For the Sanctuary of Eden is in the Camp: in the Outline,
In the Circumference: & every Minute Particular is Holy:
Embraces are Cominglings from the Head even to the Feet;
And not a pompous High Priest entering by a Secret Place.

Jerusalem pined in her inmost soul over Wandering Reuben
As she slept in Beulah's Night hid by the Daughters of
Beulah.

*

[70] And this the ⁿform of mighty Hand sitting on Albion's cliffs
Before the face of Albion, a mighty threat'ning Form.

His bosom wide & shoulders huge overspreading wondrous,
Bear Three strong sinewy Necks & Three awful & terrible
Heads:
Three Brains in contradictory council brooding incessantly,
Neither daring to put in act its councils, fearing each-other,
Therefore rejecting Ideas as nothing & holding all Wisdom
To consist in the agreements & disagreements of Ideas,
Plotting to devour Albion's Body of Humanity & Love.

Such Form the aggregate of the Twelve Sons of Albion took;
& such 10
Their appearance when combin'd: but often by birth-pangs
& loud groans
They divide to Twelve: the key-bones & the chest dividing in
pain
Disclose a hideous orifice; thence issuing the Giant-brood
Arise as the smoke of the furnace, shaking the rocks from sea
to sea.
And there they combine into Three Forms, named Bacon &
Newton & Locke,
In the Oak Groves of Albion which overspread all the Earth.

Imputing Sin & Righteousness to Individuals; Rahab
Sat deep within him hid: his Feminine Power unreveal'd,
Brooding Abstract Philosophy to destroy Imagination, the
Divine-
-Humanity: A Three-fold Wonder: feminine: most
beautiful: Three-fold 20
Each within other. On her white marble & even Neck, her
Heart
Inorb'd and bonified: with locks of shadowing modesty,
shining

Over her beautiful Female features, soft flourishing in beauty
Beams mild, all love and all perfection, that when the lips
Recieve a kiss from Gods or Men, a threefold kiss returns
From the press'd loveliness: so her whole immortal form three-fold
Three-fold embrace returns: consuming lives of Gods & Men
In fires of beauty melting them as gold & silver in the furnace.
Her Brain enlabyrinths the whole heaven of her bosom & loins
To put in act what her Heart wills; O who can withstand her power? 30
Her name is Vala in Eternity: in Time her name is Rahab.

The Starry Heavens all were fled from the mighty limbs of Albion.

*

[74] Teach me, O Holy Spirit, the Testimony of Jesus! let me
Comprehend wonderous things out of the Divine Law!
I behold Babylon in the opening Streets of London. I behold
Jerusalem in ruins wandering about from house to house:
This I behold; the shudderings of death attend my steps,
I walk up and down in Six Thousand Years: their Events are present before me . . .

*

But now the Starry Heavens are fled from the mighty limbs of Albion.

[Preface to Chap. 4]

[77] *To the Christians*

Devils are
False Religions
'Saul Saul'
'Why persecutest
thou me.'

I give you the end of a golden string,
Only wind it into a ball:
It will lead you in at Heaven's gate,
Built in Jerusalem's wall.

We are told to abstain from fleshly desires that we may lose no time from the Work of the Lord. Every moment lost is a moment that cannot be redeemed: every pleasure that intermingles with the duty of our station is a folly unredeemable & is planted like the seed of a wild flower among our wheat. All the tortures of repentance are tortures of self-reproach, on account of our leaving the Divine Harvest to the Enemy, the struggles of intanglement with incoherent roots. I know of no other Christianity and of no other Gospel than the liberty both of body & mind to exercise the Divine Arts of Imagination: 10 Imagination the real & eternal World, of which this Vegetable Universe is but a faint shadow, & in which we shall live in our Eternal or Imaginative Bodies, when these Vegetable Mortal Bodies are no more. The Apostles knew of no other Gospel. What were all their spiritual gifts? What is the Divine Spirit? is the Holy Ghost any other than an Intellectual Fountain? What is the Harvest of the Gospel & its Labours? What is that Talent which it is a curse to hide? What are the Treasures of Heaven which we are to lay up for ourselves, are they any other than Mental Studies & Performances? What are all the 20 Gifts of the Gospel, are they not all Mental Gifts? Is God a Spirit who must be worshipped in Spirit & in Truth and are not the Gifts of the Spirit Every-thing to Man? O ye Religious; discountenance every one among you who shall pretend to despise Art & Science! I call upon you in the Name of Jesus! What is the Life of Man but Art & Science? is it Meat & Drink? is not the Body more than Raiment? What is Mortality but the things relating to the Body, which Dies? What is Immortality but the things relating to the Spirit, which Lives Eternally! What is the Joy of Heaven but Improvement in the things of 30 the Spirit? What are the Pains of Hell but Ignorance, Bodily Lust, Idleness & devastation of the things of the Spirit? Answer this to yourselves, & expel from among you those who pretend to despise the labours of Art & Science, which alone are the labours of the Gospel: Is not this plain & manifest to the thought? Can you think at all & not pronounce heartily! That to Labour in Knowledge, is to Build up Jerusalem: and to Despise Knowledge, is to Despise Jerusalem &

her Builders. And remember: He who despises & mocks a Mental Gift in another; calling it pride & selfishness & sin; 40 mocks Jesus the giver of every Mental Gift, which always appear to the ignorance-loving Hypocrite, as Sins. But that which is a Sin in the sight of cruel Man, is not so in the sight of our kind God.

Let every Christian as much as in him lies engage himself openly & publicly before all the World in some Mental pursuit for the Building up of Jerusalem!

I stood among my valleys of the south
And saw a flame of fire, even as a Wheel
Of fire surrounding all the heavens: it went
From west to east against the current of
Creation, and devour'd all things in its loud
Fury & thundering course round heaven & earth.
By it the Sun was roll'd into an orb:
By it the Moon faded into a globe,
Travelling thro' the night: for from its dire
And restless fury, Man himself shrunk up 10
Into a little root a fathom long.
And I asked a Watcher & a Holy-One
Its Name? he answer'd, It is the Wheel of Religion.
I wept & said, Is this the law of Jesus,
This terrible devouring sword turning every way?
He answer'd; Jesus died because he strove
Against the current of this Wheel: its Name
Is Caiaphas, the dark Preacher of Death,
Of sin, of sorrow, & of punishment;
Opposing Nature! It is Natural Religion. 20
But Jesus is the bright Preacher of Life
Creating Nature from this fiery Law,
By self-denial & forgiveness of Sin.
Go therefore, cast out devils in Christ's name;
Heal thou the sick of spiritual disease,
Pity the evil, for thou art not sent
To smite with terror & with punishments
Those that are sick, like to the Pharisees

Crucifying & encompassing sea & land
For proselytes to tyranny & wrath. 30
But to the Publicans & Harlots go!
Teach them True Happiness, but let no curse
Go forth out of thy mouth to blight their peace.
For Hell is open'd to Heaven; thine eyes beheld
The dungeons burst & the Prisoners set free.

England! awake! awake! awake!
  Jerusalem thy Sister calls!
Why wilt thou sleep the sleep of death?
  And close her from thy ancient walls.

Thy hills & valleys felt her feet,
  Gently upon their bosoms move:
Thy gates beheld sweet Zion's ways;
  Then was a time of joy and love.

And now the time returns again:
  Our souls exult & London's towers 10
Receive the Lamb of God to dwell
  In England's green & pleasant bowers.

CHAP. 4

[Fallen Jerusalem]

[78] Naked Jerusalem lay before the Gates upon Mount Zion
The Hill of Giants, all her foundations levell'd with the dust!
Her Twelve Gates thrown down: her children carried into
  captivity,
Herself in chains: this from within was seen in a dismal night
Outside, unknown before in Beulah, & the twelve gates were
  fill'd
With blood; from Japan eastward to the Giants' causway,
  west
In Erin's Continent: and Jerusalem wept upon Euphrates'
  banks

Disorganiz'd; an evanescent shade, scarce seen or heard
among
Her children's Druid Temples, dropping with blood,
wander'd weeping!
And thus her voice went forth in the darkness of Philisthea: 10

My brother & my father are no more! God hath forsaken me
The arrows of the Almighty pour upon me & my children
I have sinned and am an outcast from the Divine Presence!
[79] My tents are fall'n! my pillars are in ruins! my children
dash'd
Upon Egypt's iron floors, & the marble pavements of
Assyria;
I melt my soul in reasonings among the towers of Heshbon;
Mount Zion is become a cruel rock, & no more dew
Nor rain, no more the spring of the rock appears: but cold
Hard & obdurate are the furrows of the mountain of wine &
oil.
The mountain of blessing is itself a curse & an astonishment:
The hills of Judea are fallen with me into the deepest hell
Away from the Nations of the Earth, & from the Cities of the
Nations;
I walk to ⁿEphraim I seek for Shiloh: I walk like a lost sheep 10
Among precipices of despair: in Goshen I seek for light
In vain: and in ⁿGilead for a physician and a comforter.
Goshen hath follow'd Philistea: Gilead hath join'd with Og!
They are become narrow places in a little and dark land:
How distant far from Albion! his hills & his valleys no more
Recieve the feet of Jerusalem: they have cast me quite away:
And Albion is himself shrunk to a narrow rock in the midst
of the sea!
The plains of Sussex & Surrey, their hills of flocks & herds
No more seek to Jerusalem, nor to the sound of my
Holy-ones.
The Fifty-two Counties of England are harden'd against me 20
As if I was not their Mother; they despise me & cast me out.

London cover'd the whole Earth, England encompass'd the
Nations;

And all the Nations of the Earth were seen in the Cities of
Albion:
My pillars reach'd from sea to sea: London beheld me come
From my east & from my west; he blessed me and gave
His children to my breasts, his sons & daughters to my
knees.
His aged parents sought me out in every city & village:
They discern'd my countenance with joy! they shew'd me to
their sons
Saying: Lo! Jerusalem is here! she sitteth in our secret
chambers
Levi and Judah & Issachar: Ephraim, Manasseh, Gad and Dan 30
Are seen in our hills & valleys: they keep our flocks & herds:
They watch them in the night: and the Lamb of God appears
among us!
The river Severn stay'd his course at my command:
Thames poured his waters into my basons and baths:
Medway mingled with Kishon: Thames reciev'd the
heavenly Jordan.
Albion gave me to the whole Earth to walk up & down; to
pour
Joy upon every mountain; to teach songs to the shepherd &
plowman
I taught the ships of the Sea to sing the songs of Zion.
Italy saw me, in sublime astonishment: France was wholly
mine:
As my garden & as my secret bath; Spain was my heavenly
couch: 40
I slept in his golden hills: the Lamb of God met me there,
There we walked as in our secret chamber among our little
ones.
They looked upon our loves with joy: they beheld our secret
joys:
With holy raptures of adoration rapt sublime in the Visions
of God.

*

Tell me O Vala thy purposes; tell me wherefore thy shuttles
Drop with the gore of the slain; why Euphrates is red with
blood?
Wherefore in dreadful majesty & beauty outside appears
Thy Masculine from thy Feminine, hardening against the
heavens
To devour the Human! Why dost thou weep upon the wind
among
These cruel Druid Temples: O Vala! Humanity is far above 50
Sexual organization, & the Visions of the Night of Beulah
Where Sexes wander in dreams of bliss among the
Emanations,
Where the Masculine & Feminine are nurs'd into Youth &
Maiden
By the tears & smiles of Beulah's Daughters till the time of
Sleep is past.
Wherefore then do you realize these nets of beauty &
delusion
In open day to draw the souls of the Dead into the light,
Till Albion is shut out from every Nation under Heaven.

[80] Encompassed by the frozen Net and by the rooted Tree
I walk weeping in pangs of a Mother's torment for her
Children:
I walk in affliction; I am a worm, and no living soul!
A worm going to eternal torment! rais'd up in a night
To an eternal night of pain, lost! lost! lost! for ever!

*

The Serpent Temples thro' the Earth, from the wide Plain of
Salisbury,
Resound with cries of Victims, shouts & songs & dying
groans
And flames of dusky fire, to Amalek, Canaan and Moab:
And Rahab like a dismal and indefinite hovering Cloud
Refus'd to take definite form; she hover'd over all the Earth 10
Calling the definite, sin; defacing every definite form,
Invisible or Visible, stretch'd out in length or spread in
breadth:

Over the Temples drinking groans of victims weeping in pity,
And joying in the pity, howling over Jerusalem's walls.

*

[The Daughters of Albion]

O sister Cambel, said Gwendolen, as their long beaming light
Mingled above the Mountain; what shall we do to keep
These awful forms in our soft bands: distracted with
trembling
[81] I have mock'd those who refused cruelty & I have admired
The cruel Warrior. I have refused to give love to Merlin the
piteous.
He brings to me the Images of his Love & I reject in chastity,
And turn them out into the streets for Harlots to be food
To the stern Warrior. I am become perfect in beauty over my
Warrior
For Men are caught by Love: Woman is caught by Pride,
That Love may only be obtain'd in the passages of Death.
Let us look! let us examine! is the Cruel become an Infant
Or is he still a cruel Warrior? look Sisters, look! O piteous!
I have destroy'd Wand'ring Reuben who strove to bind my
Will, 10
I have strip'd off Joseph's beautiful integument for my
Beloved,
The Cruel-one of Albion: to clothe him in gems of my Zone
I have named him Jehovah of Hosts. Humanity is become
A weeping Infant in ruin'd lovely Jerusalem's folding Cloud!

[n]In Heaven Love begets Love! but Fear is the Parent of Earthly
Love:
And he who will not bend to Love must be subdu'd by Fear.

[82] I have heard Jerusalem's groans; from Vala's cries &
lamentations
I gather our eternal fate: Outcasts from life and love:
Unless we find a way to bind these awful Forms to our
Embrace we shall perish annihilate, discover'd our Delusions.

Look! I have wrought without delusion: Look! I have wept!
And given soft milk mingled together with the spirits of
flocks
Of lambs and doves, mingled together in cups and dishes
Of painted clay; the mighty Hyle is become a weeping
infant;
Soon shall the Spectres of the Dead follow my weaving
threads.

The Twelve Daughters of Albion attentive listen in secret
shades 10
On Cambridge and Oxford beaming soft uniting with
Rahab's cloud,
While Gwendolen spoke to Cambel turning soft the spinning
reel:
Or throwing the wing'd shuttle; or drawing the cords with
softest songs.
The golden cords of the Looms animate beneath their touches
soft,
Along the Island white, among the Druid Temples, while
Gwendolen
Spoke to the Daughters of Albion standing on Skiddaw's top.

*

[Los's Vision of Jerusalem]

[85] Los walks upon his ancient Mountains in the deadly darkness
Among his Furnaces directing his laborious Myriads
watchful
Looking to the East: & his voice is heard over the whole
Earth
As he watches the Furnaces by night, & directs the labourers.

And thus Los replies upon his Watch: the Valleys listen
silent:
The Stars stand still to hear: Jerusalem & Vala cease to
mourn:
His voice is heard from Albion: the Alps & Appenines

Listen: Hermon & Lebanon bow their crowned heads
Babel & Shinar look toward the Western Gate, they sit down
Silent at his voice: they view the red Globe of fire in Los's
hand, 10
As he walks from Furnace to Furnace directing the
Labourers.
And this is the Song of Los, the Song that he sings on his
Watch:

O lovely mild Jerusalem! O Shiloh of Mount Ephraim!
I see thy Gates of precious stones: thy Walls of gold & silver:
Thou art the soft reflected Image of the Sleeping Man
Who stretch'd on Albion's rocks reposes amidst his
Twenty-eight
Cities: where Beulah lovely terminates, in the hills & valleys
of Albion,
Cities not yet embodied in Time and Space: plant ye
The Seeds, O Sisters in the bosom of Time & Space's womb,
To spring up for Jerusalem, lovely Shadow of Sleeping
Albion. 20
Why wilt thou rend thyself apart & build an Earthly
Kingdom
To reign in pride & to oppress & to mix the Cup of Delusion?
O thou that dwellest with Babylon! Come forth O
lovely-one:

[86] I see thy Form O lovely mild Jerusalem, Wing'd with Six
Wings
In the opacous Bosom of the Sleeper, lovely Three-fold
In Head & Heart & Reins, three Universes of love & beauty.
[n]Thy forehead bright: Holiness to the Lord, with Gates of
pearl
Reflects Eternity beneath thy azure wings of feathery down,
Ribb'd delicate & cloth'd with feather'd gold & azure &
purple
From thy white shoulders shadowing, purity in holiness!
Thence feather'd with soft crimson of the ruby bright as fire
Spreading into the azure Wings which like a canopy
Bends over thy immortal Head, in which Eternity dwells. 10

Albion beloved Land; I see thy mountains & thy hills
And valleys & thy pleasant Cities: Holiness to the Lord!
I see the Spectres of thy Dead, O Emanation of Albion.

Thy Bosom white, translucent, cover'd with immortal gems,
A sublime ornament not obscuring the outlines of beauty
Terrible to behold for thy extreme beauty & perfection:
Twelve-fold here all the Tribes of Israel I behold
Upon the Holy Land: I see the River of Life & Tree of Life
I see the New Jerusalem descending out of Heaven
Between thy Wings of gold & silver, feather'd immortal, 20
Clear as the rainbow, as the cloud of the Sun's tabernacle.

Thy Reins cover'd with Wings translucent, sometimes
covering
And sometimes spread abroad, reveal the flames of holiness
Which like a robe covers: & like a Veil of Seraphim
In flaming fire unceasing burns from Eternity to Eternity.
Twelvefold I there behold Israel in her Tents
A Pillar of a Cloud by day: a Pillar of fire by night
Guides them: there I behold Moab & Ammon & Amalek.
There Bells of silver round thy knees living, articulate
Comforting sounds of love & harmony, & on thy feet 30
Sandals of gold & pearl, & Egypt & Assyria before me
The Isles of Javan, Philistea, Tyre and Lebanon.

Thus Los sings upon his Watch walking from Furnace to
Furnace.
He siezes his Hammer every hour, flames surround him as
He beats: seas roll beneath his feet, tempests muster
Around his head, the thick hail stones stand ready to obey
His voice in the black cloud, his Sons labour in thunders
At his Furnaces; his Daughters at their Looms sing woes.
His Emanation separates in milky fibres agonizing
Among the golden Looms of Cathedron sending fibres of love 40
From Golgonooza with sweet visions for Jerusalem,
wanderer.

*

[Satan]

[89] Tho' divided by the Cross & Nails & Thorns & Spear
In cruelties of Rahab & Tirzah permanent endure
A terrible indefinite Hermaphroditic form,
A Wine-press of Love & Wrath double Hermaphroditic:
Twelvefold in Allegoric pomp, in selfish holiness:
The [n]Pharisaion, the Grammateis, the Presbuterion,
The Archiereus, the Iereus, the Saddusaion, double
Each withoutside of the other, covering eastern heaven.

Thus was the Covering Cherub reveal'd, majestic image
Of Selfhood, Body put off, the Antichrist accursed: 10
Cover'd with precious stones, a Human Dragon terrible
And bright, stretch'd over Europe & Asia gorgeous.
In three nights he devour'd the rejected corse of death.

His Head dark, deadly, in its Brain incloses a reflexion
Of Eden all perverted: Egypt on the Gihon many-tongued,
And many mouth'd: Ethiopia, Lybia, the Sea of Rephaim;
Minute Particulars in slavery I behold among the brick-kilns
Disorganiz'd, & there is Pharaoh in his iron Court:
And the Dragon of the River & the Furnaces of iron.
Outwoven from Thames & Tweed & Severn awful streams 20
Twelve ridges of Stone frown over all the Earth in tyrant
pride,
Frown over each River, stupendous Works of Albion's Druid
Sons:
And Albion's Forests of Oaks cover'd the Earth from Pole to
Pole.

His Bosom wide reflects Moab & Ammon, on the River
Pison, since call'd Arnon; there is Heshbon beautiful,
The Rocks of Rabbath on the Arnon & the Fish-pools of
Heshbon
Whose currents flow into the Dead Sea by Sodom &
Gomorra.
[n]Above his Head high arching Wings black, fill'd with Eyes
Spring upon iron sinews from the Scapulæ & Os Humeri.
There Israel in bondage to his Generalizing Gods 30

Molech & Chemosh, & in his left breast is Philistea,
In Druid Temples over the whole Earth with Victims
Sacrifice;
From Gaza to Damascus, Tyre & Sidon; & the Gods
Of Javan thro' the Isles of Grecia & all Europe's Kings;
Where Hiddekel pursues his course among the rocks
Two Wings spring from his ribs of brass, starry, black as
night
But translucent their blackness as the dazling of gems.

His Loins inclose Babylon on Euphrates beautiful,
And Rome in sweet Hesperia; there Israel scatter'd abroad
In martyrdoms & slavery I behold: ah vision of sorrow! 40
Inclosed by eyeless Wings, glowing with fire as the iron
Heated in the Smith's forge, but cold the wind of their dread
fury.

*

[90] But still the thunder of Los peals loud & thus the thunder's
cry:

These beautiful Witchcrafts of Albion are gratify'd by
Cruelty:
[91] It is easier to forgive an Enemy than to forgive a Friend:
The man who permits you to injure him, deserves your
vengeance;
He also will recieve it: go Spectre! obey my most secret
desire,
Which thou knowest without my speaking: Go to these
Fiends of Righteousness,
Tell them to obey their Humanities, & not pretend Holiness;
When they are murderers: as far as my Hammer & Anvil
permit
Go, tell them that the Worship of God is honouring his gifts
In other men: & loving the greatest men best, each according
To his Genius: which is the Holy Ghost in Man; there is no
other
God, than that God who is the intellectual fountain of
Humanity; 10

He who envies or calumniates: which is murder & cruelty,
Murders the Holy-one: Go tell them this & overthrow their
cup,
Their bread, their altar-table, their incense & their oath,
Their marriage & their baptism, their burial & consecration:
I have tried to make friends by corporeal gifts but have only
Made enemies: I never made friends but by spiritual gifts,
By severe contentions of friendship & the burning fire of
thought.
He who would see the Divinity must see him in his Children:
One first, in friendship & love; then a Divine Family, & in
the midst
Jesus will appear; so he who wishes to see a Vision; a perfect
Whole 20
Must see it in its Minute Particulars; Organized; & not as
thou
O Fiend of Righteousness pretendest; thine is a Disorganized
And snowy cloud: brooder of tempests & destructive War.
You smile with pomp & rigor: you talk of benevolence &
virtue!
I act with benevolence & Virtue & get murder'd time after
time:
You accumulate Particulars, & murder by analyzing, that
you
May take the aggregate; & you call the aggregate Moral
Law:
And you call that Swell'd & bloated Form a Minute
Particular.
But General Forms have their vitality in Particulars: & every
Particular is a Man; a Divine Member of the Divine Jesus. 30

So Los cried at his Anvil in the horrible darkness weeping!

The Spectre builded stupendous Works, taking the Starry
Heavens
Like to a curtain & folding them according to his will,
Repeating the [n]Smaragdine Table of Hermes to draw Los
down

Into the Indefinite, refusing to believe without
demonstration.
Los reads the Stars of Albion! the Spectre reads the Voids
Between the Stars, among the arches of Albion's Tomb
sublime
Rolling the Sea in rocky paths; forming Leviathan
And Behemoth; the War by Sea enormous & the War
By Land astounding: erecting pillars in the deepest Hell, 40
To reach the heavenly arches. Los beheld undaunted furious
His heav'd Hammer; he swung it round & at one blow,
In unpitying ruin driving down the pyramids of pride
Smiting the Spectre on his Anvil & the integuments of his
Eye
And Ear unbinding in dire pain, with many blows,
Of strict severity self-subduing, & with many tears
labouring.

Then he sent forth the Spectre; all his pyramids were grains
Of sand & his pillars: dust on the fly's wing: & his starry
Heavens; a moth of gold & silver mocking his anxious grasp
Thus Los alter'd his Spectre, & every Ratio of his Reason 50
He alter'd time after time, with dire pain & many tears
Till he had completely divided him into a separate space.

Terrified Los sat to behold trembling & weeping & howling
I care not whether a Man is Good or Evil; all that I care
Is whether he is a Wise Man or a Fool. Go! put off Holiness
And put on Intellect: or my thund'rous Hammer shall drive
thee
To wrath which thou condemnest, till thou obey my voice.

[The Beginning of the End]

So Los terrified cries: trembling & weeping & howling!
Beholding
[92] What do I see? The Briton Saxon Roman Norman
amalgamating
In my Furnaces into One Nation the English: & taking
refuge

In the Loins of Albion. The Canaanite united with the fugitive
Hebrew whom she divided into Twelve & sold into Egypt,
Then scatter'd the Egyptian & Hebrew to the four Winds:
This sinful Nation Created in our Furnaces & Looms is Albion.

*

[Albion's Awakening]

[94] Albion cold lays on his Rock: storms & snows beat round him,
Beneath the Furnaces & the starry Wheels & the Immortal Tomb
Howling winds cover him: roaring seas dash furious against him,
In the deep darkness broad lightnings glare, long thunders roll.

The weeds of Death inwrap his hands & feet, blown incessant
And wash'd incessant by the for-ever restless sea-waves, foaming abroad
Upon the white Rock. England, a Female Shadow, as deadly damps
Of the Mines of Cornwall & Derbyshire lays upon his bosom heavy,
Moved by the wind in volumes of thick cloud, returning folding round
His loins & bosom unremovable by swelling storms, & loud rending 10
Of enraged thunders. Around them the Starry Wheels of their Giant Sons
Revolve; & over them the Furnaces of Los & the Immortal Tomb around
Erin, sitting in the Tomb, to watch them unceasing night and day:
And the Body of Albion was closed apart from all Nations.

Over them the famish'd Eagle screams on boney Wings, and
around
Them howls the Wolf of famine: deep heaves the Ocean
black thundering!
Around the wormy Garments of Albion: then pausing in
deathlike silence –

Time was Finished! The Breath Divine Breathed over Albion
Beneath the Furnaces & starry Wheels and in the Immortal
Tomb:
And England who is Brittannia awoke from Death on
Albion's bosom; 20
She awoke pale & cold, she fainted seven times on the Body
of Albion.

O piteous Sleep, O piteous Dream! O God, O God awake!
I have slain
In Dreams of Chastity & Moral Law I have Murdered
Albion! Ah!
In Stone-henge & on London Stone & in the Oak Groves of
Maldon
I have Slain him in my Sleep with the Knife of the Druid:
O England!
O all ye Nations of the Earth! behold ye the Jealous Wife:
The Eagle & the Wolf & Monkey & Owl & the King & Priest
were there.

[95] Her voice pierc'd Albion's clay cold ear, he moved upon the
Rock.
The Breath Divine went forth upon the morning hills, Albion
mov'd
Upon the Rock, he open'd his eyelids in pain; in pain he
mov'd
His stony members, he saw England. Ah! shall the Dead live
again?

The Breath Divine went forth over the morning hills. Albion
rose
In anger: the wrath of God breaking bright flaming on all
sides around

His awful limbs: into the Heavens he walked, clothed in flames,
Loud thund'ring, with broad flashes of flaming lightning & pillars
Of fire, speaking the Words of Eternity in Human Forms, in direful
Revolutions of Action & Passion, thro' the Four Elements on all sides 10
Surrounding his awful Members. Thou seest the Sun in heavy clouds
Struggling to rise above the Mountains; in his burning hand
He takes his Bow, then chooses out his arrows of flaming gold.
Murmuring the Bowstring breathes with ardor! clouds roll round the
Horns of the wide Bow, loud sounding winds sport on the mountain brows
Compelling Urizen to his Furrow, & Tharmas to his Sheepfold,
And Luvah to his Loom: Urthona he beheld mighty labouring at
His Anvil, in the Great Spectre Los unwearied labouring & weeping:
Therefore the Sons of Eden praise Urthona's Spectre in songs
Because he kept the Divine Vision in time of trouble. 20

As the Sun & Moon lead forward the Visions of Heaven & Earth:
England who is Brittannia enter'd Albion's bosom rejoicing,
Rejoicing in his indignation! adoring his wrathful rebuke.
She who adores not your frowns will only loathe your smiles.

[96] As the Sun & Moon lead forward the Visions of Heaven & Earth;
England who is Brittannia entered Albion's bosom rejoicing.

Then Jesus appeared, standing by Albion, as the Good Shepherd

By the lost Sheep that he hath found, & Albion knew that it
Was the Lord, the Universal Humanity; & Albion saw his
Form
A Man: & they conversed as Man with Man, in Ages of
Eternity:
And the Divine Appearance was the likeness & similitude of
Los.

Albion said: O Lord, what can I do? my Selfhood cruel
Marches against thee deceitful from Sinai & from Edom
Into the Wilderness of Judah to meet thee in his pride. 10
I behold the Visions of my deadly Sleep of Six Thousand
Years
Dazling around thy skirts like a Serpent of precious stones &
gold;
I know it is my Self: O my Divine Creator & Redeemer!

Jesus replied: Fear not Albion, unless I die thou canst not
live;
But if I die I shall arise again & thou with me.
This is Friendship & Brotherhood: without it Man Is Not.

So Jesus spoke: the Covering Cherub coming on in darkness
Overshadow'd them; & Jesus said: Thus do Men in Eternity.
One for another to put off by forgiveness, every sin.

Albion reply'd: Cannot Man exist without Mysterious 20
Offering of Self for Another; is this Friendship &
Brotherhood?
I see thee in the likeness & similitude of Los my Friend!

Jesus said: Wouldest thou love one who never died
For thee, or ever die for one who had not died for thee?
And if God dieth not for Man & giveth not himself
Eternally for Man, Man could not exist! for Man is Love:
As God is Love: every kindness to another is a little Death
In the Divine Image, nor can Man exist but by Brotherhood.

So saying the Cloud overshadowing divided them asunder:
Albion stood in terror: not for himself but for his Friend 30
Divine, & Self was lost in the contemplation of faith

And wonder at the Divine Mercy, & at Los's sublime honour.

Do I sleep amidst danger to Friends! O my Cities & Counties.
Do you sleep! rouze up, rouze up, Eternal Death is abroad!

So Albiòn spoke & threw himself into the Furnaces of
affliction –
All was a Vision, all a Dream: the Furnaces became
Fountains of Living Waters flowing from the Humanity
Divine,
And all the Cities of Albion rose from their Slumbers, and
All
The Sons & Daughters of Albion on soft clouds Waking from
Sleep.
Soon all around remote the Heavens burnt with flaming fires, 40
And Urizen & Luvah & Tharmas & Urthona arose into
Albion's Bosom: Then Albion stood before Jesus in the
Clouds
Of Heaven Fourfold among the Visions of God in Eternity:

[97] Awake! Awake Jerusalem! O lovely Emanation of Albion
Awake and overspread all Nations as in Ancient Time!
For lo! the Night of Death is past, and the Eternal Day
Appears upon our Hills: Awake Jerusalem, and come away!

So spake the Vision of Albion, & in him so spake in my
hearing
The Universal Father. Then Albion stretch'd his hand into
Infinitude,
And took his Bow: Fourfold the Vision, for bright beaming
Urizen
Lay'd his hand on the South & took a breathing Bow of
carved Gold,
Luvah his hand stretch'd to the East & bore a Silver Bow
bright shining;
Tharmas Westward a Bow of Brass, pure flaming, richly
wrought; 10
Urthona Northward in thick storms a Bow of Iron, terrible
thundering.

And the Bow is a Male & Female, & the Quiver of the
Arrows of Love
Are the Children of this Bow: a Bow of Mercy &
Loving-kindness: laying
Open the hidden Heart in Wars of mutual Benevolence,
Wars of Love:
And the Hand of Man grasps firm between the Male &
Female Loves
And he Clothed himself in Bow & Arrows in awful state,
Fourfold
In the midst of his Twenty-eight Cities, each with his Bow
breathing:
[98] Then each an Arrow flaming from his Quiver fitted carefully;
They drew fourfold the unreprovable String, bending thro'
the wide Heavens
The horned Bow Fourfold; loud sounding flew the flaming
Arrow fourfold!

Murmuring the Bow-string breathes with ardor. Clouds roll
round the horns
Of the wide Bow, loud sounding Winds sport on the
Mountains brows:
The Druid Spectre was Annihilate, loud thund'ring rejoicing
terrific, vanishing
Fourfold Annihilation; & at the clangor of the Arrows of
Intellect
The innumerable Chariots of the Almighty appear'd in
Heaven;
And Bacon & Newton & Locke, & Milton & Shakspear &
Chaucer,
A Sun of blood red wrath surrounding heaven on all sides
around, 10
Glorious incomprehensible by Mortal Man; & each Chariot
was Sexual Threefold;

And every Man stood Fourfold: each Four Faces had, One to
the West,
One toward the East, One to the South, One to the North:
the Horses Fourfold

And the dim Chaos brighten'd beneath, above, around! Eyed as the Peacock
According to the Human Nerves of Sensation, the Four Rivers of the Water of Life.

South stood the Nerves of the Eye, East in Rivers of bliss, the Nerves of the
Expansive Nostrils, West flow'd the Parent Sense the Tongue, North stood
The labyrinthine Ear. Circumscribing & Circumcising the excrementitious
Husk & Covering, into Vacuum evaporating, revealing the lineaments of Man:
Driving outward the Body of Death in an Eternal Death & Resurrection, 20
Awaking it to Life among the Flowers of Beulah, rejoicing in Unity
In the Four Senses, in the Outline, the Circumference & Form, for ever
In Forgiveness of Sins which is Self Annihilation: it is the Covenant of Jehovah!

The Four Living Creatures, Chariots of Humanity Divine Incomprehensible
In beautiful Paradises expand. These are the Four Rivers of Paradise,
And the Four Faces of Humanity fronting the Four Cardinal Points
Of Heaven, going forward, forward! irresistible from Eternity to Eternity!

And they conversed together in Visionary forms dramatic which bright
Redounded from their Tongues in thunderous majesty, in Visions,
In new Expanses, creating exemplars of Memory and of Intellect; 30
Creating Space, Creating Time according to the wonders Divine

Of Human Imagination, throughout all the Three Regions immense
Of Childhood, Manhood & Old Age: & the all tremendous unfathomable Non Ens
Of Death was seen in regenerations terrific or complacent, varying
According to the subject of discourse & every Word, & Every Character
Was Human according to the Expansion or Contraction, the Translucence or
Opakeness of Nervous fibres; such was the variation of Time & Space,
Which vary according as the Organs of Perception vary, & they walked
To & fro in Eternity as One Man, reflecting each in each & clearly seen
And seeing: according to fitness & order. And I heard Jehovah speak 40
Terrific from his Holy Place, & saw the Words of the Mutual Covenant Divine.
On Chariots of gold & jewels, with Living Creatures starry & flaming,
With every Colour: Lion, Tyger, Horse, Elephant, Eagle Dove, Fly, Worm,
And the all-wondrous Serpent clothed in gems & rich array Humanize
In the Forgiveness of Sins according to the Covenant of Jehovah. They Cry:

Where is the Covenant of Priam, the Moral Virtues of the Heathen?
Where is the Tree of Good & Evil that rooted beneath the cruel heel
Of Albion's Spectre the Patriarch Druid! where are all his Human Sacrifices
For Sin in War, & in the Druid Temples of the Accuser of Sin: beneath

The Oak Groves of Albion that cover'd the whole Earth
beneath his Spectre? 50
Where are the Kingdoms of the World & all their glory that
grew on Desolation:
The Fruit of Albion's Poverty Tree, when the Triple-Headed
Gog-Magog Giant
Of Albion Taxed the Nations into Desolation, & then gave
the Spectrous Oath?

Such is the Cry from all the Earth, from the Living Creatures
of the Earth
And from the great City of Golgonooza in the Shadowy
Generation,
And from the Thirty-two Nations of the Earth among the
Living Creatures:

[99] All Human Forms identified, even Tree Metal Earth & Stone,
all
Human Forms identified, living, going forth & returning
wearied
Into the Planetary lives of Years Months Days & Hours,
reposing
And then Awaking into his Bosom in the Life of
Immortality.

And I heard the Name of their Emanations: they are named
JERUSALEM.

The End of The Song
of Jerusalem

THE EVERLASTING GOSPEL

[I]

If Moral Virtue was Christianity,
Christ's Pretensions were all Vanity,
And Cai'phas & Pilate Men
Praise Worthy, & the Lion's Den
And not the Sheepfold, Allegories
Of God & Heaven & their Glories.
The Moral Christian is the Cause
Of the Unbeliever & his Laws.
The Roman Virtues, Warlike Fame,
Take Jesus' & Jehovah's Name; 10
For what is Antichrist but those
Who against Sinners Heaven close
With Iron bars, in Virtuous State,
And [n]Rhadamanthus at the Gate?

[II]

What can this Gospel of Jesus be
What Life & Immortality?
What was it that he brought to Light
That Plato & Cicero did not write?
The Heathen Deities wrote them all
These Moral Virtues great & small.
What is the Accusation of Sin
But Moral Virtues' deadly Gin?
The Moral Virtues in their Pride
Did o'er the World triumphant ride 10
In Wars & Sacrifice for Sin
And Souls to Hell ran trooping in.
The Accuser, Holy God of All
This Pharisaic Worldly Ball,
Amidst them in his Glory Beams
Upon the Rivers & the Streams.
Then Jesus rose & said to Me
[n]Thy Sins are all forgiven thee:

Loud Pilate Howl'd, loud Cai'phas yell'd
When they the Gospel Light beheld. 20
It was when Jesus said to Me
Thy Sins are all forgiven thee
The Christian trumpets loud proclaim
Thro' all the World in Jesus' name
Mutual forgiveness of each Vice
And oped the Gates of Paradise.
The Moral Virtues in Great fear
Formed the Cross & Nails & Spear
And the Accuser standing by
Cried out, Crucify! Crucify! 30
Our Moral Virtues ne'er can be
Nor Warlike pomp & Majesty
For Moral Virtues all begin
In the Accusations of Sin.
And all the Heroic Virtues End
In destroying the Sinners' Friend
Am I not Lucifer the Great
And you my daughters in Great State
The fruit of my Mysterious Tree
Of Good & Evil & Misery 40
And Death & Hell which now begin
On everyone who Forgives Sin.

[III]

Was Jesus Humble? or did he
Give any ⁿProofs of Humility?
Boast of high Things with Humble tone
And give with Charity a Stone?
When but a Child ⁿhe ran away
And left his Parents in dismay:
When they had wander'd three days long
These were the words upon his tongue:
No Earthly Parents I confess:
I am doing my Father's business. 10
When the rich learned Pharisee
Came to consult him secretly

Upon his heart with Iron pen
He wrote, [n]"Ye must be born again.
He was too proud to take a bribe;
He spoke with authority, not like a Scribe.
He says with most consummate Art:
Follow me, I am meek & lowly of heart,
As that is the only way to escape
The Miser's net & the Glutton's trap. 20
He who loves his Enemies betrays his Friends;
This surely is not what Jesus intends,
But the sneaking Pride of Heroic Schools
And the Scribes' & Pharisees' Virtuous Rules.
For he acts with honest, triumphant Pride
And this is the cause that Jesus died.
He did not die with Christian Ease
Asking pardon of his Enemies:
If he had, Cai'phas would forgive;
Sneaking submission can always live. 30
He had only to say that God was the devil
And the devil was God like a Christian Civil,
Mild Christian regrets to the devil confess
For affronting him thrice in the Wilderness;
He had soon been bloody Caesar's Elf
And at last he would have been Caesar himself.
Like [n]Dr. Priestley & Bacon & Newton –
Poor Spiritual Knowledge is not worth a button.
For thus the Gospel Sir Isaac confutes:
God can only be known by his Attributes; 40
And as for the Indwelling of the Holy Ghost
Or of Christ & his Father it's all a boast
And Pride & Vanity of the imagination
That disdains to follow this World's Fashion.
To teach doubt & Experiment
Certainly was not what Christ meant.
What was he doing all that time,
From twelve years old to manly prime?
Was he then Idle or the Less
About his Father's business? 50

Or was his wisdom held in scorn
Before his wrath began to burn
In Miracles throughout the Land,
That quite unnerv'd Caiaphas' hand?
If he had been Antichrist, Creeping Jesus,
He'd have done any thing to please us,
Gone sneaking into Synagogues
And not us'd the Elders & Priests like dogs;
But Humble as a Lamb or Ass
Obey'd himself to Caiaphas. 60
God wants not Man to Humble himself:
This is the trick of the ancient Elf.
This is the Race that Jesus ran:
Humble to God, Haughty to Man,
Cursing the Rulers before the People
Even to the temple's highest Steeple;
And when he Humbled himself to God,
Then descended the Cruel Rod:
If thou humblest thyself, thou humblest me;
Thou also dwell'st in Eternity. 70
Thou art a Man, God is no more;
Thy own humanity learn to adore
For that is my Spirit of Life.
Awake, arise to Spiritual Strife!
And thy Revenge abroad display
In terrors at the Last Judgment day.
God's Mercy & Long Suffering
Is but the Sinner to Judgment to bring;
Thou on the Cross for them shalt pray
And take Revenge at the Last Day. 80
This Corporeal life's a fiction
And is made up of Contradiction.
Jesus replied & thunders hurl'd:
I never will Pray for the World.
Once I did so when I pray'd in the Garden,
I wish'd to take with me a Bodily Pardon.
Can that which was of woman born
In the absence of the Morn

When the Soul fell into Sleep
And Archangels round it weep, 90
Shooting out against the Light
Fibres of a deadly night,
Reasoning upon its own dark Fiction
In doubt which is Self Contradiction?
Humility is only doubt
And does the Sun & Moon blot out
Rooting over with thorns & stems
The buried Soul & all its Gems.
This Life's dim Windows of the Soul
Distorts the Heavens from Pole to Pole 100
And leads you to Believe a Lie
When you see with, not thro', the Eye
That was born in a night to perish in a night
When the Soul slept in the Beams of Light.

[IV]

Was Jesus Chaste? or did he
Give any Lessons of Chastity?
The morning blush'd fiery red,
[n]Mary was found in Adulterous bed;
Earth groan'd beneath & Heaven above
Trembled at discovery of Love:
Jesus was sitting in Moses' Chair,
They brought the trembling Woman there:
Moses commands she be stoned to death;
What was the sound of Jesus' breath? 10
He laid His hand on Moses' Law:
The Ancient Heavens, in Silent Awe
Writ with Curses from Pole to Pole
All away began to roll:
The Earth trembling & naked lay
In secret bed of Mortal Clay,
On Sinai felt the hand divine
Putting back the bloody shrine;
And she heard the breath of God

As she heard by Eden's flood: 20
Good & Evil are no more!
Sinai's trumpets cease to roar!
Cease, finger of God, to write!
The Heavens are not clean in thy sight.
Thou art Good, & thou alone,
Nor may the sinner cast one stone.
To be Good only is to be
A [n]God or else a Pharisee.
Thou Angel of the Presence Divine
That didst create this Body of Mine 30
Wherefore has thou writ these Laws
And Created Hell's dark jaws?
My Presence I will take from thee:
A cold Leper thou shalt be;
Tho' thou wast so pure & bright
That Heaven was Impure in thy Sight,
Tho' thy Oath turn'd Heaven Pale,
Tho' thy Covenant built Hell's Jail
Tho' thou didst all to Chaos roll
With the Serpent for its soul, 40
Still the breath Divine does move
And the breath Divine is Love.
Mary, fear not! Let me see
The Seven Devils that torment thee,
Hide not from my Sight thy Sin
That forgiveness thou maist win.
Has no Man condemned thee?
No Man, Lord: then what is he
Who shall Accuse thee? Come ye forth
Fallen fiends of Heav'nly birth 50
That have forgot your Ancient love
And driven away my trembling Dove;
You shall bow before her feet,
You shall lick the dust for Meat;
And tho' you cannot Love, but Hate,
Shall be beggars at Love's Gate.

What was thy love? Let me see it,
Was it love or dark deceit? –
Love too long from me has fled;
'Twas dark deceit, to earn my bread, 60
'Twas Covet or 'twas Custom or
Some trifle not worth caring for,
That they may call a shame & Sin
Love's temple that God dwelleth in,
And hide in secret hidden Shrine
The Naked Human form divine,
And render that a Lawless thing
On which the Soul Expands its wing.
But this, O Lord, this was my Sin
When first I let these Devils in 70
In dark pretence to Chastity:
Blaspheming Love, blaspheming thee.
Thence Rose Secret Adulteries
And thence did Covet also rise;
My sin thou hast forgiven me
Canst thou forgive my Blasphemy?
Canst thou return to this dark Hell
And in my burning bosom dwell?
And canst thou die that I may live?
And canst thou Pity & forgive? 80
Then Roll'd the shadowy Man away
From the Limbs of Jesus to make them his prey,
An Ever-devouring appetite
Glittering with festering Venoms bright,
Crying, Crucify this cause of distress,
Who don't keep the secrets of Holiness!
All Mental Powers by Diseases we bind
But he heals the deaf & the Dumb & the Blind;
Whom God has afflicted for Secret Ends
He comforts & Heals & calls them Friends. – 90
But, when Jesus was Crucified,
Then was perfected his glitt'ring pride:
In three Nights he devour'd his prey
And still he devours the Body of Clay;

For [n]dust & clay is the Serpent's meat,
Which never was made for Man to Eat.

[v]

Was Jesus gentle, or did he
Give any marks of Gentility?
When twelve years old he ran away
And left his Parents in dismay.
When after three days' sorrow found
Loud as Sinai's trumpet sound:
No Earthly Parents I confess –
My Heavenly Father's business!
Ye understand not what I say,
And angry force me to obey. 10
Obedience is a duty then
And favour gains with God & Men.
John from the Wilderness loud cried;
Satan gloried in his Pride:
Come, said Satan, come away
I'll soon see if you'll obey!
John for disobedience bled
But you can turn the stones to bread:
God's high king & God's high Priest
Shall Plant their Glories in your breast 20
If Caiaphas you will obey,
If Herod you with bloody Prey
Feed with the sacrifice & be
Obedient, fall down, worship me.
Thunders & lightnings broke around,
And Jesus' voice in thunders' sound:
Thus I sieze the Spiritual Prey.
Ye smiters with disease, make way:
I come your King & God to sieze,
Is God a smiter with disease? – 30
The God of this World raged in vain:
He bound Old Satan in his Chain
And bursting forth his furious ire
Became a Chariot of fire.

Throughout the land he took his course
And traced diseases to their source:
He curs'd the Scribe & Pharisee,
Trampling down Hipocrisy.
Where'er his Chariot took its way
There Gates of death let in the day, 40
Broke down from every Chain & Bar;
And Satan in his Spiritual War
Drag'd at his Chariot wheels: loud howl'd
The God of this World; louder roll'd
The Chariot Wheels & louder still
His voice was heard from Zion's hill
And in his hand the Scourge shone bright;
He scourg'd the Merchant Canaanite
From out the Temple of his Mind
And in his Body tight does bind 50
Satan & all his Hellish Crew:
And thus with wrath he did subdue
The Serpent Bulk of Nature's dross
Till He had nail'd it to the Cross.
He took on Sin in the Virgin's Womb,
And put it off on the Cross & Tomb
To be Worship'd by the Church of Rome . . .

[VI]

The Vision of Christ that thou dost see
Is my Vision's Greatest Enemy.
Thine has a great hook nose like thine,
Mine has a snub nose like to mine:
Thine is the friend of All Mankind
Mine speaks in parables to the Blind:
Thine loves the same world that mine hates,
Thy Heaven doors are my Hell Gates.
Socrates taught what [n]Melitus
Loath'd as a Nation's bitterest curse, 10
And Cai'phas was in his own Mind
A benefactor to Mankind.

Both read the Bible day & night
But thou read'st black where I read white.

[VII]

I am sure This Jesus will not do
Either for Englishman or Jew.

FOR THE SEXES
THE GATES OF PARADISE

[Prologue]

Mutual Forgiveness of each Vice:
Such are the Gates of Paradise.
Against the Accuser's chief desire
Who walk'd among the Stones of Fire
Jehovah's Finger Wrote the Law:
Then Wept! then rose in Zeal & Awe,
And the Dead Corpse from Sinai's heat
Buried beneath his Mercy Seat.
O Christians Christians! tell me Why
You rear it on your Altars high? 10

*

[Epilogue]

To The Accuser who is
The God of This World

Truly my Satan, thou art but a Dunce
And dost not know the Garment from the Man.
Every Harlot was a Virgin once
Nor canst thou ever change Kate into Nan.

Tho' thou art worship'd by the Names Divine
Of Jesus & Jehovah: thou art still
The Son of Morn in weary Night's decline
The lost Traveller's Dream under the Hill.

NOTES

SONGS OF INNOCENCE AND OF EXPERIENCE

The *Songs of Innocence* were written over several years before appearing as a book in 1789. They are in the tradition of eighteenth-century children's verse, going back to Isaac Watts's famous *Divine Songs* for children. Four-line rhyming stanzas predominate, and the pastoral naivety and emphasis on religious themes would seem normal to those who did not look too closely at the treatment of those themes.

In *Songs of Experience*, the treatment is grimmer and more economical, but B. uses the same modes and variations on the same themes. That *S E* is partly a reaction against *S I* is shown by the pairs of 'contrary' poems. In 1789 Blake had already begun to write *S E*, moving into it some of the darker poems from *S I*. The combined volume is dated 1794; he often reissued *S I* alone, but never *S E*. *S I* and *S I E* were issued many times, in a wide range of colourings, from the light, delicate tones of some of the early copies of *S I* to others much more sombre. No two copies follow the same order of poems, although certain groups of poems often recur together. The copy followed here is Keynes's 'Copy V'. For other poems of the same creative period that appear in the Notebook alongside drafts of some of *S E*, see pp. 52ff. The designs range from block illustrations of the text to a delicately elaborate interweaving of abstract, semi-abstract and allegoric patterns in and around the text. The whole is a triumph of Blake's concept of the 'illuminated book'.

Songs of Innocence

THE LAMB

18 *by his name* Jeremiah 14:9: 'thou, O Lord, art in the midst of us, and we are called by thy name'. Also 15:16 and Isaiah 43:7, but a better reference is John 10:3, 'He calleth his own sheep by name'.

INFANT JOY

5 *Joy* was not a Christian name in use in B.'s time.

THE LITTLE BLACK BOY

The agitation against the slave trade reached a climax in 1791 when a motion against it was passed (ineffectually) in Parliament.

A CRADLE SONG

Watts has a not dissimilar *Cradle Song*.

HOLY THURSDAY

Strictly, Ascension Day. This procession took place on a Thursday in May, but not on Ascension Day; otherwise it was as B. describes it.

THE CHIMNEY SWEEPER

Jonas Hanway's agitation about the plight of boy sweeps reached Parliament in 1788.

THE DIVINE IMAGE

The outlook is markedly Swedenborgian. Christ is the Divine Humanity; God is perfect human form, and our virtues are shadows of his perfection.

A DREAM

3 *Emmet* ant.

Songs of Experience

THE TYGER

The sense of line 12 is completed in a rejected version found in the Notebook: *Could fetch it from the furnace deep . . .*

THE LITTLE GIRL LOST and FOUND

These poems were originally in *SI*.

TO TIRZAH

A much later poem than the rest; Tirzah embodies female seductive power, and figures largely in *Jerusalem*. Lines 3 and 16 echo Christ's challenge to his mother before he changed water into wine at Cana (John 2:4).

THE VOICE OF THE ANCIENT BARD
THE SCHOOL BOY

These poems were originally in *SI*.

A DIVINE IMAGE

Not in any of the copies, but found as a separate, uncoloured plate. Plainly a 'contrary' poem, rejected in favour of 'The Human Abstract'.

NOTEBOOK POEMS: LAMBETH

In 1787, B.'s favourite brother, Robert, died, and B. acquired his notebook. For almost the rest of his life he used it, gradually filling it with sketches and drafts of poems of all kinds, from around 1790 to 1818. The selection here represents the variety; it is divided roughly for convenience into a group of drafts not used in *Songs of Innocence and of Experience*, but written at the same time and mixed up with *Experience* drafts. The second group (pp. 151ff.) dates from Felpham and the years following, when he was embittered by his lack of success and, as some of the epigrams show, inclined to snarl at his friends as well as his enemies.

IN A MIRTLE SHADE
Myrtle is a traditional emblem of marriage. This is one stage of a much-altered draft.

WHY SHOULD I CARE . . .
7 *Ohio* One of the newer areas into which the young USA was expanding.

THE BOOK OF THEL

Dated 1789: of the same era as *Songs of Innocence*; the theme here too is that innocence has nothing to fear, even from death. The last plate, which dramatically changes the mood of the piece, is plainly a later development; its string of rhetorical questions, implying disillusionment with the main message, echoes poems of the early 1790s, such as *Visions*. The designs are delicate, largely direct illustrations.

THE MARRIAGE OF HEAVEN AND HELL

Compiled over several years in the early 1790s, this parody of Swedenborg is a summary of B.'s early creed. The 'Memorable Fancies', and the writer's casual meetings with angels and devils, recall Swedenborg's *Memorable Relations*. Swedenborg believed in the divine humanity of God; Blake emphasizes instead the divinity of the human. B. did not long adhere to the principles stated here as they stand, but never lost his belief in the primacy of the imagination as moral and spiritual guide. B. rejected Swedenborg's attitudes, but all his life he retained many of the details of his preaching.

The designs are elaborate, though only the 'Argument' is as complex as *America*. Besides block illustrations, there are many minute but significant interlinear figures.

pl. 2.13 *Red clay* Adam was made of red clay.

pl. 3.1 *a new heaven* According to Swedenborg, history was marked by a sequence of Churches, each of which brought something new to the world, consummated it, and died, to be replaced by a better (cp. lines **4–5**, where the progress of the era is downwards, rather than upwards to a climax). He declared that the Church of Christ was about to be replaced; B. interprets the prophecy as referring to himself: it was made in the year of his birth, and he was now thirty-three, Christ's age when his ministry reached its climax.

pl. 3.4 *Edom* See Genesis 27:40, where Esau, father of the tribe of Edom, disinherited by Jacob's trickery, is told that his turn will come. But Isaiah 34 foretells vengeance on Edom. These chapters describe first Jehovah's crushing attack on nations that have not followed him, followed by a famous passage of renewal: 'The wilderness, and the solitary place, shall be glad for them; and the desert shall rejoice, and blossom as the rose.'

pl. 5.11 *Satan* In Job, Satan, as one of God's angels, appears before God as an accuser and tempter in an attempt to unsettle Job's righteousness. See pl. 17.

pl. 7.1 *corroding fires* This and similar phrases in pls. 14 and 15 allude to the engraver's use of acid to reveal writing in a copper plate.

pl. 15.1 *Hell* Here and in pl. 17, B. is carried down into Hell. Swedenborg was usually carried up into Heaven.

pl. 17.4 *Jesus Christ* See Matthew 10:24 and 25:31ff.

pl. 22.11 *Paracelsus . . . Behmen* Late-medieval mystical philosophers.

pl. 24.10 *the Bible of Hell* Probably the series of poetical works dated 1793–5: a Genesis in *Urizen*, an Exodus in *Ahania*; two Prophecies, *America* and *Europe*. (Common practice refers to all B.'s longer poems as 'Prophetic Books', but he himself used the term for these two only, because they take the specific role played by the Prophets in the Bible.) *The Song of Los* comprises two shorter poems, completing the set of continents: *Africa* fills in the history between *Urizen* and *America*, and *Asia* takes us quickly from *Europe* to the millennium. *The Book of Los* re-tells the story of *Urizen* from Los's standpoint.

pls. 25–7 *A Song of Liberty* This strongly resembles *America*, implying that the excitement of the French Revolution, following so hard on the American rebellion, was the beginning of the new world of vision that B. believed was about to dawn. Note that for B. the revolution must be spiritual before it can properly be anything else.

VISIONS OF THE DAUGHTERS OF ALBION

Visions seems to have been inspired by Mary Wollstonecraft, the founder of modern feminism, who in 1792 published her *Vindication of the Rights of*

Women. In Macpherson's *Ossian*, the Gael princess Oi-thona is abducted in her husband's absence by a rejected suitor and hidden in a cave. She disguises herself as a warrior, and is killed in the ensuing battle, because, like Lucrece but unlike Oothoon, she cannot live with the loss of her 'honour'. B. turns the situation round, not only to create a feminist tract, but also to expound his broader philosophy. Nor can he forbear to refer to other forms of political and social oppression besides sexual morality. In pl. 5.7–20 he alludes to rural distress, and perhaps to the recruiting sergeant who depopulates the land to feed war. The long sequences of rhetorical questions are characteristic of this period of B.'s writing: see *Thel*, pl. 6. The designs are slight; perhaps the book was produced in too great a haste for B. to develop the illustrations. Two short passages, totalling twenty-eight lines, are omitted.

AMERICA

For the Bible of Hell, of which *America* is a part, see *The Marriage of Heaven and Hell*, pl. 24.10n. B.'s scheme has a Swedenborgian foundation, in that earthly events are seen as reflections of the greater conflict in the immortal world. Each nation has its human form, and each mortal being has an angelic form in Heaven. This is Prophecy, showing what the earthly events mean, as the Biblical prophets did; B. used the term only for *America* and *Europe*. The chaining and escape of Orc is central to B.'s myth; he uses it in poems from *A Song of Liberty* to *Vala*.

America and *Europe* represent the highest achievement of B.'s technique of 'illuminated printing'. The design often dominates the page, with the text involved inside it. They do not always comment on one another; pl. 6 of *America* illustrates the text, but the design of pl. 7 is in idyllic mood, and pl. 8, where Orc speaks, depicts Urizen in his clouds. The total effect is a brilliant vindication of B.'s aims.

pl. 1.2 *his dark abode* Orc, like Satan, has been thrown into prison in the lowest abyss. In the design he resembles Prometheus, another victim of the repressive laws of tyrant gods. Orc's serpentine nature (pl. 1.15, pl. 8.1, and often elsewhere) alludes to Satan as the tempting serpent of Genesis and *Paradise Lost*, who – as B. saw it – was the energetic opponent of oppressive law.

pl. 3.14 *Albion's wrathful Prince* [or *Angel*] is the 'eternal human form' of the British state. He cannot defeat Orc; so, in *Paradise Lost* VI, the angels cannot defeat Satan, and God has to send his Messiah into the field.

pl. 6.1–4 These lines allude to the Resurrection.

pl. 13.2 *Bernard* Governor of Massachusetts, 1760–71.

pl. 14.4ff. Reminiscent of *Paradise Lost* VI.834ff., where the warlike Messiah routs Satan's forces.

pl. 16.2 *Urizen* This is the first appearance of B.'s Jehovah-figure, the heavenly form of all tyranny and law-making oppression.

THE BOOK OF URIZEN

B.'s Genesis, and the core work of his Bible of Hell, re-shapes the Fall and the creation of the physical universe. Urizen, like Milton's Satan, was an angel enjoying the immortal life, though among a democracy of immortals. He is not cast out for rebellion against law, but separates himself by demanding that Law be established. Los, the immortal artist, emerges to define, clarify and make sense of the disaster, by the power of imagination. B. works in many more allusions. Los becomes Adam, and Enitharmon his Eve. Orc is born to her, like Cain, but is also the Serpent. Towards the end of *Urizen*, unfortunately, B. let his myth-making enthusiasm run away with him.

As in the Bible, the text is divided into two columns and set out in chapters and verses. Designs are chiefly restricted to blocks at top or bottom of the page, often however filling more than half the page and dominating it. There are also eleven whole-page designs. The figures are often gruesome: a crouching skeleton, for example, or the blind Urizen opening his book of corruption. Earth, air, fire and water become elements of oppression and death. Only a few of the designs are lighter and more hopeful. B.'s theme now is not the overthrow of tyranny, but a horrified fascination with its origins.

Missing plate numbers are accounted for by full-page designs.

pl. 3.40 *trumpet* Not the trumpet of the Last Judgment, but the trumpet that sounded over Sinai when God gave the Law to Moses (Exodus 19:16). Jehovah, too, hid himself in darkness, in the cloud on Sinai, and then in the windowless Holy of Holies.

pl. 4.19 *I alone* Urizen has rejected community for a life of selfhood.

pl. 4.34 *Laws of peace . . .* Ironic; for B. no virtue is created by law.

pl. 10.42 *a first Age* Cp. the days of creation in Genesis.

pl. 13.51 *Pity* See p. 50; here a patronizing emotion, as against love, which unifies. In pl. 19.10, Los's pity is a false love which produces a false reaction in Enitharmon.

pl. 19.20 *a Worm* Orc is again identified with the Serpent of Paradise, but the Bible legend is altered. For B., the Serpent is not the tempter to vice, but repressed energy, chained by mankind's false perceptions. Here Orc also recalls Cain, the cursed child of Adam and Eve.

pl. 20.30–32 *Urizen . . . Explor'd* He seeks to control by reason and natural law, instead of enjoying by imagination.

VALA, OR THE FOUR ZOAS

Vala was later re-named *The Four Zoas*. It exists only in manuscript, written mostly on the back of *Night Thoughts* proofs (both are divided into nine Nights) and is chaotic in parts, a palimpsest of the several stages of B.'s reorganization of his myth and the poem. The myth changes much, but some major themes can be summarized. B. establishes a group of four spirits, the Zoas (the four beasts of Ezekiel and Revelation): Urizen, Urthona, Luvah and Tharmas, with their consorts Ahania, Enitharmon, Vala and Enion. Los is identified as the fallen form of Urthona, and the four pairs together embody in themselves the whole universe. Evil is not now purely Urizen's creation, but arises from universal disharmony caused by Vala, the spirit of female domination; when Vala's seductions corrupt Luvah, the universe falls apart. This corruption extends to all life, until the ultimate recovery of health and unity by the Zoas in the Ninth Night. Much of the Urizen–Orc–Los legend was worked into the narrative, and while some episodes fit the new myth, others remain as a mark of B.'s inability to prune exciting but misplaced material. With the latest changes, the poem becomes an expression of B.'s idiosyncratic understanding of Christianity, in which even Vala and Urizen may be redeemed and brought back into the vigorous life of the free immortals. By this time the narrative had become hopelessly confused, and B. gave up the poem, using material and ideas from it in his two final epics, *Milton* and *Jerusalem*.

The selection here represents only some of the more distinct and lyric passages, which stand apart from the legend, or legends, of the poem.

SECOND NIGHT

20 *prince of Light* Urizen, like Satan, before his fall.

100ff. B. often uses old material from *Songs of Innocence and of Experience*, *Visions* and *Europe*, but it may be that the quarrels, in *Vala* and later books, between Los (the artist) and Enitharmon, and their reconciliation, reflect tensions between himself and Catherine.

SIXTH NIGHT

1ff. This passage, B.'s equivalent of Satan's journey through the abyss in *Paradise Lost* II, expands Chapters VII–VIII of *Urizen*.

SEVENTH NIGHT

40 *fires* Los is usually an ironworker; here (l. 49) he turns into an engraver, like B. himself.

50 *Enitharmon tinctur'd it* Coloured prints had to be hand-painted, often by children. B.'s wife Catherine no doubt helped him with such work.

NINTH NIGHT

11 *Mystery* B. takes up the allusions in Revelation to the Scarlet Woman, the harlot Rahab, and develops them into a great goddess Mystery, whose devious rites dominate and corrupt mankind.

LETTERS TO THOMAS BUTTS

Thomas Butts, a minor civil servant, was a long-standing friend and supporter. B. wrote these poems to him from Felpham, the first in the enthusiasm of his arrival, the second when the situation was more strained, as B. disputed with Hayley and the dampness of the cottage affected Catherine Blake's health.

[1]62 *Ram horn'd with gold* From Daniel 8, but not a specific allusion.

[2]14–15 *Robert . . . John* B.'s younger brothers. Robert, William's favourite, died in 1787. John was the 'black sheep', and was said to have enlisted – suggesting, in a bourgeois family, that he had something to run away from.

POEMS FROM THE PICKERING MANUSCRIPT

This is a fair copy, with very few alterations, made probably *c.* 1803. It took its name from the publisher B. M. Pickering (1836–78), who owned it. All but two of the poems are printed here.

THE GOLDEN NET

There is a Notebook draft, with an alternative opening:

> Beneath the white thorn lovely May
> Three Virgins at the break of day
> Alas for woe . . .

THE CRYSTAL CABINET
Can the imagery have its source in the reflections of a triple dressing-table mirror, or of the opening glass doors of a trinket cabinet? See p. 242, l. 25.

THE GREY MONK
This, and the introductory poem to *Jerusalem* Chap. 3, have a single source in one long Notebook draft; hence the similarities.

AUGURIES OF INNOCENCE
This title may refer to the opening quatrain only.

NOTEBOOK POEMS: FELPHAM AND AFTER

MY SPECTRE . . .
For spectres, see *Milton* pl. 2.9n.

MOCK ON . . .
Democritus and Newton reduced the universe to minute, definable, rational dead particles.

FROM CRATETOS
A free translation from Crates, a minor Greek poet; B. began to learn Greek at Felpham.

WAS I ANGRY . . .
Flaxman . . . Cromek . . . Stothard John Flaxman (1755–1826), sculptor, and an old friend with whom B. had no quarrel; but in his bitterness B. cannot resist a jibe even at him. Thomas Stothard (1755–1834), another old friend, was a book-illustrator and a more successful artist than B. In 1806–7 B., at work on an engraving of Chaucer's Canterbury Pilgrims, discovered that Stothard was making an engraving on the same subject for Cromek, and came to believe that Stothard, whose engraving was more successful, had stolen his idea. Stothard is now usually given the benefit of the doubt, but Robert H. Cromek (1770–1812), engraver and publisher, might well have taken advantage of B. He had tricked B. by commissioning drawings for Blair's *The Grave* from him, and then giving the much more profitable engraving contract to the fashionable Luigi Schiavonetti.

Macklin . . . Boydel . . . Bowyer B. had done work for all of them.

WILLIAM COWPER ESQ[RE]
Cowper committed suicide in 1800; Hayley wrote a laudatory biography after his death.

YOU SAY THEIR PICTURES . . .
Titian and other Venetians, Rembrandt and the Flemish school. B., an engraver, detested their use of mass and colour to define shape, in place of firm outline.

FLORENTINE INGRATITUDE
B. worshipped Michelangelo, and detested the later Venetian and Flemish schools. In 1775 Reynolds was elected to membership of the Florentine Academy, and was required to send them a self-portrait. We have to admit that B.'s resentment of R. was largely due to envy that he had so fluently succeeded where B., for all his earnestness and his belief in his own inspiration, had been received by the public with scorn and – worse – neglect.

19 *Ghiotto . . . Apelles* Giotto was said to have been able to draw a perfect circle, and the Athenian Apelles a straight line, both freehand.

MILTON

The fully developed myth of *Milton* and *Jerusalem* grew out of *America*, *Urizen* and *Vala*, but is now profoundly changed. Although complex, and shifting in its details, it has a basic simplicity. The giant Albion, or Britain, has fallen sick, or asleep; his elements – rivers, towns, animals, people, etc. – are affected in sympathy. The theme of both poems is his awakening. His emanation, Jerusalem – for the ideal city of the Bible is not a legend, but is, potentially, our London – is despoiled, but with Albion's awakening will rejoin him 'when we have built/Jerusalem . . .' Los labours to keep the imagination alive, forcing his dark side, his Spectre, to help him. Urizen and Orc have almost disappeared. The villain is now Satan and his female counterpart, Rahab-Tirzah; as in *Job* he is the Accuser; both are obsessed with sin and war, and have the shadowy formlessness which is opposed to the human articulations of divine form. Los must give shape to these evils, so that they may be seen for what they are, and rejected.

The theme is the regeneration of the poet Milton's spirit, precursor to the regeneration of Albion. Milton is unsettled in Heaven, and still separate from his emanation, Ololon. A Bard's song brings home the errors he committed on earth, and he sets out through the abyss to rectify them. Ololon hears of his journey, and sets out from Beulah to find him. They meet in B.'s garden at Felpham; she first, in the guise of a country girl, then Milton. He takes on the form of his evil Spectre, who thus becomes visible, and is blown away like a shadow, and Albion begins to stir in his sleep. This narrative requires enlargement to make it a small epic; B. treats the Bard's song at length, creates several extensive digressions concerning Los and Beulah, and spends some time illustrating the identification of ancient Israel and Britain.

BOOK THE FIRST

pl. 1 This plate was apparently rejected by B. Before the poem is a prose passage denouncing contemporary admiration of classical models.

pl. 2.9 *Spectres* [*Shadows*] 'Spectre' is a core word, indicating much that was evil to B.; formless, dark, threatening. It is an empty human form, near to 'Non-Entity'. The Spectre is the shadow-side of a personality; it is dangerous, but can be tamed.

pl. 2.10 *False Tongue* False teaching of all kinds.

pl. 2.19 *Sixfold Emanation* Milton's Emanation, the female side of his personality, is sixfold, reflecting the six women in his life, three wives and three daughters.

pl. 6 The page is dominated by one of B.'s most striking designs: a huge Stonehenge trilithon, with a giant rocking-stone beside it, belittles a tiny horseback figure who rides through it, while moon and stars shine in a dark sky behind.

pl. 6.6 *Three Classes* See pl. 7.1–3n. The following two or three lines are intended to set the narrative of pls. 7ff. in a universal perspective.

pl. 7.1–3 *Elect . . . Redeem'd . . . Reprobate* The classes are medieval, key distinctions in theology from Augustine to Calvin. B. as usual turns the distinctions upside down. For him the Elect are the passively 'good', law-abiding people, and the Reprobate are the rebellious iconoclasts (like himself!) who are constantly doomed to be cast into outer darkness because their work is unacceptable. In both orthodox and Blakean interpretations, there is hope for the Redeemed.

pl. 7.4 *Satan* The ultimate Shadow – and yet even he was once one of the Immortals. He is the master of Law; he turns the innocent acts of the imagination into sin, and accuses humanity of it. He goes to war to maintain obedience to laws but, to B., his very insistence that 'I am God' (pl. 9.1) reveals his corruption. The narrative that follows is held to reflect B.'s conflict with his patron, Hayley, who tried to persuade B. into tasks that did not fit his convictions about his destiny.

pl. 7.30ff. B. expands the story at length in the plates not printed here. The outcome is a confrontation in which Satan confirms himself in the rigidity of his error.

pl. 9.10 *Ulro* B.'s Hell, a place not of fire but of formlessness and gloom, both qualities marking evil. In it are the lake of Udan-adan and the forest of Entuthon Benython.

pl. 9.24 *Covering Cherub* Denounced in Ezekiel 37–8; here a form of Satan, but also echoing the golden angel whose wings spread over Jehovah's throne in the Holy of Holies. See pl. 37.8n.

pl. 14.26 *claim the Hells . . .* i.e. to turn a hell into a furnace of creative fire.

pl. 15.8 *Polypus* A creature like a jellyfish; another image of formless threat, whose tentacles reach everywhere.

pl. 15.14–16 These lines recall Jacob at Beth-el (Genesis 28); he was a lost traveller with a stone for a pillow, but he dreamt of angels.

pl. 15.17 A feature of *Milton* is the infinite soul's ability to be in many places at once; thus Milton may be asleep in Ulro, journeying through space towards B.'s home, struggling with Urizen, and walking with angels in Beulah, all at once. The same infinity enables spirits to identify with one another, as later (pl. 22.13) Los enters B.'s soul.

pl. 17.2 Los and Enitharmon think that this is the old Milton, worshipper of Jehovah; hence all the Zoas (including Urizen) oppose his re-entry.

pl. 18.2 *Shadowy Female* The Shadowy Female is still, as in *America*, a hapless vehicle of great events; but now she is more firmly identified with the shadow-world of Satan and Rahab.

pl. 19.5–14 *Arnon . . . Mahanaim . . . Succoth . . . Beth Peor* Mahanaim, Succoth and Beth Peor were near Jordan to the north of the Dead Sea, into which the Arnon flows. Jacob struggled with an angel near Mahanaim (Genesis 32); Adam was made from red clay. The Israelites rested at Beth Peor before they invaded Canaan.

pl. 20.15 *Space* 'Spaces' in B.'s fallen world enable humanity to recuperate; they are usually said to be 'created' by a powerful spirit, such as Los. The 'Mundane Shell', our universe in its beautiful aspect, is a kind of 'space'.

pl. 20.27 *Og & Anak* Giant enemies of ancient Israel.

pl. 21.13 *those who Milton drove* i.e. 'those who drove Milton'.

pl. 26(27) The double numbering of pls. 25–7 indicates the two orders used by B. in different copies.

pl. 27(25).1 *Wine-press of Los* The image is taken from Revelation 14:19–20: the 'vine of the earth' is reaped, and the grapes trodden in 'the wine press of the wrath of God'; blood flows out. There is no doubt that B. had in mind, not only human suffering in general, but in particular the Revolutionary or Napoleonic War then going on. Luvah, the fiery but uncontrolled idealist, is sometimes said by B. to represent France.

BOOK THE SECOND

pl. 35.29–32 *First Heaven named Luther . . .* Swedenborg envisaged five Churches, or religious ages; B. a much more complex scheme, though he never developed it fully. *The Twenty-seven Churches* are the corrupt systems of this mortal world (see pl. 37.35–43).

pl. 37.8 *Covering Cherub* See pl. 9.24n. above. Here Milton takes on himself the Cherub's form, to prove that it is only a shadow.

pl. 37.9 *Rahab* [or Tirzah] The female Satanic principles; they maintain the false virtues of Satan's Law and denounce Jerusalem's innocence; they woo men to control them, and send them to war.

pl. 37.36–7 *Adam*, etc. B. lists the ancestors of Abraham (I Chronicles 1:1–27; Luke 3:34–8).

pl. 39.13 *Six Thousand Years* The world was said to be created in 4004 BC.

pl. 40.11–13 *Newtonian*, etc. Rationalists, deists, mockers – even Rousseau; see the Preface to Chap. 3 of *Jerusalem*, pp. 227–9.

JERUSALEM

Blake's *Paradise Lost* and *Regained*, rolled into one; his most important poem. The Giant Albion has fallen into a deathly sleep. The poem deals with the nature of his sickness; the separation from him of his emanation, Jerusalem, and her division into two, Jerusalem and Vala; the struggles of Los to rescue them; and Albion's final awakening and reunion with Jerusalem. Chap. 1 covers Albion's fall, Los's struggle with his Spectre, and the emergence out of his iron-making furnaces of spirits to care for Albion. Chap. 2 deals again with Albion's fall, and the futile struggle of Los and the friends of Albion to restrain him. Chap. 3 is a series of passages describing the evil deeds of the Sons and Daughters of Albion, and the laments of Jerusalem and Vala. The first half of Chap. 4 continues this, and adds a section on the rivalry between Enitharmon and Los. In pl. 94 Albion wakes, and all his spirits are reconciled within him, and he with the Divine Humanity, in a spirit of forgiveness. The repeated use of the word 'Then . . .' should not mislead:

after Albion's fall (recounted several times) there is no major change in the situation until he wakes. The poem consists largely of a series of tableaux, which might be rearranged without harm – in Chap. 2 B. himself does so – and that is the best way to read the poem.

CHAP. 1

pl. 4.1 *Ulro* B.'s shadowy Hell; see *Milton*, pl. 9.10n.

pl. 5.10–11 *Hand*, etc. The Sons of Albion, representing the modern spirit of the nation, corrupted by Albion's sickness. The names are taken from B.'s enemies: the Hunt brothers (*Hand*), who sneered at him in their *Examiner*; Hayley (*Hyle*), who, B. thought, used him under a pretence of helping him; Cromek (?*Coban*) swindled him. The soldier Scholfield accused him of sedition in 1803, and most of the other names represent soldiers supporting Scholfield.

pl. 5.14 *Entuthon Benython* The dark forest of Ulro.

pl. 5.20 *Jerusalem and Vala* In this poem, Jerusalem is Albion's emanation, or female part; Vala is her shadow. Together they are the good and bad sides of Jerusalem, but when she is divided her two parts are at odds with one another, and Vala constantly attacks Jerusalem. They must be reunited before either is whole, and before Jerusalem can rejoin Albion – the theme of the poem. *Division* of a soul into conflicting entities is a major symptom of fallen humanity.

pl. 8.20 *Babel & Shinar* Babylon and Assyria, the cruel superpowers who overwhelmed biblical Israel.

pl. 8.27 *London Stone* Supposedly the base-milestone for the Roman road system; now on Cannon Street.

pl. 9.10 *Spaces of Erin* Erin is a favoured inhabitant of Beulah, where 'spaces' are created for struggling souls to rest in.

pl. 15.10–11 *Loom of Locke . . . Newton* The works of the principal eighteenth-century rationalists.

pl. 15.20 *Valley of the Son of Hinnom* Where children were sacrificed in the fire to Molech (Jeremiah 19).

pl. 20.24 *Veil* A major symbol: Vala casts the shadowy veil; cp. the veil in the Temple (Exodus 25) that separated man from God, the human from the divine. The veil also suggests modesty and coyness, and in line 34 (see also pl. 44(30).13–20; pl. 69.20–22), the hymen.

pl. 21.14 *Gwendolen & Ragan* Names of two of the Daughters of Albion, counterparts of Hand, Hyle, etc., and legendary women in Albion's history. Others are named in the following lines.

pl. 21.21 *Tabernacle . . . Cherubim* B. often uses the secrecy of the forbidden inner sanctum of the Tabernacle and Temple (see pl. 20.24n. above; also Exodus 25:17–22; Leviticus 16:2) as an image of secret sexuality, both representing the evils of suppressed imagination and its joys.

pl. 21.22 *Sabrina* The Severn; another Daughter of Albion.

CHAP. 2

The Preface, 'To the Jews': B. follows contemporary antiquaries in finding a primeval universal religion, ancestor of Judaism and Druidism alike. Jerusalem, the Holy City of the Bible, is thus the 'Emanation of the Giant Albion' (as in the famous prefatory poem to *Milton*). This poem follows.

pl. 34(38) The plates in this chapter are found in two different orders in different copies. The alternative numbers indicate this.

pl. 43(29).9 *Reactor* A term used here only.

pl. 45(31).3 Los here takes a walk from the northern outskirts of London down to the river.

pl. 45(31).25 *Bethlehem* Literally, 'house of bread'; Bethlehem Hospital, or Bedlam, the notorious 'madhouse'.

CHAP. 3

pl. 52.13 *remnant of Druidism* This was considered a reasonable speculation in 1810.

pl. 59.1–8 *Daughter of Los*, etc. This passage may reflect the sweated labour of the children's orphanages in Lambeth. The imagery is taken from the prescription for the hangings in the Tabernacle (Exodus 26).

pl. 59.18 *Rahab & Tirzah* B.'s great image of female evil.

pl. 59.30 *Goats'-hair . . . Linen* Material of the Tabernacle (Exodus 25:4).

pl. 60.1 *Jerusalem . . . Babylon* She is imprisoned in the workhouse, identified with the Dungeons of Babylon, but her soul is safely cared for in Beulah.

pl. 60.22 *thou bindest*, etc. Job 38:31.

pl. 61.31–3 *Euphrates . . . Pison* The four rivers of Paradise (Genesis 2:10–14).

pl. 62.9–10 *I know*, etc. Said by Martha to Jesus on the death of Lazarus (John 11:24). *in my flesh* Cp. Job 19:26.

pl. 66.5 *Victim* of Rahab-Tirzah's perversion of Love, in religion, sex, philosophy, idealism; affecting humans as individuals, groups, or even nations.

pl. 66.10 *King of Canaan* An echo of Judges 4:2–3, adapted to the mockery of Christ.

pl. 66.26–8 *a burning flame . . . night* Biblical visions of the sun: Moses on Horeb (Exodus 3:2); the Israelites in the desert (Exodus 13:21, etc.); the vision of Ezekiel; and the rationalist view of a dead globe.

pl. 66.38–9 *they seem remote . . . Deep* A polypus is made up of a number of independent organisms which only seem to be one body.

pl. 69.11 *Leah & Rachel* The sisters Leah and Rachel, Jacob's two wives, were rivals for his bed; each gave him her maid as concubine to thwart the other.

pl. 70.1 *form of mighty Hand* A huge trilithon dominates the plate. Three diminutive figures in a rural landscape walk beneath it, and a moon shines through it. 'Hand' represents the three brothers Hunt, who sneered at B.'s work, and thus sum up the blindness of the Sons of Albion.

CHAP. 4

pl. 79.10–13 *Ephraim . . . Og* Philistea and Og were enemies of Israel. Ephraim was a sacred city and capital of the northern kingdom; Shiloh was the site of the Tabernacle for a long time before it was moved to Jerusalem, the ultimate capital and sacred city.

pl. 79.12 *Gilead* 'Is there no balm in Gilead? Is there no physician there?' (Jeremiah 8:22).

pl. 81.15 Above this line, most of the plate is filled by the Daughters of Albion, nude; Gwendolen has her back to us, and is pointing out to the rest the motto (in mirror-writing): *In Heaven the only art of Living / Is Forgetting & Forgiving / But if you on Earth Forgive / You shall not find where to Live*. Beside this, also reversed: *Especially for the Female*.

pl. 86.4ff. The imagery of this passage is based on the vestments of the High Priest (Exodus 28); the phrase *Holiness to the Lord* is inscribed on a gold plate on his forehead.

pl. 89.6–7 *Pharisaion . . . Saddusaion* The Pharisees, Scribes, Elders, High Priest, Priest and Sadducees.

pl. 89.28–9 *Above his Head . . . Os Humeri* A parody of the fittings of the Holy of Holies; these are iron, not gold.

pl. 91.34 *Smaragdine Table of Hermes* The Emerald Table of Hermes Trismegistus, a fabled mystical philosopher. B., mistakenly, identifies it as another tablet of laws.

pl. 98.34 *terrific or complacent* Terrifying or pleasing.

THE EVERLASTING GOSPEL

B. never made his final decisions about these unfinished pieces, written *c.* 1818 on widely separated pages of his now nearly full Notebook. He wrote the title above 'Was Jesus Humble . . .', which was certainly not the first section to be drafted. Most of the major pieces are included here; 'If Moral Virtue . . .' is not the first, but is marked 'This to come first'.

I. 14 *Rhadamanthus* A legendary figure, an ideal of justice.

II. 18 *Thy Sins . . .* Mark 2:5, when Jesus healed a paralysed man.

III. 2 *Proofs* B. detested rational proof.

III. 5 *he ran away* See Luke 2:41–52.

III. 14 *Ye must be born again* John 3:3.

III. 37 *Dr. Priestley* Deist minister and scientist (he discovered oxygen). B. would detest his rationalist religion much more than his science.

IV. 4 *Mary . . . Adulterous* B. conflates (as does some Christian tradition) Mary Magdalene, 'a sinner' (John 12:3, Mark 16:1–9) with the unnamed adulteress of John 8:1–11, the scene alluded to here. The commandment of death is in Leviticus 20:10.

IV. 28 *God* First reading, *Devil.*

IV. 95 *dust and clay* See Genesis 3:14.

VI. 9 *Melitus* One of the accusers who demanded that Socrates should die for perverting the minds of youth.

FOR THE SEXES: THE GATES OF PARADISE

In 1793 B. issued a little emblem-book of allegorical designs with brief captions, entitled *For Children / The Gates of Paradise*, depicting the evil effects of restricting the imagination, when life becomes a dreary progress to a sad grave. Much later, perhaps *c.* 1818, he reissued it, tying the designs into his mature thought and imagery, with added captions, a set of cryptic interpretations, and these poems as Prologue and Epilogue. The altered title means that the book is now directed, not to the innocent, but to mortals tied to the restricted life of this world.

SELECT BIBLIOGRAPHY

Facsimiles

The Complete Graphic Works of William Blake, compiled by David Bindman and Deirdre Toomey, Thames & Hudson, 1978.

The Illuminated Blake, annotated by David V. Erdman, OUP/Anchor, 1975. (All the 'illuminated books', in monochrome.)

Songs of Innocence and of Experience, intro. Sir Geoffrey Keynes, OUP, 1970.

America. A Prophecy, intro. G. E. Bentley, London, 1974.

The Marriage of Heaven and Hell, intro. Sir Geoffrey Keynes, OUP, 1975.

The Book of Urizen, ed. Kay Parkhurst Easson and Roger R. Easson, Thames & Hudson, 1979.

The Four Zoas, ed. David V. Erdman & G. Canelli, OUP, 1988.

The Pickering Manuscript, Pierpont Morgan, 1972.

Blake's Notebook, ed. David V. Erdman, OUP, 1973.

All Blake's 'illuminated books' were reprinted individually in colour facsimile in their original size for the Blake Trust by the Trianon Press. *Jerusalem* was also reproduced in a black-and-white copy.

Writings about Blake

Gerald E. Bentley, *Blake Records*, OUP, 1971.

David Bindman, *Blake as an Artist*, Phaidon, 1977.

Joseph Bronowski, *William Blake and the Age of Revolution*, Routledge & Kegan Paul, rev. edn, 1972. (Original title, 1947: *William Blake, a Man without a Mask*.)

Martin Butlin, *William Blake*, Tate Gallery, 1978.

David V. Erdman, *Blake, Prophet against Empire*, 3rd edn, Princeton, NJ, 1977.

Northrop Frye, *Fearful Symmetry*, Princeton, NJ, 1947.

Alexander Gilchrist, ed. Ruthven Todd, *A Life of William Blake, Pictor Ignotus*, new edn, Dent (Everyman), 1982.

John Holloway, *Blake: the Lyric Poetry*, Edward Arnold, 1968.
W. J. T. Mitchell, *Blake's Composite Art*, Princeton, NJ, 1978.
Kathleen Raine, *Blake and Tradition*, Phaidon, 1967.

INDEX OF TITLES AND FIRST LINES

READ MORE IN PENGUIN

In every corner of the world, on every subject under the sun, Penguin represents quality and variety – the very best in publishing today.

For complete information about books available from Penguin – including Puffins, Penguin Classics and Arkana – and how to order them, write to us at the appropriate address below. Please note that for copyright reasons the selection of books varies from country to country.

In the United Kingdom: Please write to *Dept. JC, Penguin Books Ltd, FREEPOST, West Drayton, Middlesex UB7 OBR*

If you have any difficulty in obtaining a title, please send your order with the correct money, plus ten per cent for postage and packaging, to *PO Box No. 11, West Drayton, Middlesex UB7 OBR*

In the United States: Please write to *Penguin USA Inc., 375 Hudson Street, New York, NY 10014*

In Canada: Please write to *Penguin Books Canada Ltd, 10 Alcorn Avenue, Suite 300, Toronto, Ontario M4V 3B2*

In Australia: Please write to *Penguin Books Australia Ltd, 487 Maroondah Highway, Ringwood, Victoria 3134*

In New Zealand: Please write to *Penguin Books (NZ) Ltd,182–190 Wairau Road, Private Bag, Takapuna, Auckland 9*

In India: Please write to *Penguin Books India Pvt Ltd, 706 Eros Apartments, 56 Nehru Place, New Delhi 110 019*

In the Netherlands: Please write to *Penguin Books Netherlands B.V., Keizersgracht 231 NL–1016 DV Amsterdam*

In Germany: Please write to *Penguin Books Deutschland GmbH, Friedrichstrasse 10–12, W–6000 Frankfurt/Main 1*

In Spain: Please write to *Penguin Books S. A., C. San Bernardo 117–6° E–28015 Madrid*

In Italy: Please write to *Penguin Italia s.r.l., Via Felice Casati 20, I–20124 Milano*

In France: Please write to *Penguin France S. A., 17 rue Lejeune, F–31000 Toulouse*

In Japan: Please write to *Penguin Books Japan, Ishikiribashi Building, 2–5–4, Suido, Tokyo 112*

In Greece: Please write to *Penguin Hellas Ltd, Dimocritou 3, GR–106 71 Athens*

In South Africa: Please write to *Longman Penguin Southern Africa (Pty) Ltd, Private Bag X08, Bertsham 2013*

READ MORE IN PENGUIN

A SELECTION OF POETRY

American Verse
British Poetry Since 1945
Caribbean Verse in English
Contemporary American Poetry
Contemporary British Poetry
English Poetry 1918–60
English Romantic Verse
English Verse
First World War Poetry
German Verse
Greek Verse
Irish Verse
Japanese Verse
Love Poetry
The Metaphysical Poets
Modern African Poetry
New Poetry
Poetry of the Thirties
Scottish Verse
Spanish Verse
Women Poets